Tess had done some crazy things in her life, but nothing even remotely like this.

God knew what crime she could be charged with. Kidnapping? Aiding and abetting?

Jack's fingers flexed against the throb in his shoulder. "What the hell just happened?" He looked past her out the darkened window of the car. "Who were they?"

Tess steepled her hands over her mouth to stay the bubble of hysteria that threatened to burst. "Cops." Her voice had risen an octave. "Or not. I don't know. All I do know is they meant to kill you and possibly me."

He reached out and took her shaking hand in his. For reasons she couldn't imagine, she allowed it. That solitary, silent gesture spoke volumes and dissipated a large chunk of the terror that had lodged in her throat. Whatever was going on, they were in it together now.

Dear Reader,

Happy holidays! In honor of the season, we've got six very special gifts for you. Who can resist *The Outlaw Bride,* the newest from Maggie Shayne's bestselling miniseries THE TEXAS BRAND? Forget everything you think you know about time and how we move through it, because you're about to get a look at the power of the human heart to alter even the hardest realities. And you'll get an interesting look at the origins of the Texas Brands, too.

ROYALLY WED, our exciting cross-line continuity miniseries, continues with Suzanne Brockmann's *Undercover Princess.* In her search to find her long-lost brother, the crown prince, Princess Katherine Wyndham has to try life as a commoner. Funny thing is, she quite likes being a nanny to two adorable kids—not to mention the time she spends in their handsome father's arms. In her FAMILIES ARE FOREVER title, *Code Name: Santa,* Kayla Daniels finds the perfect way to bring a secret agent in from the cold—just in time for the holidays. *It Had To Be You* is the newest from Beverly Bird, a suspenseful tale of a meant-to-be love. Sara Orwig takes us WAY OUT WEST to meet a *Galahad in Blue Jeans.* Now there's a title that says it all! Finally, look for Barbara Ankrum's *I'll Remember You,* our TRY TO REMEMBER title.

Enjoy them all—and don't forget to come back again next month, because we plan to start off a very happy new year right here in Silhouette Intimate Moments, where the best and most exciting romances are always to be found.

Enjoy!

Leslie J. Wainger
Executive Senior Editor

Please address questions and book requests to:
Silhouette Reader Service
U.S.: 3010 Walden Ave., P.O. Box 1325, Buffalo, NY 14269
Canadian: P.O. Box 609, Fort Erie, Ont. L2A 5X3

I'LL REMEMBER YOU

BARBARA ANKRUM

Silhouette®

INTIMATE™ MOMENTS®

Published by Silhouette Books

America's Publisher of Contemporary Romance

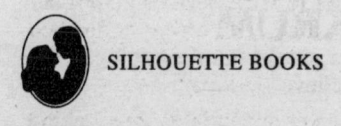

SILHOUETTE BOOKS

ISBN 0-373-07972-9

I'LL REMEMBER YOU

Copyright © 1999 by Barbara Ankrum

Visit us at www.romance.net

Printed in U.S.A.

Books by Barbara Ankrum

Silhouette Intimate Moments

To Love a Cowboy #834
I'll Remember You #972

BARBARA ANKRUM

says she's always been an incurable romantic, with a passion for books and stories about the healing power of love. It never occurred to her to write seriously until her husband, David, discovered a box full of her unfinished stories and insisted that she pursue her dream. Need she say more about why she believes in love?

With a successful career as a commercial actress behind her, Barbara decided she had plenty of eccentric characters to people the stories that inhabited her imagination. She wrote her first novel in between auditions and she's never looked back. Her historicals have won the prestigious Reviewers' Choice and K.I.S.S. Awards from *Romantic Times Magazine,* and she's been nominated for a RITA Award from Romance Writers of America. Barbara lives in Southern California with her actor/writer/hero-husband and their two perfect children.

For David, my own warrior—
this one's for you, my love.

Prologue

Dusk seemed to hold its breath as the gunshot's echo reverberated against the canyon's rocky walls. Birds fell silent. Even the steady coastal breeze, which had only moments earlier relieved the thick summer evening, stilled as the two men stood at the top of the precipice, staring down into the well of darkness below.

"Dammit!" snarled the bulkier of the two. Decapitating a clump of weeds near the edge of the road with one well-placed kick, he punched the air like a shadowboxer. "What did I tell you?"

"I hit him, *bato*," argued the second in a voice born of the barrios east of the city. Smoke still trailed from the gun in his hand as he peered over the edge of the shrub encrusted slope. Dragging a hand through his black hair, he searched the darkness. "I know I did."

"You know? You *know?*" The older man stopped dead in his tracks, staring incomprehensibly at his companion. "Then maybe you know what the boss is gonna do to us when he finds out we lost the bastard over the side of a cliff!''

A low growl rumbled deep in the second man's throat and he rolled one shoulder with a grimace. "He's dead. The fall alone would've killed him."

The shadowboxer glared over the steep incline below them, fingering his bleeding knuckles and pondering whether luck was indeed with them.

"Well, wouldn't it?" the other man pressed. Shadows clung to his chiseled features, carving them with fatigue.

His partner turned and locked eyes with him, clamping a hand against his shoulder as a big brother might a dim-witted sibling. "How many times I gotta tell ya? Head shot. It's clean. It's fast, it's—"

"*Basta, ese bato.* I aimed for his head. How was I supposed to know the crazy bastard would turn and jump off the cliff?"

"Hell, I should've done it myself."

"You're the one who decided to beat the truth out of him first. We should'a just popped him—"

"Before he told us where it was? And leave both our butts swinging in the wind?"

"Yeah, well, he told us exactly nothing."

"And maybe," the older one conceded, "that was everything."

The second man shrugged his shoulders inside his black leather jacket. "I hit him good. I saw it knock him backward." He shook his head and gave a gesture of dismissal with his hand. "Ah hell...he's dead all right. No man could've survived that fall."

The eerie screech of an owl from across the canyon evoked a shiver in both men. As one, they looked at each other, then peered silently over the side of the sage and juniper dotted cliff, listening. Nothing but the heavy flap of wings overhead broke the unnatural hush that had blanketed the night. No sound of movement or life came from the depths of the blackness below.

The older of the pair muttered and shook his head. "Stupid bastard."

"*Loco.* You think we ought to—"

"—go down and check?"

There was a long pause. "Yeah."

Loose dirt skidded down the treacherous slope from beneath the weed kicker's foot. With a curse, he leaped backward. "Whad'ya think I am? A suicide waitin' to happen? I say he's dead and that's the end of it."

"Right."

"That's our story and we stick with it."

"Yo."

The two men knocked knuckles and exchanged an almost violent handshake of solidarity, cast one last glance toward the darkness below, then retreated to the dark sedan waiting nearby. The engine ground to life—a punctuation mark to the end of a very unpleasant evening.

The tires crunched gravel as they edged off the shoulder, then squealed against the asphalt as the car pulled away, speeding down the road toward the constellation of city lights that haloed the distant hills. In its wake was a deathly silence, broken only by a breath of wind skidding down the canyon.

That, and the faintest scrape of rocks against loose dirt from somewhere far below the deserted road.

Chapter 1

"Of course, I'm all right. What did you think I was going to do? Throw myself off the nearest bridge?"

Tess Gordon cringed at the forced lightness in her voice, certain that her boss, Daniel McCaffrey, wasn't for a moment fooled. She tightened her grip on the cellular phone, staring at the dark canyon road winding before her.

"Nothing as dramatic as that," came Daniel's measured reply. "Just tell me you're not going to...I don't know...go *bungee* jumping, or diving off some cliff in Acapulco."

"Hunh. I pro-miss nozzing," she said in her best Garbo imitation, half enjoying the concern in Daniel's warning. "Besides, I don't recall any stipulations on exactly *how* I should spend this enforced vacation of mine. As a matter of fact, as I recall, the beach was one of your suggestions."

Daniel laughed. "Remind me about your literal nature next time, will you?"

She could picture his kind, hazel eyes sparkling as he bantered with her over the airwaves. His interest in her was something he didn't even try to conceal anymore. She was grateful for his friendship, but for her, it would never be anything more than that.

It couldn't be. With anyone.

"My literal nature is the reason you hired me in the first place," she pointed out, following her headlights around a pitch-black curve in Angelo Canyon. "You need me, Daniel. The project needs me. Which is exactly what I tried to tell you when you—"

"Uh-uh! Don't even go there," he warned. "We both know you're invaluable on this team. We would never have gotten as far as we have without your work. But we need you alive, Tess. And frankly, you're starting to worry me."

Here it comes, she thought. "Daniel—"

"You need this vacation, Tess," he interrupted before she could argue anymore. "You need twenty-four solid hours in a real bed—as opposed to, say…your office couch?—to erase those little Morticia Addams smudges around your eyes. You need three squares a day prepared by room service in some ridiculously luxurious hotel. You need maid service and frou-frou drinks with little umbrellas propped beside some five-star lagoon. Relax. Contemplate your navel." He paused deliberately. "Hey, here's a thought. Have some fun. Remember fun?"

"No," she replied glumly as the fleeting image of her forehead connecting repeatedly with a brick wall flickered through her mind. Gripping the steering wheel hard, she rounded a sharp curve fast enough to make her tires squeal. The high-pitched whine echoed off the steep canyon walls, then slipped down the sheer cliffs that hugged the road.

Only passingly aware of that sound, Tess focused on the more obvious one—the distinctive thud of the proverbial "other shoe" dropping.

Okay, so things had been going too well. She should have seen this day coming. Braced herself for it. But how did one prepare for being dropped like an egg from fifty stories without so much as a parachute?

Work had become her sanctuary, her sanity. Didn't Daniel know that? For the last two years, the lab and the research had been the glue that had held her together. Without it she might just crumble like a stale cookie.

The sharp tang of damp eucalyptus filtered through her open window and the crisp night air slapped against her skin. Daniel was talking again.

"...your own good...let me..." Static sputtered in her ear. "...when you...there, will ya?"

She shook the cell phone. Damn. Her battery was dying. She must have forgotten to charge it. Again.

"Daniel?" she said loudly. "You're breaking up. I— hello? I can't hear you!"

"Nice try, Elroy," he said, obviously unconvinced by the dead-battery ploy. "I ex...postcard...when you—"

"No, Daniel, really." She was shouting now. "My battery is—"

"...three weeks...hear me? ...not a minute—" *Sshhh.*

Tess pulled the receiver away from her ear with a wince, glared at it, then tossed it down with more force than strictly necessary onto the seat beside her.

She blew out a breath. Damn technology.

Damn Daniel.

Just because he had a point about the dark circles under her eyes and about the crummy cafeteria food she'd been subsisting on, that didn't make him right.

She couldn't be bothered to go home to cook for one. She considered that a waste of time. The work was what mattered. And they were close. So close.

Shifting down as she approached another lonely curve of road, she thought of the hours, days, *months* she'd put into the research project they were working on. She'd put her body and soul into it, alongside the rest of the team. Like them, she'd sweated blood over each failure, and reveled in every inch forward they'd made.

So she'd reveled quietly and alone. So she had yet to join in one of Kiki Rader's poolside celebrations, replete with laughing children, barking dogs, husbands and wives.

"Is that a crime?" she asked the perfectly dead phone that lay on the seat beside her.

Tess sighed. Why, she wondered, did people think that she'd lost her ability to manage her own life the day she'd lost Adam?

Tess clenched her jaw, staring into the darkness ahead. Well, so be it. She'd go home, collect her things, head for the airport and fly somewhere. Anywhere. She'd dive into a good book, explore a pyramid, lose herself in a crowd. She'd do anything, in fact, *but* contemplate. Swimming with sharks sounded safer than that.

As a matter of fact, swimming with sharks just might appeal to her sense of—

By the time she caught sight of the figure stumbling into the cone of her headlights, it was nearly too late. She slammed her foot against the brake pedal and jerked the wheel to the left.

Her Honda fishtailed violently sideways.

The sound of squealing tires shattered the inky silence of the canyon. In horror, she watched the guardrail that separated the road from the steep-walled ravine below rush toward her.

Wrenching the wheel hard to the right, she heard the left rear fender of the car scream against the metal as an explosion of sparks arched into the darkness behind her.

Adrenaline rocketed through her like a punch of heat. Desperately, she fought the road for control. The tires spit gravel against the underbelly of the car as it left the shoulder and swerved back to the right side of the road. The car swam sideways one last time toward the sheer sandstone cliffs that walled in the canyon, then, miraculously, skidded to a grinding stop.

Her thundering pulse slammed against her eardrums. She threw the car into Park and dropped her face into hands that had begun to shake violently.

"Ohmigod..."

No more than eight seconds had lapsed from start to finish—the longest eight seconds of her relatively short life. Long enough for every glaring mistake she'd made to flood past her in the dark.

Enough of those for two lifetimes.

Shaking, she tipped her head back against the headrest and looked in the rearview mirror, surprised by the unnatural pallor of the face that stared back. Dismissing it, she turned her attention to the darkness behind her. Only moon shadows occupied the empty road. Nothing else but the briefest notion that someone had been there.

A man.

Another punch of adrenaline squeezed through her chest. Had she imagined it? It could have been a deer or a bear—

"In Levi's?" she said aloud.

Turning fully in her seat, she peered out the back window.

Who was she kidding? It had been a man. A tall man. And despite the color-robbing headlights and her fractional glimpse of him, she'd had the distinct impression of blood. And he hadn't been just walking along the road.

Lurching was more like it. Staggering like he was drunk. Or hurt.

There was no sign of him now.

Every instinct screamed at her to put the car back in gear and get the hell out of there. She was a woman alone, for heaven's sake. And even *she* watched the eleven o'clock news on occasion. No one would blame her for driving away. It was the sensible thing to do.

Still, she hesitated, cursing Daniel for forcing her to leave the lab at all tonight. If only she'd followed her normal routine, she'd be safely ensconced on her lumpy office couch counting genetically altered sheep.

Maybe another car will come by.

She glanced at the clock on her dashboard. Eleven forty-five. This road became deserted after ten. It would be morning before residential commuters used it again. By then, who knew? The stranger could be dead.

The paranoia that had become a part of everyday life here was something she loathed. More than that, she detested her own impulse to walk away from someone who might need her help.

Automatically, she reached for the cell phone, then threw it back down again.

Damn technology!

Still shaking, and with a reluctance that bordered on panic, she shoved the car into Reverse and made a three-point turn until her headlights pointed in the other direction. As she inched forward, the words of Gil Castillano—her late husband's partner and now a dear friend who had talked her into buying the cell phone in the first place—echoed in her head.

"I worry about you, Tess," he'd said in that brotherly tone of his. *"Living alone out there in the middle of nowhere. Humor me, will you, and take precautions?"*

"Precautions," she muttered. *A little late for that.* If she'd had any sense at all, she'd be dialing 911 like a sane person instead of driving intentionally into trouble.

In the distance, something moved in the dim frame of her headlights. It was little more than a lump of darkness that pushed itself up off the ground and started to stagger in an erratic way down the road.

She bit hard on her lower lip as she inched forward. A hundred feet down the road she caught up with him. His once-white shirt flapped open at his sides like a flag of surrender in the evening breeze. He seemed oblivious to her, or to the lights illuminating the uneven ground he was walking on. The dark stain on his shirt had a reddish cast in her headlights.

"Ho, boy," she mumbled, chewing on her lower lip. *Scratch falling-down-drunk as a possibility.*

She ducked her head out her window. "Hey!" No response. "Hey! Mister—"

Like a switch had been flicked off, his knees buckled and he crumpled to the ground again like a load of bricks.

Tess gasped and threw the car into Park. Yanking her keys out of the ignition, she closed her fingers around the pepper spray that dangled from her key chain. She grabbed a flashlight from the glove compartment and raced toward him.

He didn't move as she approached. Aiming her flashlight until the beam struck his face, she fought the instinct to run. Her heart slammed against the wall of her chest.

Dear God.

Whatever had happened to him, it had been bad. Clinically, she assessed the nasty swelling that had formed around the bloody gash above his left temple, automatically calculating the number of stitches required to close it and the distinct possibility of head trauma. The left side of his face and chest were covered with blood.

Crimson glistened across the swollen cheek and eye of what she suspected was a wickedly handsome face. His skin was pasty looking, and what wasn't covered with blood glimmered with a sheen of sweat. She crouched down and gingerly palpated the pulse at the side of his throat, relieved to feel a thin, reedy throb beneath her fingertips. His skin was clammy and cool. Shocky. No surprise, considering the amount of blood he'd already lost. She let the arc of light drift down the rest of him.

She'd been right. He was tall. Very tall. Six-three if he was an inch, and though his clothes were a mess, this man was no drifter. Expensive jeans hugged long, muscular legs, and his cowboy boots—though scuffed and dirty as the rest of him now—were crafted of fine leather. The buttons had somehow been ripped loose from his ragged shirt, which was wound halfway around his back, exposing a truly impressive set of abs amid a mass of purplish bruises. He looked as if he'd been dragged behind a horse.

He was Montgomery Clift and a young John Wayne, with a brooding dash of James Dean etched in the dark crescent of lashes shadowing his high cheekbones. Sweat dampened his hairline, forcing his straight, dark hair to hang in spiky hanks against his brow. The lines bracketing the firm set of his mouth appeared grim, unrelenting. The overall effect actually made her forget to breathe for a minute, in a profoundly unprofessional way.

Shaken, she purposefully redirected her light back at the road he'd just navigated. Could be a car accident, she reasoned, tightening her shaking grip on the flashlight. Cars plunged over the sides of this canyon on a disturbingly regular basis. Had he gone over and climbed up out of the ravine on his own?

Some darker instinct warned this was more complicated than a car wreck. She'd seen enough accidents, enough battered faces to recognize the difference between an accident and fist-inflicted damage. But more worrisome was her suspicion that even the gash on his forehead couldn't account for all this blood.

Gently, she touched his arm. "Hey…can you hear me?"

He groaned, but didn't move. He lay sprawled half-on, half-off the road's shoulder. Any car rounding the curve just ahead would not have time to avoid him.

She cursed silently. "No way I'm moving you alone," she muttered, knowing she'd have to do just that if he didn't wake up. For a moment she could only stare at the labored rise and fall of his rib cage, wondering how a man in such prime condition had wound up in such a state.

A wave of dizziness accompanied that thought. Survival had less to do with conditioning than it did with luck. That point had come home two years ago when Adam's luck had flat run out. Since that awful night she'd worked feverishly to forget a life's calling that seemed determined to rear its ugly head again tonight. That night she'd sworn off trying to fix broken bodies. She thought she'd made that abundantly clear to the universe.

The man groaned and half rolled to his right.

Apparently, not clear enough.

Her beam of light flickered across his upper chest, then stopped dead. His movement had shifted the fabric of the shirt bunched around his shoulders. What she saw there made her knees hit the pavement with a dull *thwack*.

A neat, black hole.

Her lips went numb. She snapped her eyes shut, inhaled sharply and braced a hand on the dew-slick asphalt. Fear— cold, puddling fear—gathered in her belly. The kind that had woken her in clammy sweats for the last two years.

Now it threatened to close her throat.

She gulped the cool night air as if she were about to plunge underwater. *Calm, Tess,* she told herself. *Calm. You've seen worse. Much worse.* But that did little to allay the rush of panic churning inside her.

Ironic, she thought, that a gunshot wound used to seem almost passé. Dozens, hundreds of them came through the ER where she'd worked. In fact, never once before that night had the sight of one sent her pitching headlong for a bedpan. All that, of course, had changed after Adam had died. And it was common knowledge in the rather insulated community of physicians that Tess Gordon had lost her nerve.

She closed her eyes and counted to five. *Breathe,* she told herself firmly. *Just breathe. He needs your help. There is no one else.*

She went down the automatic checklist in her head: D5W, Ringers, at least two units of o-neg, CT, CBC—none of which she could provide for him here. She had to get him to a hospital. And soon. He was leaking like a rusty pail.

Her hand was still shaking as she reached forward to lift his shirt away from the wound. The soaked fabric sucked at his skin as she peeled it back.

There it was, an inch and a half below the clavicle. Neat, probably a .38. She slid her hand under his shoulder to check for an exit wound. Nothing. The bullet was still inside him. She raised the heavy black flashlight higher. If he was very lucky, the bullet had missed his lung. If not, he'd—

The flicker of his eyelids was her only warning.

His hand closed around her wrist and jerked her toward him.

A squeak of terror lodged in her throat. In the space of a heartbeat, her world shifted. Her flashlight and key chain went flying and the pavement slammed against her back.

His weight pinned her hard to the ground and he levered a steely forearm against her trachea. She gagged and gasped. Above her she heard him snarl something at her, but she couldn't comprehend it. He said it again, more demandingly this time, but his voice sounded even farther away.

Everything she'd learned in that stupid self-defense class she'd taken last year promptly exited her brain as white lights flashed behind her eyes. A pathetic gurgling sound issued from her throat. Pinned there helplessly with her wrists trapped above her head and the rest of her immobilized by his unyielding weight, she realized that she was about to die.

But inexplicably, as blackness circled in on her, an earthy epithet sounded from somewhere above her, followed by an unflattering observation about her gender. Then the pressure on her neck abruptly lifted.

Like water rushing into an empty vessel, her lungs sucked air past the fiery pain in her throat. She coughed and gagged and gulped more air. Blood pounded in her ears.

He was a shadow hovering above her, haloed by the moonlight behind him. He still had her trapped beneath him, but the brutal force he'd applied only moments ago was gone. He held his weight slightly off her with the concern of a misguided lover.

Anger flooded past the oxygen pumping through her veins. Her eyes burned and she clenched her teeth to keep from letting tears slide down her cheeks. He could kill her, but she wouldn't give him tears. She wouldn't!

He swore again. *"Hold…still."*

She bucked underneath him. *"Let…me…go!"*

"Who are you?" Violence simmered in his eyes and thickened his voice with all the finesse of a carpenter's rasp. "Who sent you?"

His iron-like grip hadn't relaxed, but for the first time, she felt his muscles quaking with the effort to hold her.

"Tell me, dammit!"

"Nobody *sent* me."

She'd be a fool to discount the force of will that had brought him this far against odds that would have crushed a weaker man. And a fool to think that luck would have the guts to rear its head tonight after deserting her so long ago.

The panic that had seized her only moments ago leaked

away as years of training kicked in to some still-functioning part of her brain.

"So, what are you going to do?" she asked in a hoarse whisper. "Kill me? I'd say you've got another thirty seconds of strength left before your body gives out. So you better do it now."

His expression hardened dangerously. "It…would be a mistake…to underestimate me."

"I'm hardly in a position to underestimate anything, am I?" she replied, casting a glacial look at his hands clamped against her wrists.

"Then we…understand each other." His voice shook slightly, belying the steely set of his mouth.

"Oh, I wouldn't go that far."

Amusement flickered in his expression, before the deadly flatness returned to his eyes. "Just…how far would you go?"

She blinked. "What?"

"Club me while I'm unconscious? Maybe just—" he swallowed thickly "—run over me with that car? Make it look like an accident?"

She jerked angrily against his hands. "Make it…? You almost ran *me* off the road! I had to swerve to avoid you!"

"Give me a name, lady. You got three seconds."

She felt the warmth of his blood seeping against her breasts. A name? What name? Who did he think she was? Someone hired to kill him?

His eyes rolled slightly with his half-lidded blink. "One."

She had no doubt that he could, *would* kill her. That he had killed before. Every steely inch of him seared her flesh. He could crush her if he wanted to. Or worse.

She squeezed her eyes shut. Regrets flooded her: for the babies she'd never had; for the months that had gone by since she'd spent time with her mother; that she hadn't had the guts to listen to Adam's voice that night months after he'd died, when she'd imagined she'd heard him tell her everything was going to be okay.

It hadn't been. She hadn't let it.

"Two—"

The word sliced into her like a scalpel. Every nerve in her body tingled to life in reaction. "Tess," she blurted. "Tess Gordon."

He blinked down at her, his face only inches from her own. Confusion deepened the lines of pain bracketing his mouth.

"M-my name," she explained. "My name is Tess."

Sweat trickled past his eye and cut a path through the grime on his cheek. She could almost hear him rifle his memory banks in search of her name, coming up, naturally, empty. He shook his head slowly, his unfocused gaze circling in on her mouth. "Tha's...wrong."

"Wrong?"

His lips pulled back in a snarl. "No...more...games."

"I'm not—look, I can help you. I'm a doc—"

"Give me a name, dammit!"

"I don't have a—!"

"Two," he repeated through gritted teeth, weaving above her like a hissing balloon.

She rocked her head against the cold asphalt. "You already said two. You're losing it. Can't you see you're bleeding to death?"

He wiped his sweaty face against the shoulder of his shirt. "Okay." One side of his mouth lifted in a dangerous leer. "Three."

A sound of utter frustration wrenched from her. "*Nobody* sent me. That's what I've been trying to tell you." Her breath rasped against the sudden dryness in her throat. She had to make him understand. "Listen to me carefully. I was just driving by. I—only—stopped—to—help—you!"

* * *

The words slammed into him like a cold blast of water. *Stopped to help you…help you…help you.*

That's how muddled his brain was. That possibility hadn't even occurred to him.

Had she? Stopped to help?

The pain in his head intensified and he squeezed his eyes shut to ease the throb. *Gordon. Tess.* The name lay like a stone in his memory—hard, cold, useless. He didn't even remember her face. And those eyes…he'd never have forgotten eyes like hers. But how was she connected to—? His mind went blank. To whom? He cursed silently.

If only he could think. Turn down the rush of noise in his head. Nausea clawed at his gut and fire branded his shoulder with every breath.

Beneath him, the woman's soft curves molded against the hard angles of his body, which was doing a good imitation of a California aftershock. It crossed his mind to simply sink into her softness and disappear. Let the earthquake come. Roll over him.

But the woman's wrists felt fragile, bird-like in his hands. And warm. So warm. He inhaled her scent—the smell of summer rain—a distant memory flitting by him like the moon scudding behind the clouds.

Gone again.

Her eyes never left his face. They were wide with fear. Fear of him. With good reason. Suddenly, he knew she was telling the truth. She was too damned scared to be one of them. Whoever they were. *Hell.*

He glanced back at the car parked across the road, whose headlights still cut a swath of brilliance across the canyon. He turned back to her. "Your keys."

"M-my *keys?*"

"Give 'em to me."

She gestured with her chin toward the still-shining flashlight that lay some ten feet away. "Over there. I—I lost them when you grabbed me."

He saw the dull glint of them in the moonlight. The thought of moving that far made bile rise in his throat.

"What are you waiting for?" Her voice had gone flat and cool. "Go get them. They're right there. Easy to reach."

He pondered telling her to go get them, but discarded the idea as idiotic. The last he'd see of her would undoubtedly be her backside.

Pain shot through his temple as he crawled off her, ignoring the fire in his shoulder and the nausea in his gut. He heard her scramble to her knees behind him.

"How far do you think you'll get?" she taunted. "Even if you make it as far as the car, how long before you pass out again behind the wheel and go right over the edge of one of these cliffs?"

He ignored her, focused solely on the glint of metal in the dark.

"You're bleeding to death." Her voice shook as she spoke. "You are going to *die*."

Five feet. Only five more feet and he'd have them. The keys slipped in and out of focus. His left arm shook as he inched forward.

"You *need* a hospital."

No! he heard himself say. At least he thought he said it. Three feet. His head throbbed and his throat felt like ground-up glass.

Then a pair of scuffed white tennis shoes appeared where the keys had been an instant before. Despair rocked through him as he watched her stumble a few steps backward.

"Give'm to me, dammit!" he croaked at her.

She thrust something in his direction from above, with her finger poised above a trigger. "Don't come any closer," she warned. "I mean it! I've got pepper spray!"

He let his head dangle between his splayed arms, contemplating the ground below him and the mess his life had just become. He swallowed thickly. "I'd...appreciate it if you'd wait till I pass out again before you...use that on me. Don't think I could...handle...puking my guts out right now."

"Well, maybe you should have thought about that before you tried to kill the only person who's given a damn about you all night," she said, backing up. Peripherally, he was aware of the sound of tears in her voice.

Right. Should've. Would've. Ah, hell. Two of her swayed before him, making him feel oddly off balance. He had to get the hell out of here, get to some cover. But the ground rose up to meet him as he rolled onto his back in a boneless sprawl. Black spots swam through his vision. The cold asphalt stung his damp back and deepened the chill that had begun to work at his insides. "Go then. Get outta here."

The woman sent a helpless look around her, uncertain what to do next. "Go?"

He ran his tongue over his parched lips. Even breathing was getting harder. His gaze circled in on her and he could think of only one thing to say. With an effort, he lifted his head off the ground and looked right at her. "You got bad timing, cupcake," he said. "Amazing eyes...but...lousy timing."

"Don't call me cupcake."

"Get outta here," he said, dropping his head to the ground again. The pain in his shoulder stole his breath momentarily. At some gut level, he understood now why wolves crawled off to die alone, to spare themselves the humiliation of exposing the weakness that was settling over him like a two-ton shroud. And still she stood, waiting for some answer he couldn't give her.

"Go!" he barked in a voice that didn't seem to belong to him. "Get outta here!"

She stumbled backward a couple more steps. "Bastard."

He wasn't sure if she'd said the word or it had simply echoed in his brain. Out of the corner of his vision, he watched her hesitate, then move toward her car.

The world began to spin in a slow, sickening spiral, like water being sucked down a drain.

Stars. Clouds. Him.

All but the nagging suspicion that there was something he'd needed to do. Something important. But down it went with everything else. Like bad water.

He could feel himself dying. And his last hope was backing away like a frightened cat. *Go,* he told her silently. *Run.* Before you get caught in the whirlpool.

But some other instinct, welling up from the depths of him, was stronger. The same force that had willed him up out of that canyon and onto the road, clawing back toward life.

He heard himself call her name.

She turned. The moonlight spilled over her stunned expression.

With the last of his strength, he spoke two words as foreign to him as surrender. "Help...me."

And then everything went black.

Chapter 2

Tess watched him sleep.

The overhead fluorescents cast stark shadows across his eyes. Eyes that moved beneath their lids, following some dream he wrestled with in silence. Beyond that, he was absolutely still, hauling himself steadily back from the precipice he'd nearly fallen off. Thin lines of fluids dripped into his veins with the steady rhythm of his breathing.

She had no idea what compelled her to sit here with him. By rights she should have dumped him in the lobby of the ER and walked—no, *run*—away. But her reasons for sitting beside him now had less to do with logic than with emotion. An emotion so foreign to her she couldn't even identify it. She told herself it was simple curiosity. That she'd never been one to let a mystery go. And this man was something more than a mystery. He was an enigma.

But it wasn't even that that held her here at his bedside. Nor, she had decided, was it simply the duty she felt as a physician to follow his case to its logical conclusion. It was something else. Something…stronger. It was the look in his eye when he'd called out to her back on that road. The loneliness she'd glimpsed. The desperation. She couldn't explain why, but she didn't want him to wake up here alone. For the first time in years, someone needed her.

"You got bad timing, cupcake. Amazing eyes, but lousy timing."

Tess dropped her head into her hands. *Cupcake.* What kind of a man called a woman like her cupcake? A doctor whose reputation was so by-the-book that residents had made jokes about her sensible earrings being screwed on a little too tight. And whose idea of fun for the last two years was staring at strands of DNA through an electron microscope.

And he was right about her timing. It was consistently, undisputably bad. But she couldn't help but wonder how he'd known that about her. And what he'd meant by it. That, had she come only a few minutes later, he would have been dead and none of this would have happened?

Tess moaned in self-reproach. That the question had even found a voice in her thoughts appalled her. This man was dangerous. Most likely a criminal. Certainly no one she had any desire to know. God only knew who he'd thought she was, who he'd been waiting for out there. No one good, that was certain. And yet…

She found herself still here, long after his vital signs had stabilized. Why? Was it purely Hippocratic duty that kept her here? Or—and the thought actually frightened her—did she actually hope that he would look at her one more time the way he had out there on the road? Was she really so pathetic that a simple plea from a desperate stranger could leave her clinging to a feeling she'd thought she'd never have again?

It occurred to her then that Daniel may indeed have been

right about her needing a vacation. She was definitely in trouble here.

"You all right, Dr. Gordon?" asked the plump RN holding the silver chart at the foot of the bed. "You wanna call somebody to come get you?"

"Thanks, Earline," she said, forcing a smile. "I'm fine." She stood, stretching the stiffness out of her back. "I should go."

"Yeah, you should," Earline agreed with a musical lilt to her earthy voice. "You're not doin' anybody any good stayin' here with him. You should be home in your own bed, gettin' some rest. It's been a bad night for you."

That, Tess thought, was something of an understatement. She'd contemplated calling Gil, but decided the hour was too late, and saw no point in upsetting him in the middle of the night when she was perfectly capable of—

"Don't you be worryin' about him, now," Earline continued, laying a hand against the arm of the man on the bed. Her dark skin was in sharp contrast to the pallor of his. "We'll take good care of him."

"And who's doing the surgery?" Tess asked, frowning.

Earline smiled patiently, moving toward the hallway. "Waltrip. He's on his way."

"Right," she said automatically. Earline had told her that ten minutes ago. Dean Waltrip was a perfectly capable surgeon. Thorough. Exacting.

And pompous as hell.

He'd overseen her surgical rotation in residency. Oh, he'd have a good laugh over her involvement in this whole thing. Tess, the chickenhearted, in over her head again.

What did that matter? After tonight, what happened to this stranger would be Waltrip's problem, not hers. And personally, she could think of no sweeter revenge.

Flame exploded from the barrel of the snub-nosed .38, hammering him with all the sound and fury of a cannon and sending him flying.

He jolted awake with a guttural gasp, the blast still ringing in his ears. Hands pressed him backward. Agony exploded in his shoulder. A voice said something from far away, but he couldn't comprehend it. An antiseptic smell assaulted his senses.

Dark figures swam through the overhead lights that were blinding him, and instinct warned him back toward that darkness he'd just left. That haven of nothingness appealed.

Then he heard her.

That throaty, familiar voice. A tether he reached for, linking him to something. Anything recognizable.

"He didn't tell me his name," he heard her say. "Let me try."

He blinked at the feel of a hand on his arm. Warm. Don't stop, he thought, forcing his eyes to focus.

"Hey, can you hear me?"

Shadows coalesced into form. Chocolate-brown eyes peered down at him from a face that he could only compare with a valentine—heart shaped, delicate, angelic.

He remembered then: the headlights; the violent chill of the pavement. The woman. *She hadn't left him.*

"Cupcake?" he croaked.

A breath of relief escaped her. "Close."

"Where—?" His voice rasped in his throat like sandpaper.

"You're safe now. Don't worry." She glanced up at the little baggies of fluid strung above him, somehow connected to his arms. "Just lie still. You're gonna be okay."

Okay? His shoulder burned like a son of a bitch and he felt like a piece of Swiss cheese, full of black holes and questions. He couldn't remember anything after he'd passed out back there on that road. "How did I...get—"

"You don't remember? I brought you here." She tugged on her lower lip with her teeth. "How do you feel?"

He swallowed thickly. "Like roadkill."

A reluctant smile escaped her.

He remembered her name now. Tess. Tess with the voice like Tennessee whiskey, and guts to match. The overhead lights hurt his eyes. His hand encountered the gauzy bulk of a bandage wrapped against his skull. Beneath it, a tenderness that throbbed its way back to a dull ache.

The pale green walls and sterile curtains surrounding them reminded him of something. He couldn't think what. Something stiff was pressed under his nose, blowing air up his nostrils. He clawed it off as the situation sank in.

IVs. Antiseptic.

Hospital.

His pulse galloped into overdrive and pinged like a depth charge from some machine out of his view. Damn! She'd taken him to a hospital!

"Don't take that off," she scolded, pushing him back with surprising ease and readjusting the annoyance under his nose.

He cursed silently at his pathetic lack of strength. He needed to tell her. Warn her. This was all wrong. "Listen to me—"

"Try to relax." Her hand circled his bare forearm. "I promise I won't leave until I'm sure you're okay."

Okay? What the hell was *okay?* And would she know it if she saw it?

"Get the hell out of here," he told her, shoving himself up onto one elbow as the room took a slow spin.

She looked vaguely insulted. "What?"

"I mean it."

She shook her head. "You're upset. That's expected. You've had a terrible—"

Expected! He threw his covers off, only to feel the cold, telling rush of air against his bare skin.

"Damn!" he growled, looking down at himself.

He heard her gasp and saw the flush of color tint her cheeks as she took in the sight of him in the altogether.

Yanking the sheet back over him, he swore again. "Where the hell are my clothes?"

Her gaze jerked guiltily back up to his face. "Um, they're…" She jerked a thumb toward a closet behind her, then pressed her lips together and stiffened her shoulders. "Don't worry about your clothes. You're not going anywhere."

He grabbed that bird-like wrist of hers and drew her closer. The sight of his blood on her pale blue T-shirt crystalized his urgency. "I gotta get out of here."

"You're scheduled for surgery in—"

"They'll find me," he interrupted. "And when they find me, they find you."

Tess's lips parted in shock.

"You okay, Dr. Gordon?" a female voice asked from the doorway. As he released Tess's wrist, a plump nurse with skin the color of fine Swiss chocolate appeared, narrowing a look at him. He wondered who she was talking to, and he searched past Tess's shoulder for the bastard who'd hooked him up to all these tubes.

"I'm fine, Earline. He's just upset," Tess answered, as if the nurse had directed the question at her. "He's still a little disoriented."

He was definitely a little slow on the uptake, but he blinked up at her, comprehension dawning. "You— you're…a doctor?" he stammered.

She shrugged with a guilty little lift of her shoulder.

"She saved *your* sorry behind tonight, and that's a fact," Earline interjected. "You were one lucky man, my friend.

Um-hmm. She's one of the best ER docs around, no matter what she calls herself these days."

Tess studied the floor. "I don't think your patient is particularly interested in my personal life, Earline."

On the contrary, he thought. This was just getting interesting.

Duly chastised, Earline concentrated on a syringe she was filling, but the "you-can-deny-it-all-you-want" look on her face remained.

When Tess leaned over him, she'd recaptured her professional cool. "Do you remember what happened tonight?"

He squeezed his eyes shut and moistened his cracked lips with his tongue. They felt as swollen and raw as his thought processes. Her question tumbled over and over in his brain until he forgot what she'd asked him. He felt certain of only two things: the gnawing feeling that if he didn't get the hell out of here now, he would never leave this place alive, and the certainty that she was neck-deep in it beside him.

Above him, Earline was doing something to his IV, eyeing him like a wildcat trainer would an unpredictable animal. He returned the favor.

"Not very grateful, is he?" Earline remarked.

Tess's mouth lifted in a crooked smile. "He's not the grateful type."

He turned his scowl on her. "We need to talk." He swung a dark, impotent look at Earline, then deliberately back at Tess. "Alone."

Tess hesitated for only a moment. She cleared her throat. "Earline, could you, um, excuse us for just a second?"

"Ohh…" Earline frowned. "I don't know…. You sure, Dr. Gordon?"

"It's okay."

"Well, all right, but you call if you need me, hear?"

Tess didn't take her eyes off him. She simply nodded. When Earline had gone, she lifted the slender guardrail at the side of his bed with a deliberate clank, placing it firmly between them.

Gauntlet thrown, shields up. All right then.

His gaze slid up to her face. His first impressions out there in the dark hadn't been wrong. She had the kind of face painters search for, with dark, soulful eyes that belied the cool restraint she showed the world; pale, flawless skin that seemed almost translucent under the harsh hospital lights; and a mouth that undid all the straight laces she'd wound around herself. And as she regarded him now, those lips trembled ever so slightly, searching for control.

"You're afraid of me," he said. It wasn't a question.

She stiffened. "Should I be?"

"Hell, yes," he said, his eyes never straying from hers. "You should'a left me there."

"Hindsight is the better part of valor," she retorted, then looked away. "Besides, I couldn't."

"Why not? Hippocratic oath?"

The phrase had an edge of sarcasm that made her blanch. "Something like that."

"There's a comfort."

Her knuckles whitened on the rail. "You asked me to help you."

"I was out of my head." His gaze fell to the telltale bruises on her throat. He'd put them there.

"You were *dying*. Do you think you're the first out-of-it patient to wake up disoriented, and blindside me?"

He remembered the crush of her breasts against his chest and he wondered if her lips were just as soft. Ruthlessly, he shoved those thoughts from his mind with the knowledge that had she been damned lucky he hadn't killed her tonight.

"I want you t'leave," he said, ignoring the thickness

spreading through his bloodstream like blackstrap molasses. "Take yer name off the charts an' go."

She frowned. "I—I'm not the attending. I…I don't even practice anymore."

"Who…signed me in?"

"I did, but—"

"Tess, gimme my clothes."

That brick-wall look crept back into her expression. "I can't do that."

"Goddammit!" He rolled to his side. She promptly stopped him.

"Who did this to you? Who are you afraid of?"

Fuzziness was stealing into his brain. His lips, his fingers, his legs tingled with the odd sensation. "Yer init now, too," he said, hearing the words slide together. "Disappear, Tess. Don' tell 'em wha'chu know."

"What?" She blinked uncomprehendingly, fear etched in her expression. "I don't know anything. I don't even know your name!"

His name…his name…

Frowning, he looked at the closet across the room. It looked a thousand miles away. But he shoved himself up and pulled the IV needle ruthlessly from his arm.

She gaped at him. "Wh-what do you think you're *doing?*"

He yanked the sheet out of its moorings and threw his legs over the opposite side of the bed as Tess scrambled around the end of it. The room tipped dangerously.

"Don't even think about trying to—"

He lurched to his feet, sure he could make it as far as the damned closet, but the floor seemed to shift under his feet like the deck of a boat. He clamped a hand against his throbbing head and skewered the IV with a black look. "What? Did'yu *drug* me?"

Tess was there then, wrapping her arms around his naked

chest, holding him up. He groaned at the contact against the mass of bruises on his ribs and kept a precarious hold on the sheet dangling around his hips.

"You idiot," she said, catching her breath against his shoulder. "Of course we drugged you! What are you trying to do, kill yourself?"

He sent her an ironic look. "Tha's funny, Tess. Really…funny." Stumbling backward as the room started a slow rotation, he held on to her as a drunkard would a lamppost. Only Tess was no lamppost, and the way she felt in his arms was something even his hazy brain couldn't ignore.

Maybe it was the drugs buzzing through his veins, or the soft press of her breasts against his chest. Maybe it was just that he felt so damned alone. But it stunned him how much he wanted her to hold him, how much he didn't want her to let go.

But she did.

Tess siphoned him backward onto the bed. "Is there someone I can call for you?"

Her voice had an echo that throbbed at the back of his head. The room continued its slow sickening spin. Who should he call? *A friend. A friend would help him.* His brain ached. He couldn't think. Couldn't remember a friend. Did he have any?

"What's—yoourr—naaame?" she asked oh-so-slowly.

He blinked. Numbness stole through him. His name? Hell, it was right on the tip of his tongue. Couldn't spit it out. An image of a hand slipping into a pocket flitted through his mind, then vanished. Closet. *Look in my jacket,* he wanted to say. *It's all there. It must be. I'm somebody.*

"Yoourr naaame," she repeated more urgently. "Tell meee your naaame."

"Jacke—" Jacket. *Jacket.*

Surprise spread across her heart-shaped face. "Jack? Your name's Jack?"

Oh, hell.

Blackness circled in on him again, a dark wing flapping away any arguments. Another voice slipped into the swirl of noise. He strained to hear it.

"Dr. Gordon? The police are waiting outside to talk to you."

And then there was only silence.

The two men standing near the window turned as she entered the waiting room. The taller one, a thick-waisted man of fifty with graying hair and a nose like a hammer, smiled at her. She supposed it was meant to be friendly, but she was too tired to respond in kind.

"Dr. Gordon?"

"Yes," she answered, taking the man's extended hand, and hoping he couldn't feel the tremble in hers. She looked down at the blood still smeared on her T-shirt and caked under her fingernails. "Sorry," she said.

"No problem," he said. "Detective Bruener, ma'am. This is Detective Rivera." He pointed to his partner. The other man, a slightly younger version of Robert DeNiro, was all swagger and pecs. "We understand that you were the one who found the gunshot victim up on Angelo Canyon?"

"That's right. Can I see some ID, gentlemen?"

They exchanged looks and reached into their pockets. Both flashed badges at her, then withdrew them. "We understand it's been a trying night, ma'am, so we don't want to prolong it." He flipped open a small notebook and took a pen from his pocket. The younger detective lit up a cigarette and half turned toward the hallway leading to the ER.

"If you could just give us your full name, phone number and address for our records—"

Uneasiness flared through her. "There's no smoking in here, Detective Rivera."

The man didn't seem to hear her immediately, then spun around guiltily. "What?"

"Your cigarette."

"Geez, Rivera," Bruener snapped. "You know better than that. Snub that out."

Rivera did. "It's been a long night," he said in his own defense.

"Dr. Gordon," Bruener began again. "Your address? For my report."

"What division did you say you were from?" she asked.

Bruener narrowed his eyes. "Santa Monica. Have you talked to the victim, ma'am? Has he given you any indication of how he was shot? Or...who shot him?"

Disappear, Tess. Don't tell them what you know. Tess blinked. Tell who? Surely he didn't mean the police? Still, she said, "He hasn't talked much at all. He's quite ill."

Bruener looked at Rivera. The younger detective looked away and flicked at his fingernail with a click-click-clicking sound.

"We're anxious to talk to him."

"That's impossible right now. He's going up to surgery soon."

"You his doctor?"

"I don't practice anymore, Detective."

"No? How come?" Bruener gave her a blank, detective stare.

"I hardly think that's relevant."

"Kind of a coincidence, you finding him up there, you bein' a doctor and all," Rivera commented in a voice that betrayed his East L.A. roots.

"How's that?" she asked. "Do you mean that if I hadn't been a doctor I wouldn't have stopped?"

Rivera smiled at her. "No ma'am, I didn't mean that at all."

Bruener interrupted again. "Approximately what time did you stop for him, ma'am?"

"Around eleven forty-five."

He scribbled that down. "You sure about that time?"

"I looked at my dashboard clock after I nearly ran off the road swerving to avoid him." She glanced at her wristwatch. Little more than an hour had passed since then. For the first time since it all happened, fatigue pressed in on her. She longed to close her eyes.

"And he didn't say what happened to him?"

"I was more concerned with saving his life than interrogating him, Detective."

"Sure. Naturally."

Glancing distractedly at his book as he scratched out something in ink, she thought of Jack lying unconscious in that bed. Uneasiness tugged at her. His words had frightened her, but they could have been nothing more than disoriented rantings. Still, instinct argued that point. Someone had done their damnedest to kill him tonight. What if what he said was true? What if she was in danger? What if they both were?

"—who'd been beaten and shot wouldn't be in much of a mood to talk," Bruener was saying, still writing in his notebook.

Tess blinked. "I'm sorry, what?"

The older cop looked up. "Just saying it's not uncommon to get very little out of a shooting victim at the scene. These things are usually related to some kind of crime, and the perp, if he's conscious, has no reason to spill his guts."

"Perp?" she repeated incredulously. "As far as I'm concerned, Detective, he's a victim. Now if there's nothing else—"

"You never gave me your phone number and address, ma'am."

She hesitated. *Don't tell them anything.*

Rivera swiveled his head, looking at her intently. Bruener's pen sat poised above the paper.

"Tell you what. I'll come down in the morning and give you a full statement. I'm tired. I want to go home. Santa Monica, you said?"

Bruener's mouth opened and closed, then he shrugged. "That's a lot of trouble for you."

She smiled thinly. "No trouble at all. Ten o'clock, then?"

He flipped his notebook shut with a look at Rivera. "Ten is fine."

"Good night, gentlemen."

"Ma'am," both men said as she turned and left the waiting room.

She walked past the nurses' station, down the hallway toward Jack's room. Her head ached. She suddenly wanted to put this whole ugly night behind her, go home and sink into a hot, steaming tub of water. She didn't want to think about guns, or blood, or Jack. Or the niggling sense that something was wrong.

Of course something is wrong, idiot, she berated herself. *Your life is a Clint Eastwood movie, gone awry!*

She ran a hand through her hair as she passed her reflection in a door. God, she looked like hell. Ten o'clock would come early tomorrow. She should have just given them her address and been done with the whole mess.

She slowed her step. Why hadn't she? Tess stared at the granite speckles on the polished linoleum floor. Because they'd made her uncomfortable? Because she didn't like the way Rivera looked at her?

"A guy who'd been beaten and shot wouldn't be in much of a mood to talk."

Bruener's words echoed in her head. *Beaten and shot.* She frowned. Listening to the rush of blood in her ears, she felt a sick sensation work its way up her throat. No one had said a word about "beaten." She certainly hadn't. And they hadn't had a look at Jack yet. How would they know that?

An orderly hurried by her, rattling a crash cart. A flurry of activity moved to the other end of the hall.

And the detectives hadn't asked her one question about where in Angelo Canyon she'd found him. She was familiar enough with police procedure to know that they would yellow tape the area to investigate. Maybe even take her back up there to point out the place. But Bruener and Rivera had seemed more concerned with what the man had said to her. Why?

Tess squeezed her eyes shut and braced her hand against the wall. She was probably being ridiculous. What she knew about police procedure had come secondhand through Adam, and he rarely talked about his work to her. But something didn't feel right.

She'd seen enough badges to recognize a phony one when she saw it. Theirs had been the genuine article. She was just being paranoid. Looking at shadows and seeing monsters. Maybe one of the nurses had told them about Jack's face and the bruises there. That had to be it.

Still, something niggled at her.

In her mind's eye, she kept seeing Rivera light up that cigarette. In itself it meant nothing, except what cop in Los Angeles didn't know better than to light up in a public building?

Silly, ridiculous worries, she reasoned, pushing away from the wall. This was real life, not television. Not a Clint Eastwood movie. Bruener and Rivera were just cops doing a hard job. And Jack had simply found himself in the wrong place at the wrong time.

She headed toward the sliding glass doors at the end of the hallway. In the reflection, she saw Rivera leave the waiting area, heading toward the bank of phones near the nurses' station at the end of the hall. He hadn't turned in her direction, but glanced around the empty hallway ahead of him.

Tess stopped walking. Nothing in her experience urged her to do what she did next. In fact, little conscious thought went into it. Adrenaline drove her. That and the stupid promise she'd made to Jack. *I won't leave until I'm sure it's okay.*

Making an abrupt about-face, she walked silently to the now-empty nurses' station, turning sharply into the carousel while watching Rivera, whose back was still toward her. He was only five feet away. Pulling a chart from the stack, she lowered it behind the counter, then bent as if to pick it up. She heard him punch in a number and wait.

"Yeah, it's me, *jefe,*" he said softly after a moment. "We got him. Yeah. Son of a bitch is still alive."

Cold shock fingered up her spine. She froze against the file cabinets, out of sight, and forgot to breathe. Rivera had fallen silent, absorbing the verbal attack even she could hear coming from the other end of the line.

"I don't know," he said tightly when it was over. "I— I mean…we're not sure. She's one tight-assed *chica.*"

Outrage puckered Tess's mouth before the obvious dawned on her. He wasn't just rude. He was wrapping her into this whole horrid conversation he was having about Jack as if she were part of the whole, unbelievable package!

"Right," Rivera continued. "Uh-uh. Don't worry, he won't get by us this time. Send Ajax."

Chapter 3

Tess hardly heard the detective's footsteps recede after he hung up the phone. She crouched, staring at a black smudge on the floor, afraid to move. Nausea roiled her stomach. They were going to kill him!

If they find me, they'll find you, he'd said. *Disappear, Tess. Don't tell them what you know.*

Jack had warned her. He was afraid. Afraid of this very thing. Had she listened? No, she'd walked right up to the lion's mouth and pried open its teeth!

Somewhere above her, the station phone gave a muffled beep. Someone would come to answer it. She had to get out of here.

On her hands and knees, she crawled toward the opening. The waiting room was directly opposite. She could hear voices from within. Rivera was talking to Bruener, saying something she couldn't make out.

Her heart thundered against the wall of her chest as she peeked around the corner. Coast clear. She shot to her feet and hurried toward Jack, without the faintest idea what she would do. A nurse rounded the corner and gave her a strange look as she walked hurriedly past her. Flashing her a smile, Tess veered down the same corridor the nurse had come from, passing room after room of patients.

Think. Think! What to do? Call the police? A hysterical laugh nearly tumbled out of her. They *are* the police!

Or were they? How could she know? She could call Gil. Gil would know what to do. He was her best friend. She would trust him with her life.

But if she told him, would she be putting his life in danger as well? Undeniably. Could he get here in time to prevent whatever "Ajax" was going to do?

These guys weren't messing around. If they were cops, they were bold enough to talk face-to-face with a witness. If they weren't, it could only mean one thing. That they didn't care if she saw them or not. Because they meant to kill her, too.

Your phone number and address for my records, Dr. Gordon?

She sucked in air. Dear God. They knew her name. Finding her house would be child's play. Except it was listed under her married name. Hackford. That might slow them down.

She had to get out of here. She had to get Jack out of here! That would be a good trick, considering that he had ten milligrams of Vistarel cruising through his veins. She rounded a corner and nearly tripped over a wheelchair parked there.

Rubbing her knee, she stumbled into the curtained area where Jack lay. Earline jerked a surprised look up at her. "Dr. Gordon?"

Out of breath, she smoothed a hand down her unruly hair and smiled. "Oh. Hello."

"Is everything all right?"

"Fine," she answered, gulping down her hysteria. "How, um, how's our patient?"

Earline sent her an easy smile. "Sleepin' like a baby."

Tess let out a breathless laugh. "Good…good." *Damn!* She rubbed a hand across her mouth, thinking, staring at the thick padding of bandage taped across his shoulder.

Earline raised her eyebrows and grinned a little wickedly at her. "He may be ungrateful, but he's not hard on the eyes, is he? My, my, my…"

Taken aback, she glanced at the nurse, then at Jack and the masculine dusting of hair that veed down toward his taut abdomen. Indeed, he *wasn't* hard on the eyes. Asleep as he was, the dangerous planes of his face softened to simply appealing and gave him the sort of boyish charm women like her ran from.

"Must be somebody missing him," Earline mused aloud with a shake of her head. "Man like that, he gotta have somebody home waitin' for him."

Did he? Tess wondered suddenly. A wife? A girlfriend? A family?

"You get his name?"

Tess jerked her gaze up at Earline. "Uh…he said…Jack."

"Jack." Earline nodded. "Well, at least that's better than John Doe."

Tess nodded distractedly. "Listen, Earline, I—I can stay here for a while. Watch him. I'm sure you've got a million things to do."

The plump nurse frowned at the chart in her hands, tempted. "Nah, that's okay."

"No, really. You know I can handle it."

She sighed. "We all miss you here, Doc. You know we do."

A smile flickered on Tess's mouth. "Thanks. I miss it sometimes, too," she lied. "I haven't lost my touch. Look, he's in la-la land. I'll call you if anything happens. Why don't you go grab a cup? It's the witching hour."

Earline glanced down at Jack, tugging the light blanket over him. "Well, I suppose he's not goin' anywhere. You sure you're okay here? I thought you wanted to go home."

"I do," she said quickly. "I—I just thought I'd wait till he goes up for surgery. I'm fine. Really. Go."

The nurse replaced the chart. "Thanks. Back in five."

"Don't hurry," Tess told her lightly.

The curtain had hardly swished shut before she was leaning over him, her hands curled into the flimsy blanket covering him. "Jack?" she whispered, shaking him. "Jack, wake up!"

He mumbled something from the twilight zone.

"Jack, I'm not kidding. Wake up!" *Oh, please wake up.*

He stirred restively against the pillow.

"This is life or death, Jack. I mean it. This is no time to be sleeping."

"Cupcake?" he muttered.

"Yes!" she almost crowed. "It's me! Cupcake! Wake up, now. You have to open your eyes, Jack."

Slowly, he did. "Huh?" he said, frowning at her, trying to blink away the drug-induced grogginess.

"Oh, you were *so* right, Jack," she said, yanking IV needles out of his arms and the tape that held them there.

"Ow!"

"Sorry," she mumbled. "Ho, boy, I'm definitely going to lose my license over this." She took his face between her hands, forcing him to look at her. "Jack, I should never have brought you here. We've got to get out of here. You think you can walk?"

He blinked at his feet.

"What am I thinking? Of course you can't."

Jack silently agreed as he watched her yank open a drawer full of bandages and packages of surgical gloves, and stuff a few in her purse. From a pushed-aside tray on wheels, she took some medieval-looking instrument whose purpose he didn't want to think about and shoved that into her purse as well. He blinked hard, trying to clear his head.

She yanked his clothes from the closet, but shoved his arms into a hospital gown. He thought to protest that if they were going somewhere, he wanted his pants on, but she didn't give him the chance.

She disappeared through the curtains and returned hauling a wheelchair. "C'mon," she said, reaching out to him. "Don't ask me what the hell I'm doing. Committing professional suicide," she said in answer to her own question.

His head whirled. He felt a little giddy as she forced him up, and he smiled at her with a silly grin. She was so damned pretty.

She tilted a look at him. "You're in no pain, right? Amazing what a little Vistarel'll do, huh? Oh, one last thing." Mercilessly, she ripped the heart monitor patches from his chest.

"Oww!"

"Sorry again," she said with a distinct lack of sincerity. "Okay, here we go."

He scowled at her, but had the impression that she wanted him to stand up, so he did. At least he tried. His legs didn't seem to get the message. Catching him, her arms went hard around his ribs and her face flattened against his chest as she shoved him back against the bed. He felt like a mizzenmast—all top-heavy and listing. And she…? Hell, she felt spectacular. All warm and soft and—

"Jack," she said, breathing hard. "Listen to me. Right next to you is a wheelchair."

Her skin, he noticed, was pale as porcelain. He wanted to drop his mouth against it. Taste it.

"*Jack!* Concentrate!"

He blinked hard. She was trying to tell him something,

but he couldn't focus. Not with her breasts against him like they were. And why was she calling him Jack?

"One—two—three!"

She pushed him backward and he fell. Something caught him at the knees. The impact stole his breath. The fire in his shoulder leaped back to life and he grabbed it with his hand. Black spots swam before his eyes, and, intermittently, so did her face as she propped his feet up somewhere beneath him.

"Sorry, Jack. Don't pass out on me now. I need you."

Need you. Need you. Those words rattled endlessly in his head as she shoved his boots and shirt and pants into his lap and sped down a hallway at warp speed toward a service elevator whose doors whooshed open for them. He forgot where they were going. But he trusted her to take him there. He had no other choice.

The monitor alarm at the nurses' station went off just as Earline wandered back from the coffee room. She was stirring in the amaretto-flavored nondairy creamer with a swizzle stick as the warning alarm sounded. She glanced at the board, immediately identified the patient and swore.

"Code blue!" she shouted to an orderly slouching against a laundry hamper nearby. "Code blue, dammit! Stat!" The man leaped into action, scrambling for the nearest crash cart.

The two men in the waiting room watched Earline dump her coffee on the desk and run in the direction of their man. Rivera and Bruener exchanged glances and followed, hard on her heels.

She tore open the curtain, ready to do battle. A perfectly empty bed was the last thing she expected to find. Openmouthed, she stared at it as if it were a spaceship dropped in for a landing. "Uh-oh."

Bruener skidded to a stop beside her. "Tell me this isn't our boy's bed."

"Oh-hh, yeah," she said.

The detective snarled something colorful as his partner reached the door.

"Where'd he go?" Rivera demanded, out of breath.

Bruener didn't answer as he bolted down the hallway. They both knew where he'd gone, and more importantly, with whom.

She'd done some crazy things in her life, but nothing even remotely like this, she thought as she crammed Jack's well-muscled frame back into her car. God knew what crime she could be charged with. Kidnaping? Aiding and abetting? Not to mention what she'd stolen.

She slammed the passenger door and raced to the other side. Before she could duck into the driver's seat, however, she saw the service entrance doors fly open with a bang and the two detectives charge out, guns drawn, into the circle of light below the parking lot floodlight. Her heart jumped into her throat.

She ducked into the car, shut the door quietly and turned the key. Jamming the car into Drive, she peeled out of the parking lot without her lights, praying that they wouldn't be able to read her license. In her rearview mirror, she watched them run for a car in the parking lot. Then she lost sight of them.

She gunned the car down the road, squealing the tires and fishtailing onto Arizona.

"Hang on," she told Jack, who braced his hand against the dashboard, his eyes riveted to the road. She tore down Arizona, swung left on Seventeenth, then right on Washington. Minutes ticked by. All the while, her gaze flicked up to the rearview mirror, catching glimpses of headlights a quarter of a mile back.

Damn!

She wrenched the wheel to the right, slipping down a small alleyway between a row of upscale Santa Monica apartment buildings. The engine raced loudly and the Honda flew over a speed bump in the alleyway seconds before she spotted the ungated parking slots beneath the last building.

Slamming on her brakes, she backed up, maneuvered into a spot and cut the engine. Ducking down, she watched the alleyway to her left for the detectives' car to pass. In a few seconds, it did. And it didn't come back.

Tess released the breath she didn't realize she'd been holding and tilted her head back against the headrest. Her hands were shaking and she couldn't hang on to the wheel. She let them fall in her lap and slid a look at Jack. He sat staring wordlessly at her. He looked pale, but better than he'd looked back on the road little less than two hours ago, thanks to the fluids they'd pumped into him in the ER.

"You okay?" she asked, her voice shaking.

His fingers flexed against his throbbing shoulder. "What the hell just happened?"

She propped her hands over her mouth to stay the bubble of hysteria that threatened to burst. "I think," she said, "I just threw away about nine years' worth of medical school."

He looked past her, out the darkened window. "Who were they?"

"Cops." Her voice had risen an octave. "Or not. I don't know. All I do know is they meant to kill you and possibly me, unless my overactive imagination has conjured this whole thing up. Has it, Jack? 'Cause I'm way out on a limb here and I hear the darned thing cracking underneath me!"

He reached out and took her shaking hand in his. For reasons she couldn't imagine, she allowed it. That solitary, silent gesture spoke volumes and dissipated a large chunk of terror that had lodged in her throat. Whatever was going on, they were in it together now.

"Not," he said in answer to her question, "unless we're both imagining this." He glanced pointedly at his shoulder.

She blinked at the feel of his thumb rubbing back and forth against the back of her hand, then pulled away. "You've got to be straight with me. What happened out there and who are those guys?"

He squeezed his eyes shut. "I don't know."

She'd been prepared for a lot of possibilities, but certainly not denial. "*What?* Don't play games with me here! It's only a matter of time before they swing back this way and find us, but I swear to you I'm not moving until you tell me what's going on!"

His large fist clenched along his thigh. "I'm being straight with you. I don't know."

She blinked twice, reining in her quickly rising temper. "Are you trying to tell me that—that you have no idea who those guys who shot you are? That they decided to kill you for no particular reason? And then pursued you into the emergency room of a reputable hospital with every intention of—" She broke off, unable to finish.

"No. Yes." He tipped his head backward. "I'm trying to tell you that I don't...remember."

"*What?*"

The pain was ebbing back to his shoulder in dull waves and he stared out the darkened window, trying to grasp the truth himself. "I don't remember. Anything."

She gaped at him for a full ten seconds. "Y-you mean about tonight? About what happened?"

"Anything," he repeated, sliding a look of desperation at her. "Where I live...what I did yesterday, or the day before that." The weight of it settled like a stone on him as he realized the full implications for the first time.

Her gaze didn't stray from his face. "Some memory loss

is normal on presentation of a head injury like yours. Missing minutes. Even hours..."

"It's a blank, Tess! My whole damned life is one big black hole! I don't even exist! Do you understand?"

He was scaring her, and she shrank back against the seat. In a small voice, she said, "But you said you thought they'd come for you. How did you know?"

"I just knew. Instinct maybe." He stared at her, unflinching. "I was right."

A full ten seconds ticked by. "If you're lying to me—"

"Why would I lie?"

She narrowed a look at him. "You told me your name was Jack."

"No, I didn't."

"Y-you're Jack. You told me. That's your name."

He shook his head. "I don't even remember telling you that."

"You told me in the hospital, as the Vistarel was taking eff—" Her eyes went wide. "Ho, boy."

She braced both hands on the steering wheel, then dropped her cheek on top of them. "Well, if that's not your name, who the heck is Jack?"

With an absurd grin, he shook his head. "Hell if I know."

A bark of semihysterical laughter escaped her. She collapsed helplessly against the steering wheel, her shoulders jerking rhythmically. But it wasn't long before he saw tears dripping off her face and onto her lap.

Oh, damn. "Hey." He reached out with one hand to comfort her. "Don't cry."

She sniffed, finally lifting her head. Her eyes were red, her nose puffy. "You're right. What's the point? It's only a career. I mean, those people on the *Twilight Zone* never cried when they woke up in an alien world, did they? Or when they discovered they were just characters whose lives were being tapped out by some typewriter on the roof. Right? But that's what I feel like. Like I've just stepped out of my life and into somebody else's.''

She looked at him, wiping her cheeks. "My life is very…*ordinary,* you know? I mow my lawn. Pay my taxes. This sort of thing just doesn't happen to people like me."

He wished he knew if it did to people like him. *Hell.* He put his hand on the door handle. "It's over," he said. "I go, you drive to the police station, tell them I forced you. Tell them whatever you want. Then forget you ever saw me."

He was offering her a way out. Whether or not it made any sense, the offer meant more to her than the possibility of walking back toward the reality she'd left almost two hours ago.

The door clicked open.

"No." Tess reached across and pulled it shut. Heaven only knew what she was getting herself into. But whatever was out there waiting for him was not going away. And she was in it now, too. "No," she said more firmly. "You wouldn't make it half a mile."

"I'm okay."

"Yeah, 'cause you've been pumped full of fluids and drugs. But in a while those'll wear off. And then…" She noted the sweat beading above his lip. "I'm not leaving you."

He gave her his full attention then, sliding his unfathomable gaze from her eyes to her mouth and back again. "You always been this stubborn, Doc, or is it just me that brings out this unreasonable streak?"

The night's events had roughened his voice, but she imagined the raw sex that vibrated from him was a natural part of who he was. Whoever he was.

"Don't flatter yourself," she said lightly. "I don't take orders well. It's a long-standing character defect of mine."

"Why doesn't that surprise me?"

"Because I suspect we're very much alike in that regard."

With his face only inches from hers, she could hardly miss the intensity that darkened his eyes and troubled his expression. Not gratitude, or even apology. More like an anarchy of emotion. She couldn't blame him. She felt nearly as confused as he must. Slowly, she eased away from his closeness.

"That bullet in your shoulder's not going anywhere on its own." She took a deep breath and stared past him into the darkness of the alley, the hollow ache of a tremor coiling inside her. "We're just going to have to trust each other for now. That's all. Take it one minute at a time. All right?"

He rolled a look at her with those Paul Newman blues. "Anybody ever tell you you're certifiable?"

"Anyone ever tell you that flattery was not your strong suit?" A hint of a smile tugged at her mouth.

"I wish I knew."

"Right," she said, taking in the glistening pallor of his skin. "So...Jack. May I call you Jack?" He shrugged in reply. She turned the key in the ignition until the Honda purred to life, then she backed out into the alley. "So, Jack," she said, shoving the car into gear, "I've been thinking.... L.A. is getting a little crowded lately. What do you say we make ourselves scarce?"

Chapter 4

Dawn tinged the horizon before they reached their destination. Late August heat lurked over the mountains, waiting for sunrise, and the air blowing against Tess's face through her window carried the redolent scent of summer. She watched the ponderosa pines that picketed the sides of the road pass by in a blur as memories of other trips up this winding highway replayed in her mind like photographs.

Click.

Cara, her best friend, laughing and boogying behind the wheel to the beat of some eighties disco band, which had made Tess laugh and fear for their lives as the steep edges of the road had loomed ever closer.

Click.

Adam, teasing a kiss from her on the night of their wedding, with the gearshift poking her hip and the two of them falling into a hopeless fit of giggles.

Click.

Silent rides with Adam as the years edged them farther

and farther apart. The mountain trips, their last-ditch efforts to repair the damage done.

Tess tipped her head out the window and inhaled deeply. The wind tore at her hair and burned her eyes. The moisture there, she told herself, was from the sting of the wind, not the memories she'd worked so hard to put behind her.

She turned off the main highway onto the familiar unpaved road that wound through a stand of paper birch. The deep green leaves shimmered almost magically in the dawn light, reminding her why she'd brought Jack here. It was part of her. The place she'd always come to heal.

A car passed them from the other direction, and she saw Jack shrink down in his seat and turn his face the other way. The driver gave a friendly wave. She returned it, hoping whoever it was didn't recognize her or her car. She was practically a local here, she'd spent so much time at Cara's cabin in the last few years. Cara was in Brazil on a film shoot, teaching Matthew McConaughey how to samba in her off-hours as a dialogue coach. She'd called to rub that juicy fact in less than a week ago. So there was no chance she'd drop in for the weekend. But Tess wondered how Cara would feel when she found out her best friend had involved her in this whole mess.

She couldn't think about that now.

Her left front wheel caught the edge of a pothole in the dry gravel road. From beside her, she heard Jack hiss in pain.

"Sorry," she said, looking over at him. He sat with eyes closed, head tilted back against a too-low headrest. He'd barely moved or spoken during the whole ride. "You okay?" Stupid question. He chose to ignore it.

"How long?" His eyes rolled beneath his closed lids and he swallowed thickly. "Till we get there."

"We're here. It's just down the road. Hang on."

He was. By his fingernails. The drugs had, indeed, worn

off, as had the fluids they'd pumped into him. Time was against them. That bullet had to come out. Blood had seeped through the bandage at his shoulder and he was shivering. Dear Lord, she couldn't think about that, either. She cranked the heat up to high and gunned the car toward the end of the lane, where Cara's cabin peeked through a stand of pine.

The driveway wound around the side of the house and ended with a spectacular view of the lake. Smooth as glass, with morning fog still drifting over it like smoke, the lake looked the same as it always had. The pines around it hadn't changed, nor had the place where the sky met the tree line beyond. But somehow everything looked different. And she had the distinct and uneasy feeling that the same was true for the rest of her life.

Tess parked and came around to Jack's side. She helped him out and he staggered against her, woozy and unbalanced, before finding his feet. Dawn lent color to the unnatural pallor of his face.

He glanced out at the lake. "Where are we?"

She helped him up two worn wooden steps. "My friend Cara Barrington's cabin. I come here a lot."

That brought his head slowly around. "Who else knows that?"

She shrugged. "No one will know where I am, if that's what you're thinking. Cara's out of the country. Her husband's an ex, and I don't really talk about this place much. It's kind of...well...private."

"What about th' neighbors?"

"Weekenders. Not many permanent residents up here."

He pressed his back against the doorjamb, eyes squeezed shut, as she felt beneath the potted geranium for the key Cara always left there. Sweat was trickling down the side of his face and drawing crescents of moisture beneath his armpits. She fumbled with the key.

"Tess—"

"This dumb lock always sticks," she said, wrestling with it.

"Hey…Tess—" His voice was a little weaker this time.

"I'm getting it. It's almost—" She practically fell through the door as it swung open. Jack followed her. But not the way she'd hoped.

Behind her, she heard a loud thud. She turned to find him sprawled facedown on the black-and-white linoleum floor. Out cold.

"*Ohh,* Jack. This is not good."

The sight of him lying there had numbness spreading up her legs and moving toward her throat. She'd been doing all right until a minute ago. Now the whole awful night pressed in on her like a giant fist, shutting her down one function at a time. She stood frozen in the empty kitchen with the stainless steel Paul Revere teakettle winking at her in the morning light and the stale scent of old pine fires hanging in the cool air. Another day, another moment like this, sneaked into her consciousness:

"Don't go in there, Tess," Paul Wyler, her second-year resident, warned her. "Somebody is on the way."

She couldn't breathe. Why couldn't she breathe?

Through the glass, she could see the nurses and paramedics swarming around the man on the ER table. A chin. A profile. Like a brick, it hit her squarely in the center of her chest.

Oh, God. Not Adam. It can't be Adam.

She could feel Paul tugging at her arm.

"Who?" she'd shouted. "Who's coming? When? He's dying! Let me go!" Paul couldn't, perhaps wouldn't, hold her. She pulled rank, barged in, took over. The other attending was gone. Surgery, they said. It was up to her to save him. Only her. Oh, God, Adam! Don't die. Don't die!

In Cara's kitchen, Tess shivered, her breath coming in

shaky gasps. It was a nightmare that visited her regularly at night, but rarely like this in the light of day. Tears welled up in her eyes. Dammit! Don't cry.

Swiping at the moisture in her eyes, she wondered what had made her think she could do this by herself. What crazy impulse had told her to steal this man out of a hospital with the looney notion that she could help him? She couldn't even get him in the house, much less do what she needed to do to save his life.

"Jack?" She touched his back, felt the slow rise and fall of his breathing. "Don't you dare die on me now. We've come too far for this. I mean it. I'll never forgive you. Jack? *Wake up!*"

He didn't so much as twitch.

She pressed her lips together and sat back on her heels. "Great. Thanks a lot for your help. I can see that you're going to leave this all up to me. Well, let me just tell you something here, pal. I'm no good at this. You know? I'm really not. In fact, I'm so bad at it that I quit it. Long ago."

Tess got to her feet and stalked out to find a quilt in the blanket chest by the couch. "That's right. Quit. *Q-U-I-T.* Get it? Finished. Never to so much as touch the frail human body again with a scalpel."

She stomped back to him and spread the quilt on the floor beside him. "And you know, Jack, that was…that was the right decision. I'm really happy in research. Content, you know?" Tess rolled Jack over onto his back on the quilt. He didn't blink an eye.

"No torn ligaments," she continued, "no stab wounds at three in the morning. No compressed skull fractures or battered wives with cheekbones that look like broken egg-shells on the X rays."

Gathering the quilt in her hands, she pulled hard, and miraculously dragged him a couple of feet. "Nope. None of that. Just…me and my microscope. And my—uhh—research. You know? *That's* productive. I can really make a difference in people's lives that way. I don't do this anymore, Jack. You get it?''

She tugged backward, nearly stumbling over her own feet as he slid across the linoleum. ''If I'd wanted to keep losing this battle, I would have gone back to practice myself. Long ago.'' She hit the carpet in the living room, and Jack's forward movement screeched to a halt like a bad brake job. She put all her weight into the effort. She heard stitches in the quilt rip as she slowly pulled him across the floor.

''So, I want you to know that I really appreciate the help you're giving me here. I had high—uhh—expectations of you, Jack. And here you are. Out cold. Not so much as a 'Buck up. Be brave. I know you can do it, Tess.'''

''I know you can do it, Tess,'' he mumbled as she pulled him to a stop in front of the river-rock fireplace.

Breathing hard, Tess slipped backward and landed hard on her behind. An embarrassed flush crept up her cheeks. ''How much of that did you hear?''

He ran his tongue over his dry lips and gave her a half-hearted grin. ''Got any whiskey?''

They stared at each other for a protracted moment, until she had to look away. He'd heard enough. And for some reason that mortified her.

''Whiskey. Great idea.'' She got to her feet and headed toward the kitchen. ''I could use a drink.''

''Tess...''

She stopped, but didn't have the nerve to look back at him. ''What?''

''I trust you.''

''You shouldn't, you know,'' she said, suddenly very tired. ''Ask anyone.''

The roaring fire spit heat into the cold room where Jack was easing into intoxication the way any man who'd lost the volume of blood he had would—*quickly*. Tess sat with her back to the fire, absorbing the warmth and watching the bottle meet his mouth.

It was, she thought without impunity, the sexiest mouth she'd ever seen on a man. Full, sensual lips that curved naturally up into a "frankly-my-dear, I-don't-give-a damn" grin, even when he wasn't smiling.

Like now.

She dragged her gaze away from his mouth and turned her attention to the mass of bruises on his bare torso. It made her shudder to think what he must have gone through. "Somebody really worked you over."

He drew one jean-clad knee up gingerly as if to alleviate the pressure on his bruised ribs. "Either that," he said, wincing, "or somebody mistook me for a landing strip." He followed her gaze to the myriad of scars on his torso.

"That looks like an old knife wound," she said, running her finger along the ridge of skin. "Someone did a bad job of stitching it up. You in the habit of having near death experiences?"

"You tell me."

"I think so. The question is, why?"

He lowered the half-empty bottle, grimaced as the whiskey went down, and let his head fall back against the pillow she'd put there. Perspiration beaded his upper lip, where a dark shadow of stubble blended with the bruises on his battered face. "You think too much, Doc. Why don't you get this bullet out of me now?"

Pulling her gaze away from his chest, she asked, "Are you drunk yet?"

"Since I still understan' the question...no."

"I want you unconscious."

He hummed in amusement. "Bet you say that to all the guys."

She wrinkled her nose with a false smile.

"Yer hands're shaking."

Tess clenched them in her lap. "No, they're not." She glanced up through her lashes at him. "Okay, maybe they are. I haven't done this in a long time."

"What? Watched someb'dy get drunk?"

She tipped her head sideways, annoyed that he could be making light of this, considering what she was about to do. "This is no laughing matter, Jack."

"No? What the hell is it, then? A funeral?" He took another gulp.

"I don't think that's funny." Tension slid up the back of her neck. The nausea that had been threatening roiled earnestly now in the pit of her stomach, while her nerve folded up like a piece of origami. Fear took hold, the certainty that she would fail—fail herself, fail the promise that she'd made to herself never to risk another person's life, and worst of all, fail Jack.

Tess shot to her feet and paced to the window with her fingers pressed over her mouth. "This is crazy," she said. "What are we doing here? I could kill you just trying to get the damn thing out. I have no equipment, no anesthetic...." And the antibiotics they'd given him at the hospital weren't working as well as they should. He had a fever. That meant infection. If nothing else should have compelled her to take him back, that should have. "Look," she said, "I shouldn't even be operating on you with—"

Halfway to his mouth, the bottle stopped. "Tess—"

"—a fever, which I can't treat here. I should take you back to a hospital."

He dropped his head against the pillow and shut his eyes. "Ahh, geez."

She shook her head. "I'm sorry. It's true. I'm not equipped. I thought I could do it, but I—"

"Forget what you don't have." He gritted his teeth. "Use what you've got. You're a doctor, for crissakes."

"Was!" she almost shouted. "*Was* a doctor."

He let out a snort of derision. "What're you so damned scared of? Any two-year-old could do this."

A bark of laughter escaped her. "Oh, you think so? Any two-year-old?" She gestured at the pine-plank door. "Maybe I should try to find one. Surely there must be an available toddler in some nearby cabin!"

For a long moment, he just stared at her, comebacks poised on the tip of his inebriated tongue. In the end, he simply lifted one side of his mouth in a lopsided grin before allowing his eyes to slide shut again. "I like you better mad than...scared."

She shifted uneasily, hands on her hips. "Are you finished?"

"I dunno," he mumbled. "Are you?"

The anger leaked out of her. Damn him for being right. There he lay, with a bullet festering in his shoulder, while she complained about something she could no more change than she could stop the day from coming. This wasn't about her or her cowardice. The only thing that mattered was saving his life. *Forget what you don't have. Use what you've got.* His words rang truer than he could have ever imagined.

"You're right," she said. "I am scared." She walked over and knelt beside him. His skin was flushed and warm. Too warm. "Because I may just finish what that bullet started."

His hand wrapped around her wrist and held her fast, the teasing gone from his expression. "Then so be it. But if you don't try I might as well've...given it up on that damned road last night. 'Cause I'm gonna die. And I'm gonna do it on the friggin' floor of your friend's cabin. Is that what you want?"

"I'm sorry," she said, shaking her head. "Very bad form for a doctor to…scuttle a patient's confidence that way. I, um, I want you to know that I've done this very operation dozens of times." Unfolding the towel beside him, she stared down at the sterilized instruments she'd stolen from the hospital. *Just not without anesthetic and all the amenities of an operating room.* "I can get that bullet out, Jack, but we're going to have to trust each other. Can you do that, Jack?"

"Stop talking and do it, cupcake."

She released a shaky sigh. "All right. Since you apparently have an unnatural capacity for alcohol, we're going to have to do this the hard way. You must hold very still. I know that'll be hard." She paused. "In fact, it'll be damn near impossible. But you can't grab my arm. Understand?"

He nodded.

"Do you—do you want something to bite on?"

Those eyes of his did a quick, suggestive sweep down her. "You offering?"

A nervous laugh erupted from her. "Ha, ha."

His smile faded. "You can do this, Tess."

"I'll go as fast as I can."

He blinked in reply, then looked away, mentally girding himself for what was to come. She pulled the halogen desk lamp close and switched it on. One thing she had on her side was the X ray they'd taken at the hospital. She'd seen it and knew where the bullet had lodged. Its trajectory had been deep, but constant. The challenge was to avoid the major artery that ran millimeters from the location of the bullet.

After pulling on surgical gloves and swabbing his shoulder with whiskey, Tess lifted the scalpel she'd pilfered from the ER. She willed her hand to stop shaking as she poised it above his wound.

Jack's eyes were squeezed shut, his whole body braced

for the first cut. When it came, he stiffened and inhaled sharply, but didn't move. A four letter word hissed past his lips. Sweat broke out instantly on his chest and his chalk-white face.

"Sorry," she whispered as she probed past the incision with the tip of the scalpel. Seconds ticked by. A minute.

Nothing. The only sound in the room was the harsh rasp of his breathing. Fresh blood welled up in the wound. She prayed she hadn't nicked something. She followed the path of the scalpel with the forceps, but there was nothing of substance beneath the tips.

"Hang on, Jack. Just a little longer." *Where the hell is it?* Her palms prickled and the instruments grew slick in her hands.

She went deeper. A guttural sound escaped from his throat. With every millimeter, his breathing became shallower and faster.

"I know," she told him. But she knew she didn't, couldn't. "Almost there." *Please.*

Concentrating solely on breathing in and out, he clenched the rumpled quilt until his knuckles went white.

She was working blind. She'd done this surgery a thousand times, but this—this was different. Nausea climbed in her throat. Moisture broke out on her brow. She needed suction, cautery—

He gasped and arched backward, his hand clamping over her arm like the jaw of a mad dog.

Her heart slammed against the wall of her chest. *"Don't!"*

His lips curled back in a snarl that any sane woman would have shrunk from. But she couldn't quit now. She couldn't do this again. "Let go, Jack," she said carefully, holding the scalpel perfectly still. "You have to let go."

If she'd been a fly, he would have squashed her. But some small particle of rationality lingered yet behind the haze of pain he was swimming though. Against every instinct he held dear, he released her arm. An animal-like sound of surrender erupted from his throat.

Her breath returned in jerky gasps. "Good," she murmured. "Good, Jack. I know it's bad. I know it. But if I stop now I'll have to start over. Should I stop? If you can't take any mo—"

He shook his head. *"Do it."* The muscle in his jaw clenched and unclenched until she was sure she would hear his teeth crack. Sweat poured off his face. Rationality was rapidly losing the battle with the instinct to fight the invading pain. She had to hurry or all the promises in the world wouldn't matter.

It had been years since she'd prayed. But as the small bit of metal evaded her every attempt to find it, she sent up a prayer that he would pass out.

Less than ten seconds later, that prayer was answered. His eyes fluttered back and the tension flowed out of him like a wave receding from the shoreline.

Tess let out the breath she hadn't realized she'd been holding and sent up a thank-you to whoever was listening.

With the tip of the probe, she eased aside torn muscle and reached deeper. The probe touched something hard and she heard the blessed scrape of metal on metal. A shudder of relief coursed through her.

"There you are…you little bugger." She eased the blunt tips of the forceps around the edges of the bullet. "Gotcha."

After a moment, the mashed piece of lead released its hold on the deep muscle of his shoulder and appeared at the end of her forceps. A .38, from the looks of it—whole and unfragmented. Lucky, she mused, fighting to keep the bullet in focus as tears of relief blurred her vision.

She'd done it. And he was still breathing. In terms of where she'd been once, what she'd done this morning would seem relatively benign. But here, now, with the sun pouring through the east-facing window onto Jack's face, and warming the chill in her bones, she knew that it was no small victory in a battle she'd never again thought to fight.

And he was breathing.

She swiped at her damp cheeks, embarrassed by the breakdown of her normally iron-fisted control. Training and experience kicked in as she discarded the bullet, reached for the whiskey and poured it into the wound, cleaning it out as much as she could. She pressed a thick pad of clean torn sheet against the wound to stop the bleeding. Primitive but effective. When the bleeding slowed to a stop, she replaced the sheeting with bandages stolen from the ER, then immobilized his arm against his chest. It was then she noticed the tattoo on his left forearm. It was odd looking—eight arrows bound together by something that looked like a seabird, with "25th" entwined there.

She checked his pulse against her watch. Thready and too fast, but his breathing had the slow rhythm of deep sleep. It was the best place for him. He needed rest to heal and to battle the fever that had already taken hold. Not once had Jack moved, or so much as blinked. The fight had gone out of him. He'd retreated to where the pain couldn't reach him.

She covered him with two more blankets and sat watching him for the next hour. She left him briefly to clean up and trade her own bloody clothes for clean ones from Cara's closet. His fever held steady. Then she watched Jack some more. That he'd lived through that poor excuse for an operation said more about the man than about her skill. He'd already taken more than most men could and hadn't complained once.

"Strange," she murmured aloud, brushing back the hair from his damp forehead. "You're a strange one, Jack.

Whoever you are." She pulled the blanket up under his neck. "You rest. I won't let you die. I promise you that." She prayed it was a promise she could keep. Right now, there was something she had to do she couldn't put off any longer. She grabbed her car keys off the counter and slipped quietly out the door.

The pay phone outside Winston's Pharmacy and Drug was encased in an old-fashioned wood and glass booth, complete with a hinged door and a curved wooden seat. The number she dialed rang twice before the deep voice on the other end answered.

"Detective Castillano."

"Gil?"

"Tess? Is that you?"

She heard the smile of recognition in his voice and felt instantly better. In fact, she hadn't realized until this very moment how much she counted on him. Gil had been her rock since Adam's death. Adam had always told her that Gil, a fifteen-year veteran with the credentials of men twice his age, was the kind of man you'd want by your side in a fight. Her husband had been right. And she couldn't think of anyone she would trust with her life more than Gil. He also had the uncanny ability to always calm her down. And right now, she needed calming. "It's me."

"Hey, I tried to call you last night," he said lightly. She heard the shuffling sound of papers. "You weren't home. And don't tell me you were at the lab. I tried there, too. They said you were on vacation."

That, she mused, sounded less and less like a punishment, considering the past eight hours or so. "Not exactly."

"What's that mean, 'not exactly?'"

"Well, you might call it a getaway. On the other hand..." The rest drifted off as she came very close to betraying the quiver in her voice. She could almost see the frown bisecting his brow.

"What's going on, Tess? Are you all right?"

"Yes. I'm—I'm fine. Really."

"Why don't I believe you? What did you do? Forget the security code on the alarm at your house again?" He waited for a pithy comeback. It didn't arrive. "Tess?"

She'd rehearsed what she was going to say to him a hundred times on the way into town, and now everything she'd practiced sounded idiotic. She owed him the truth, but she also owed it to him to keep him out of whatever danger she'd stumbled into herself.

She chose her words carefully. "Promise me that this will stay between us."

"*What?*"

"You have to promise, Gil. It's important. My life could depend on it. A man's life absolutely does."

She heard him rearrange the phone against his ear. "Now you're scaring me."

"I'm sorry." She was. More than he would ever know.

"Whatever it is, you can trust me, Tess. I hope you know that."

She turned her back on the couple strolling arm in arm down the sidewalk past the phone booth, and cradled the phone against her shoulder. "That's why I'm calling you, Gil, and no one else."

"What's happened?"

"It's a long story. Are you sitting down?"

She told him about finding Jack on the road, and about what had followed at the hospital. She recounted the hair-raising chase by the two officers and the slug she'd dug out of Jack's shoulder. Even to her own ears it sounded like she'd fallen off the deep edge of paranoia. The tale lost critical mass in the translation. And she was so tired she stumbled over even important details.

A brief silence followed, before he said, "And you're...where?"

"Don't ask me that. I can't tell you."

"The hell you can't. Give me five minutes and I'll be on my w—"

"No! You can't come. And I can't tell you where I am. You'll just have to trust me. I don't want you in the middle of this."

Even years of training couldn't hide the anger in his voice. "I'm a cop. That's right where I'm supposed to be."

"He trusts me, Gil. I promised him. I need time to figure this whole thing out. And so does he."

"*Judas Priest!* He could be a serial killer for all you—"

"He's not."

A snort of laughter resounded from the receiver. "Oh, yeah? That's what they all say. 'Oh, him? He was such a quiet boy...he seemed so normal....'"

"Nothing about this is normal. That bullet was intended to kill him. And those two cops had every intention of finishing him off."

"You're in way over your head," he said quietly.

"I know." She closed her eyes against the morning sun streaming through the heated glass. Fatigue pulled at her. She wanted nothing more than to let Gil take this whole thing off her shoulders. But she couldn't, wouldn't, do that to him.

"You sure they were cops?" he asked finally, his voice grim.

"Detectives. Their badges looked real," she answered, "but I don't know. The younger one, Rivera, lit up a smoke right there in the lounge. Don't you think that's odd?"

"I wouldn't hang my case on it." She could hear him scribbling down notes. "Santa Monica, you said?"

"Yes. But, Gil, be careful. Don't stir up any dust on this.

I don't want them to know you're checking on them. If they find out—''

"Hey, I do this for a living, remember? I'll be careful," Gil said, his voice tight and controlled. She knew him too well. He was angry. Not so much with her, she suspected, but with the fact that he wasn't in control of the situation. "And this guy claims to have no memory?"

"None," she answered. "But considering the wallop he took on the head, that's not unheard of. I believe him."

"I don't. This Jack character is trouble with a capital *T*," Gil said. "And he's dragged you into it."

Silence stretched between them. Finally, Tess spoke. "I have to go, Gil. I have to get back to him. I'll call you in twenty-four hours."

Gil exploded. *"Twenty-four—!"*

"Sooner if I can. But listen, there's one more thing. Gil?"

There was another pause as he reined in his temper. "What?"

"There's a tattoo. On his forearm."

Gil sighed. "This gets better and better."

Tess rubbed her eyes. "I don't know if it means anything, but it's an odd-looking tattoo. Sort of an insignia." She described it to him. "Does that sound like anything you've ever seen?"

"No, but that doesn't mean anything. I can run it through the computer. See if any hits come up."

"Thanks, Gil," she said. "I have to go. I'll call you."

"Tess?"

"Yeah?"

She heard him swallow hard. "You watch yourself. Don't turn your back to him, you hear? I don't like it. The whole thing smells bad. And it starts with your boy, there."

No matter how she felt about Jack, she knew Gil was right. It began, and apparently ended, with Jack. And she had no idea how or why. "I'll be careful," she promised. "Try not to worry."

He laughed humorlessly. "Yeah? Go tell it to somebody who doesn't give a damn."

Tess's mouth trembled into a smile. *Bless him.* "Thanks, Gil," she said, and carefully hung up the phone.

Chapter 5

*H*eat.

Unrelenting.

Pounding him down against the hot, damp floor of the jungle. Above him, the canopy of green shifted like a kaleidoscope, changing shape and dimension as it blotted out the sunshine beyond. His fingers curled into the thick rotting earth as he pulled himself forward, snake-like, through the undergrowth. Razor-sharp banana leaves sliced at his skin. Insects buzzed around his eyes and hummed in his ears and clustered at every bloody rivulet streaming from his arms.

Behind him, he could hear them coming. He could hear the metallic rattle of M-16s; the muffled thudding of boots against the jungle floor; the jumbled Spanish imperatives, dampened by the sound-sucking vegetation.

He wanted to run but the heat held him like a fist. His knees scrambled at the slippery slope he lay on, and the white-hot pain slapped him back down again.

His fingers closed around the cool, thick handle of his knife and he slid it from its sheath. Wherever the hell he was going, he swore silently, he damned well wasn't going alone.

Closer. Closer. Standing practically on top of him. Why couldn't they see him?

Then another sound invaded his consciousness. Fainter, but growing closer. It was... He frowned. It didn't belong here. He couldn't identify it at first. Then somehow, it dawned on him. A dog. Barking. Louder. Louder.

What the hell was a dog doing in the middle of—?

Jack's eyes snapped open and the jungle vanished, replaced by thick, rounded logs and the vague shape of a room. Warm sunshine from a nearby window poured over him. Dust motes swam in the morning sun and drifted upward—toward the sound of the barking dog outside the window.

He tried to sit. Pain sizzled up his arm and landed in his chest like a blast from a howitzer. He swore viciously and pressed his head back against the pillow under his head. What the hell—?

Then he remembered.

The bullet. His shoulder throbbed in remembrance. Tess must have...

He looked around the room. It was empty. He lay still and listened. Nothing. No sound of her.

"Tess?" His voice sounded pathetic, like an eighty-year-old man's. He cleared his throat. "Tess?" Though it sounded stronger this time, he still got no reply.

How long had he been out? Where the hell did she go? To the police? No answers came to him.

And that damned dog kept barking.

Jack eased slowly up on one elbow, blinking away the dizziness and watching the room swim. His brain felt scrambled. If she'd left him to go to the cops, he had no choice. He had to get out of here.

Easier said than done, a voice told him. He felt as weak as he sounded and in no shape to go anywhere. And worse, he was trussed up like a turkey ready for Thanksgiving.

He rolled slowly to his knees and stayed there, unwinding the gauze from his shoulder and releasing the arm he needed. Damned woman. He should've guessed she'd take off on him. Then again, who could blame her, considering what had happened? He'd just thought—hoped…

Dammit! He couldn't worry about her now. He had to get the hell out of here.

Jack staggered to his feet and crashed into the lamp that was poised inconveniently nearby on a stack of books. He heard the shattering of glass as the bulb hit the floor. He clutched the thick, oak mantel on the fireplace and braced himself there until the room stopped turning. Remnants of a fire still crackled in the fireplace. The room was hot and he longed to make his way outside to fresh air.

Slowly, he edged toward the sunlight pouring through the window. The light hurt his eyes and he squinted through the glass at the huge golden retriever standing twenty feet away, staring at him. The damned thing woofed at him. Jack blinked, wondering how the hell the animal knew he was here.

The dog just looked at him for a moment, panting, tongue lolling out to one side, then turned around and trotted off. Disconcerted, Jack stared at the now-empty lawn.

Had that been real or a figment of his imagination, too? He blinked hard as the world swam in and out of focus. A fierce heat was crawling up his skull and tangling his thoughts. Water. He needed a drink.

He edged across the room, pausing to catch his breath. Last night's ordeal had left him more than weak. It had stolen his equilibrium. He felt like he was walking on one of those bridges that floated on—what was the word?—pontoons.

He paused, leaning on a ladder-back chair. *Pontoon.* Was that a memory? A bridge with pontoons? And what about the dream? The jungle? Was it the fever, or was he remembering something that had happened?

He squeezed his eyes shut. *Why* couldn't he remember? His name. Last night. *Something.* How could a whole lifetime of memories be simply blotted out in the space of a night? He had to believe it would come back sooner or later. It had to. It was his only hope.

Right now, he had more immediate worries. He scanned the room. No phone. At least not in here. Not that he knew who to call. He needed a drink and he needed a way out. But most of all, he needed an edge.

Tess had stopped at Ned Wilton's Pharmacy for supplies, feeding Ned a story about how she'd cut herself on a piece of barbed wire fencing and needed bandages and antibiotic ointment. She hadn't dared write a prescription for Jack. Ned's pharmacy was linked to the rest of the world by computer and prescriptions could be easily tracked. She'd have to make do with what she had.

Thick ominous clouds had moved in from the west by the time Tess pulled up to the cabin. At seven thousand feet, the mountain air held the promise of an early fall. The weather matched her mood, she thought, as the first fat drops of rain splatted against the flagstone path that led to the porch. She ran the rest of the way, fumbling again with the key in the stubborn lock.

Her conversation with Gil kept surfacing in her thoughts, pricking her conscience. She knew he was angry he couldn't jump in the car and rescue her. And God knew, she needed rescuing. But there was something about Jack—something she couldn't even articulate—that made her want to help him. She prayed she'd done the right thing, not telling Gil where she was. She would have to deal with his anger later, after she figured out how to get out of this mess. And Jack? She had no intention of telling him about her conversation with Gil until she found out where she stood. What he didn't know couldn't hurt him. What *she* didn't know, on the other hand, could kill her.

Finally, the lock gave. She pushed the door open and went absolutely still at the sound of a gun cocking beside her ear.

Tess gasped and dropped the bag in her hands. At the other end of the gun stood Jack, wearing nothing but a half-buttoned pair of bloodstained jeans and a deadly look on his face. His aim was shaky, but unnervingly accurate.

"Jack…"

He was breathing hard, leaning against the wall. His size alone was enough to intimidate her—all two hundred-odd pounds of rock-hard muscle.

"Jack!" she whispered. *"Please. Put it down."*

A four-letter expletive hissed from his lips. He dropped his injured arm to his side and tipped his forehead heavily against the wall.

"Give me the gun," she said, carefully extending her hand toward him.

It took him agonizing seconds to even respond. Then, he eased the cocking mechanism safely back into place and handed the weapon to her.

She took it gingerly between two fingers like a smelly piece of fish and sent it skidding across the kitchen island, far from his reach.

He rolled his back against the wall, then slid down it like warm taffy until he reached the floor. He clutched his shoulder and went utterly white.

"Jack?" She knelt down beside him.

Through a sweep of dark lashes he glanced at her. "I

thought you left. I thought maybe you went to call the cops.''

Outside thunder rumbled across the sky. ''No. I needed some things.'' She reached for the bag she'd dropped and pulled them out to show him. ''For you. Supplies. Bandages. Groceries. Why would I do that after all we've already been through? Look, you're not thinking straight. We…we have to trust each other, Jack.'' It was a despicable untruth, considering she'd already broken a promise to him by calling Gil. ''Where did you get that gun?''

His blink was slow and unfocused. ''Found it.''

Cara was keeping a gun here? ''Well, you obviously know how to use one.''

He tipped his head tiredly against the wall. ''Apparently.''

Tess ripped open a small red box and flicked the lid on the bottle of Ibuprofen open. She yanked out the cotton filler, and pills scattered across the floor. She ignored them. Shaking out two, she handed them to him and stood to get a glass of water. ''Take those. Your fever's up.''

He just stared at the two little red-and-yellow pills in his palm as she hurried to the sink. Running the water cold did little to stem the panic she was starting to feel. She handed him the glass and watched him force the pills down his throat. The water he attacked as if he hadn't tasted it in years. Outside, rain slapped against the window.

''You should be in bed.'' Tess took the glass from him, but didn't move. ''You're bleeding again.'' She reached for a fresh bandage and tore open the protective paper around it.

''I wouldn't have blamed you.'' She looked up questioningly from the bandage she was pressing against his chest. He explained, ''If you hadn't come back.''

Pulling a length of gauze from the roll, she drew him forward to wrap it around his back. ''I told you I would.

Anyway, do you think I went to all this work so you could die alone here in my best friend's house?" She leaned him back and ripped the gauze so she could tie the ends. "Cara would never forgive me."

He smiled thinly. "That's real comforting, Doc."

Her own smile faded as she watched him. The very real possibility of that happening was too disturbing to ponder. "That's why I get the big bucks," she quipped. "My winning bedside manner."

That practically earned her a chuckle. But his smile vanished almost as soon as it appeared. She laid the backs of her fingers against his forehead, and this time he let her. No thermometer was required to tell her he was too hot. She had to get his fever down and soon, or all of the bandages in the world weren't going to help him.

"C'mon," she said. "Let's get you moved before I have to drag you to the bedroom." She tucked his arm around her shoulders and helped him up. "I'm not sure I could do that again."

"Keep that gun close," he said hoarsely as they passed it on the countertop. "Promise me, Tess."

"That gun—" she began tightly, but checked herself. "No one's going to find us here, Jack. No one. I promise. Just concentrate on resting. That's all you have to do."

They shuffled through the living room in an awkward three-legged dance as Jack grew weaker and weaker. He started to shiver. Outside, the rain beat harder against the tin roof.

As they moved into the guest room, she aimed him toward the bed. Glancing up at him, she noted that his face, mere inches away, was a study of grim resolve. "Let's take this slow," she said. "Now, I'm gonna back you up to the bed and—"

He wasn't listening. His entire focus had already shifted to the cool, inviting mattress dead ahead. In fact, his whole being seemed to surrender at the sight of it, and she felt him listing toward it before she was able to stop his momentum.

"Wait," she gasped. "No—uh-oh!"

Down they went. Tess managed to avoid landing directly on him, but he didn't manage the same feat with her. He landed on her arm, pinning it beneath his naked back.

"You ever do anything the easy way?" she asked him under her breath. He didn't reply, and she rolled toward him.

His face was a study of cool concentration as he focused on breathing in and out. The only outward sign that he was in pain was the rhythmic pulse of the muscle in his jaw and the shiver that was working its way down his body with some regularity. She wondered if he'd learned that somewhere—how to control his reaction to pain, how to push it out of his mind.

She started to pull her arm out from under him, but he stopped her.

"Stay," he whispered hoarsely.

"Jack—this isn't—"

"Just f-for a minute. I'm so…c-cold."

His skin was so hot it nearly burned her. Hesitantly, she eased her cheek down on his good shoulder and wrapped an arm carefully around his bare torso.

It had been years since she'd shared warmth with a man or felt the brush of a naked shoulder beneath her cheek. Not since Adam. She wondered now if that had been her mistake. Cutting herself off from this sort of intimacy, denying herself the very comfort that Jack now craved. How odd that she would choose this time to think of it, with Jack so perilously close to death, when his need for her meant only that he was cold. But lying here, she felt like a woman. And that was something she hadn't felt in a long, long time.

She tightened her arm around his waist and listened to the steady thud of his heart. How long they lay that way, Tess didn't know. But when she felt his arm relax over her back and heard the steady, even rhythm of his breathing, she knew he'd fallen asleep again.

Pulling her arm from beneath him, she lifted his legs fully onto the bed. Somehow she managed to drag the down comforter from underneath him so she could get him in after undressing him. That he'd even been upright was a miracle. The fever and blood loss were sucking the life from him. She doubted he'd have had the strength to pull the trigger if his life had depended on it.

She stripped off his jeans and his boxers and tried not to look at the all too tangible evidence of his masculinity.

That proved harder in practice than in theory. She'd seen hundreds of men. Patients. After her years as a resident, she'd thought nothing of it. Patients were patients.

Jack, on the other hand, was Jack. A warrior in a warrior's body. Nothing about him was routine or ordinary. Not the way her heart skidded against her chest as she took in the Michelangelo form beneath his clothes, nor the kick-in-the-gut feeling she got as she imagined losing the battle for his life.

She told herself she didn't need any good reason to try to do that. It was her job. Her duty. But something more than that connected them, something more elusive. He needed her. And in a strange way, she needed him, too. A point of honor, she told herself. If he survived, then somehow she'd have survived these last two harrowing years, skill intact. If he died, it would simply prove all her doubts about herself were justified.

That's what she told herself.

But as she ran her fingers down his muscled arm to the pulse on the inside of his wrist, and felt the fierce life force burning inside him, she knew it was more than that. She

needed him to survive because for the first time since Adam
died, she felt alive.

And she needed to know why.

*The swirling sand enveloped him like a whirlpool, in-
vading every orifice, hampering every lungful of air he tried
to drag in. The inferno-like heat sucked him dry and blis-
tered his tongue. His mouth seemed incapable of forming
words, but he wanted to cry out, "Help me!" No one could
hear him. The storm raged around him, and his men were
too far away. Dying wasn't all it was cracked up to be, he
thought, fighting the shifting sand for footing, though it
beckoned him downward with a soulful howl. In the distance, the thunder of guns and tanks drowned out the sound
of his struggle.*

*A young man appeared beside him, smiling with a tilted
grin that was so familiar. His name teetered on the edge
of Jack's memory, then eluded him. Crouched there with
his forearms poised on his fatigue-covered knees, the man
seemed to be waiting, unconcerned by Jack's efforts to drag
himself through the sand.*

*"Remember?" the soldier said. "Her name was Sheila.
Best damned dog we ever had."*

Dog?

*"Used to do tricks. Remember? She could play dead for
hours in the heat. Try it. You'll sink slower."*

*Like a ball of yarn sent spinning from its end, Jack felt
himself unfurl. He stopped struggling and let the stinging
sand drift over him. He was so damned tired. Maybe he
would die now. Just swallow sand until there was no more
air. But as the sand piled deeper, he felt the soldier's hand
behind his head, holding him up.*

Chapter 6

Tess's eyes drooped as she wrung out the washcloth for the hundredth time since dawn had broken. Mind-numbing fatigue manacled her movements as if she'd been caught in a slow-motion sequence of a movie. She ached with the need for sleep, but didn't allow herself even a moment of it. Her movements had become automatic somewhere after the first twelve hours of battle.

Dunk. Wring. Fold. Lay the washcloth on his forehead.

Dunk. Wring. Wipe down his chest and arms and watch the steam practically rise off his body.

She'd run out of ice quickly. The automatic ice maker couldn't keep up after she'd packed him in the stuff. She'd scavenged Cara's bathroom cabinets and found a partially used bottle of antibiotics, which she'd crushed up and forced down Jack. There weren't enough for a full course, but they couldn't hurt him now. For hours he hadn't so much as moved a muscle, retreating to some dark place where none of this could touch him. During the darkest part of the night, however, all that had changed.

The restlessness that had begun with terrible sounds coming from his throat dissolved into a full-blown wrestling match, in which Tess had come out the loser. She had the bruises on her cheek and upper arm to prove it. He was astonishingly strong for a man so weakened by fever. But caught in the throes of some terrible dream, he had struck out at her as if she were the enemy he was fighting. His fist had sent her sailing halfway across the room. Stars clattered through her vision and for a minute, she lay there, simply trying to breathe again.

After that, she'd tied him down. Naturally, he hadn't been keen on the idea, even unconscious. He made his protest clear by fighting the restraints with every toss and turn. But restraining him made the rest almost manageable.

Except that the hours without sleep preyed on her now. And even lifting the washcloth onto his forehead seemed an unreasonable task to ask of her body. She was going on forty-eight hours without sleep and the toll was inevitable.

But she couldn't sleep. If she did, he would die. Of that she was sure.

So she dunked the washcloth again in the tepid water, wrung it out and ran it slowly over his heated body. She moved the sheet aside to access one long, muscled leg and ran the washcloth down his firm, bruised thigh. Dampness tangled with the silky hair that grew there. A runner's legs, she mused. Or legs that were familiar with running. Tess sighed, covered his limb and turned her attention to his chest.

In the last few hours, she'd become familiar with the flat brown discs of his nipples and the way his skin quivered as she passed the cloth over his taut abdomen. She'd memorized the geography of the bruised and battered chest with its dark triangle of hair trailing down in an ever-narrowing V to disappear beneath the sheet at his hips. She'd become intimately familiar, too, with the L-shaped scar that bisected his good shoulder to curve lazily around his collarbone, and the puckered one she'd noticed before, three fingers below his last rib on the right. That one was either from a bullet or a knife, she guessed. She traced one finger lightly around its outline, wondering about it. About him.

Who was he and what sort of a life had he led before yesterday? She gazed at his torso, which, despite the battering he'd gotten, was beautiful: a perfect balance of form and substance. No bulky gym-junkie's body, his physique had been forged like fine steel. A tan line marked his thick upper arms, as if he wore T-shirts often. If she had to guess a history for him, she'd pick some job that kept him outside. Construction, maybe? The tattoo would fit there. Maybe even the scars. But his hair didn't quite fit that image. It was shorter than most construction workers' she'd seen, who seemed to prefer loose and casual. There was nothing loose or casual about this man.

She smoothed a hank of hair off his forehead. Dark and soft, it sifted through her fingers like damp silk, and she followed the movement with the washcloth. This time he seemed to press his heated face into the coolness, like a cat craving a rub.

"Feels good, huh?" she asked hoarsely, her voice roughened from lack of sleep. "Why don't you wake up and tell me so?"

He tossed his head with a moan when she picked up his hand to smooth the washcloth over his arm. His fingers curled around hers with something close to desperation.

"Jack?" she whispered, shaken by what she felt in his grip.

"Don't—" The syllable was invested with a need she couldn't begin to comprehend.

"What is it? Don't what?"

"Don't go," he mumbled hoarsely.

The fear in his voice was almost tangible. Tears pricked

her eyes. Even in the short time she'd known him, she sensed how much he would despise being so vulnerable. She shook her head. "I'm not. I'm here." But he wasn't talking to her. His eyes were closed and he was talking to someone who wasn't even there.

"Should've seen it...should've..." Jack came up off the pillow. "Joe—no—!" he cried, tightening his fingers suddenly and painfully around hers. "Don't—! Damn you—!"

"Shh," she said, dreading the next round. "It's all right. You're safe."

He muttered something else she couldn't make out. Something ugly.

Tess frowned and braced herself against his arms. She straddled his hips and pinned him to the bed. "Jack!"

He tossed his head from side to side, gasping for air. He thrashed around as if water was closing over his head. "Nooo!"

Alarmed, Tess pressed down harder. "Jack, stop! You're going to start bleeding all over agai—"

He opened his eyes and looked right at her. Ancient ice, those blue eyes, muddied with a fury that transformed his face and scared her right down to her bones.

"Tell him!" he growled. "He's a dead man. You hear me?"

His intense gaze shifted to a point somewhere behind her. She'd ceased to exist.

"He's a dead man," he breathed, falling back against the pillow, exhausted. He mumbled something that sounded like Benedict—or Benedicto—then slipped back into the darkness from which he'd emerged.

Tess let out the breath she'd been holding. She stared down at him, knowing it was over. For now. Shaken, she smoothed her fingers gently along his arm. The hatred that oozed from him was real. The violence in his voice was real, too.

Tess pressed four fingers over her mouth. What was she doing tangled up with this stranger? What had he been before last night? And who did he want to kill? Who or what was Benedicto? It sounded Italian or South American. Were the memories real, or were they some figment of his fevered imagination? And how could he remember those things unconsciously, if his conscious brain could not?

More importantly, how did she even know that he hadn't been lying to her about his amnesia? What if he remembered everything, even that man he wanted dead? Her eyes fell to the nasty swelling near his left eye. She'd operated on instinct for most of her adult life. Now that same instinct told her that he wasn't lying. Whatever memories were coming back to him now were the first trickle in the floodgate she hoped would open for him soon.

For the rest of the day, she waged war against the infection bent on killing him: rounds of struggle, forcing liquids down him until he would once more slip into a deep sleep. Without antibiotics, she was obliged to try some alternate methods of treatment. She'd concocted a drawing poultice of hot milk and the linseed oil she'd found in the cupboard. It required changing every few minutes to stay hot. The repetitiveness of the job kept her awake.

Hours ago, she'd stopped kidding herself that her motives for saving him were purely altruistic, or had anything to do with the oath she'd taken. This battle was personal now, and his death something she would not accept. Sometime in the dark of night, she'd admitted that winning wasn't a goal in itself, but a means to an end—his survival. She didn't know why. She couldn't explain what it was about him that made her care. Perhaps the desperation she saw in his eyes. Or maybe it was the lack of artifice. A man with no memory had no walls and no defenses. Perhaps it was that lack of defense that made her want to protect him.

She wrung out the cloth again and placed it on his fevered brow. No, she admitted, it was more than that.

The intimacy that had grown between them was more than simply physical. She wanted Jack to live for selfish reasons, none of which she was prepared to explore.

She forgot the time. Sunlight had faded hours ago, and with it her ability to think coherently. She moved automatically from one task to the next, hardly seeing what she was doing. He'd been resting quietly for more than an hour when she rolled her tense shoulders and made the mistake of leaning one elbow on the mattress to reach the poultice bowl. She stalled there, unable to contemplate moving any farther.

Collapsing on the soft comforter, she told herself that she'd close her eyes for just a moment. She was so tired. If he woke again, she'd know. Resting her hand against Jack's arm, she let her eyes slide shut.

It was light when Tess opened her eyes. At first she thought she'd left the light on, but morning was pouring through the six-paned widow to her right and birds were chirping outside it. Languidly, she rolled onto her back and blinked up at the cabin ceiling, pondering how long it had been since she'd slept like that.

She gasped and bolted upright. *Jack!*

On all fours she crawled up the mattress to him. He was absolutely still. Dread moved up her spine.

"Jack?" She touched his forehead. It was cool.

Cool!

"Oh, no...Jack! Don't be dead. Please don't be dead. I'm so sorry. I was just so tired. Jack?" As her fingers found the pulse at his throat, his eyes fluttered open.

She jumped back with two hands over her mouth, her eyes brimming with a burst of unexpected tears. "Oh! Thank God, you're alive!"

Jack blinked at her, then frowned. "Tess?" His voice was a croak. "You look like hell."

With her hands still clamped over her mouth, she laughed. "Oh, you don't know how good it is to hear you say that." She reached out and brushed his arm to convince herself that he was really alive, then pulled it back. What she really felt like doing was hugging him. Getting emotional over a patient was unprofessional and unlike her. But she felt like crying and laughing all at once.

"How long—?" he asked.

"Two days."

He rolled his eyes. "Ah…damn."

"You should be thanking your lucky stars. You nearly died."

A moan escaped him as he shifted on the bed. "You absolutely sure I didn't?"

A laugh escaped her. "Not unless we're both there." She smoothed down her hair. "How do you feel?"

"Steamrollered," he murmured, rubbing his temples.

"Thirsty?"

He grunted an affirmative reply, but she'd barely turned her back before she heard, "What the hell?" He was tugging at the bonds around his wrists. "You tied me down?"

Tess bit her lip. She'd forgotten about the ties. "It's not what you think." She reached for the knot on his left wrist and began untying it.

She knew the moment his gaze found the ugly bruise on her left cheek. Her hand went reflexively to the spot.

He swore viciously under his breath. "Did I do that?"

She freed his right wrist. "It wasn't your fault. You were out of your mind with fever. I just got in the way. You weren't aiming at me." She leaned over him to untie the other.

He looked sick. "I'm sorry, Tess."

"Don't be." She reached for a glass and held it up to his lips.

It made him dizzy to sit up, but he drank greedily, despite the bitter taste of the water. It had a familiar taste, as did the feel of her hands against the back of his neck. There was something else, too, he thought.

It struck him then why she looked like she'd been dragged under the same steamroller he had. Because she hadn't let him die. She'd willed him alive.

His gaze scanned her perfect heart-shaped face, dragged down by fatigue, and the emotion still written there, despite her best attempts to deny it.

"Why?" he asked.

"Why what?" She looked away.

"Why did you bother? You don't even know me."

She looked almost fragile standing there, as transparent as parchment. "I don't have to know you," she said, tilting her chin up. "I'm a doctor. It's what I do."

"Bull. A hundred other doctors would have let me go. Why didn't you?"

She flinched and started to turn away. "I'm going to get you something to eat."

He stopped her with a hand on her arm. She was trembling and he needed to know why. "Tess?"

"Because I couldn't," she said simply.

"So then, was it me, or just the principle of the thing?"

She regarded him with a slow, ironic grin. "I suspect no one's ever mistaken you for a principle, Jack."

Chapter 7

Gil Castillano slammed into the precinct and drew the uneasy stares of the desk sergeant and two beat cops as he took the stairs two at a time to the second floor.

"Hey, Gil, where you been? Sullivan's lookin' for you." The stacked brunette who'd spoken to him was already ten feet behind him and talking to his back. "What, did we forget your birthday or something?"

"I wish it was that simple, darlin'," he called back to her. He squeezed between two detectives and a hooker hashing it out in the hallway, and ignored their curious expressions.

As he passed the reception desk, the plain-looking girl named Annie shot to her feet with a fistful of messages in her hand. "Gil!" she called, following hard on his heels. "The captain's been looking for you. He's called here three times and I told him what you told me to say, but he wasn't biting—"

She bumped smack into his back as he came to an abrupt

halt near his desk. He turned around and grabbed her by the upper arms before she could teeter and fall. She had that wide-eyed puppy dog look in her eyes as she peered up at him through those damned odd-looking, black-rimmed glasses of hers.

"Oh!" she said. "Sorry."

He set her away from him as his phone rang. "Thanks, Annie. Was there anything else?"

She shook her head as Gil picked up the receiver. Annie placed the last of the messages on his desk and headed back to her desk.

"Detective Castillano," he said into the receiver.

"It's me," the voice on the other end said.

Relief lurched in his chest. "Tess! Where the hell—!"

"Please don't yell," she pleaded. "You have no idea how much I wished I could've called you earlier."

He took a deep breath. "Are you all right?"

"I'm fine. Just tired. I couldn't call before—I was a little busy trying to keep Jack alive."

Gil frowned. "Is he—?"

"He made it. He almost didn't, though. The fever almost killed him. He's tough. Tougher than most."

"Tough as you?" He stared at his desktop, piled high with unfiled paperwork, wondering what strength she was drawing from in all this.

"I'm not."

He smiled despite her denials. "That's why they made you a doctor. Only the strong survive."

She made a sound of disagreement. "I'm a little shaky in the survival part, as the last two years have proven."

"The last two years have proven that you're human, Tess. That's all."

He listened to the long silence on the line and could almost hear her gathering up her voice again.

"What did you find out?"

"Okay," he said. "Are you sitting down? There's no record of a gunshot victim being brought into the hospital three nights ago."

"What?"

His sentiments exactly. "Nothing. Zippo. Nada."

"Oh, my God. That can't be. They can't just erase the records. Someone would know. There were others on the floor that night."

"You certain it was Santa Monica?"

"Gil—"

"Okay. Just checking. I looked at the sign-in sheets myself. You're not there." He could almost hear the gears shifting in her head.

"Waltrip," she said.

"What?"

"A surgeon. Dr. Dean Waltrip. He was scheduled to do the surgery on Jack. They had to call him in. Talk to him. He must know something."

Gil scribbled down the name. "Okay, I'll check with him. Next, I just heard back from the charge nurse I called earlier. Seems your nurse, Earline Bradberry? She left yesterday on an extended vacation. No forwarding number."

The sigh Tess heaved sounded shaky. "This is bad, isn't it?"

"Uh, it's not good." He leaned back in his chair and looked around the squad room. A handful of detectives had their noses buried in paperwork. Peter Kimbrough sat chewing on a pencil, staring vacantly in his direction. Gil swiveled his chair around. "That's not the worst of it."

Tess sighed, bracing herself. "Let's have it."

"There's an APB out on a man with your boy's description all over it. He's wanted for murder in the death of a mid-level drug dealer named Ramon Saldovar."

"Drugs?" she repeated incredulously.

"It's bigger than that. This ring has its hands in more

than one candy jar. Seems Saldovar might have been connected to a car theft ring run out of L.A. into Mexico City by some genuinely unsavory characters.''

The name Jack had called out—Benedicto—leaped to her mind. But despite the implied connection, she discarded the possibility as ridiculous. It could mean nothing. ''I don't believe it,'' she said flatly. ''It's not him. It's not.''

''There was no name on the wire. Just a description.'' Gil paused pointedly. ''It could be someone else.''

''Yes. Or someone else could be setting Jack up,'' she said. ''Isn't that possible? Look at the lengths to which someone's already gone to erase that night.''

''It's possible. But why?''

Frustration vibrated her voice. ''I don't know!''

''There's more.''

''Tell me.''

''The tattoo you described? It sounds military, circa the Gulf War. And if my source is correct, it's Special Forces—SEALS.''

''As in…*Navy* SEALS?'' she asked incredulously.

''That's the one.''

She'd heard about the SEALS. Who hadn't? The most elite branch of Special Operations for the Navy. They were reputed to be ruthless killers. Loyal to the death, they were commandos so fearless they went places other soldiers didn't have the guts or the wherewithal to go. It made a strange kind of sense. After all, Jack had survived injuries few other men would have, and when she found him he was still on his feet. But it didn't explain what he was doing out there all alone, involved in something like this.

''So,'' she summarized, ''he's a military, drug-running car thief? That makes no sense to me.''

''Or it could make great sense. I don't like the idea of you being alone with him.''

''He won't hurt me,'' she said. ''I know it.''

Gil's sigh was filled with more than sheer frustration. "Rose-colored glasses were never really your style, Tess. Let me help you. I think I can hazard a guess where you are."

"Don't say it!" she said, loudly enough to make Gil pull the phone away from his ear. "Your phone could be tapped."

Gil glanced at the phone receiver before he decided how absurd that was.

"Anyway, I'm not where you think I am," she said.

He didn't believe her. In the background, he could hear a Steller's jay squawking, could practically smell the crisp mountain air. "C'mon, Tess, I could easily trace your call."

"No, you can't."

That meant she was on her cell phone. "Fine, then I'm coming."

It took a moment of self-control before she could answer. "Gil, they may even be watching you. You could lead them right to us."

They? "You're sounding—"

"Paranoid?" she finished for him.

He paused, glancing around the squad room again, feeling the first traces of it himself. Kimbrough was staring down at paperwork on his desk. J. C. Daniels, Kimbrough's partner, was laughing about something with Dan and the only female detective in the squad, Maria Bellanetti. All of them seemed to be looking right at him. Gil swiveled back, shrugging off the ridiculous notion that any one of them could be involved. Hell, all he needed now was to get spooked by ghosts where none existed.

Ten minutes from now, he'd be in his car, on his way to the mountains where he knew she was. But he wouldn't tell her that. She was too involved to see straight.

"All right," he said at last. "You win. I'll wait. But I

want to hear from you again by tonight. Got it? No more forty-eight hour gaps with me thinking you're lying on some road somewhere.''

He heard her breathe a shaky sigh of relief. "Thanks, Gil. I will. Promise. I just need some more time. Okay?''

Gil listened to the dial tone buzz in his ear and felt his back teeth grinding in an unconscious response. He didn't know why she was being so stubborn about this, but he'd damn well protect her whether she wanted it or not. He owed it to her. Moreover, he owed it to Adam.

Tess crammed the cell phone into her purse on the way back into the house and felt like she'd just dodged a bullet herself. She never should have dragged Gil into this. Of course he would want to come. Even if Gil had figured out where she was, she believed he'd keep his word and give her more time. Time to figure out who Jack was and how to get out of this mess. Gil couldn't protect them if he brought them in. No one could.

Jack was sitting at the edge of his bed, looking pale and wobbly, by the time she made her way back to his room. The covers were dragged across his naked lap.

"What are you doing?'' Tess hurried to him, worried that he was about to topple over.

"Where are my pants?'' he growled.

"You shouldn't be getting out of bed. You're too—''

He swiveled a look up at her, effectively silencing the rest of what she'd been about to say. "It's a matter of some urgency that you hand me those damned pants,'' he said, "unless you're lookin' for a cheap thrill, cupcake.''

Understanding dawned.

With a smile, she opened a drawer and handed him the Levi's she'd washed earlier. "Ah, and humble, too,'' she quipped. "But you should know that after the last two days, I've seen just about everything you've got, pal.''

A slow, sexy grin tilted his lips as he started to rise. "Not everything."

She did the prudent thing and turned around before he could see the heat she felt spring to her cheeks. Behind her, she could hear the rustle of the stiff denim as he tugged the jeans on, and the effort he expended doing it. She listened to the snick of copper buttons sliding into place, the rattle of the nightstand as he bumped against it and his subsequent curse—her cue to turn back.

For more than a moment, she forgot to breathe. He was so right. She hadn't seen everything. Standing upright and alert, Jack hardly resembled the man whose fever-ravaged body she'd coaxed back from the edge these past days. Her gaze traveled unbidden down the length of his broad chest to the rippled definition of his belly disappearing below the waistband of his jeans.

Lord have mercy, she thought. *He's beautiful.*

"Where's the head?" He steadied himself against the nightstand.

She blinked in confusion. "The head?"

"The facilities," he clarified.

She pointed down the hallway. "On the right. Second door." Watching him leave, she was reminded of a wounded cat, his natural grace hindered by days of inactivity. But nothing could erase the prowling essence of his movements, nor the danger inherent in them.

It took her a moment to settle her jangled nerves. His effect on her shouldn't have come as a surprise, but it had. The medical blinders she wore out of necessity when it came to patients of the opposite sex had lost their power in this situation. She had somehow allowed herself to become emotionally involved with him. When she looked at him, she no longer saw a wound in need of healing, but the whole, complicated, vulnerable man instead. That, she knew, was dangerous territory for both of them.

Still, as she pulled his sheets off his bed to change them, the memory of his solid, oh-so-masculine warmth beneath her cheek as she held him replayed in her mind. She tried to reconcile the gentleness she'd felt from him with the picture Gil had painted of him. Drug smuggling car thief? She couldn't wrap her brain around it. Like someone else's clothes, these descriptions didn't fit the mental picture she had of Jack.

Tess pulled fresh sheets from a dresser drawer and snapped the first one over the mattress like a wind-filled sail.

She could be wrong, of course. God knew, people who ended up in prison didn't always look like criminals. They looked like the man next door, or the teacher you had in high school. They didn't, however, look like Jack. Here was a man with everything going for him—looks, brains and, indisputably, brawn. Why, she wondered, tucking the second sheet under the mattress, would a man like him resort to dealing drugs from a Central American cartel? Or stealing cars for some underworld ring?

Why would someone be trying to kill him?

These questions, as usual, dead-ended in her head. There would be no fast answers until Jack's memory returned.

"You didn't have to do that."

His voice came from behind her. Tess turned to find him braced against the doorjamb, looking shaky and unwell. The dark smudges under his eyes stood out in stark contrast to the chalkiness of his skin.

She spread the comforter quickly over the bed. "You'd better lie down before you fall down."

He didn't even argue. For a moment, she feared his fever had risen again, but one touch of his forehead eased her mind. "It's going to take a few days before you're up to full speed again," she told him, tucking the comforter over his chest. "Are you hungry?"

He made a face. "No."

"Good, I'll be right back with some soup."

"I'm not hungry," he repeated.

She simply smiled at him and exited with the pile of sheets in her arms. Before he could fall asleep again, she was back with a steaming bowl of fragrant broth. He turned his head away.

She sighed. "You won't get stronger if you don't eat."

He flashed an annoyed look at her. "You always this pushy?"

A smile crept to her mouth. "I think we've already established my stubborn streak."

Surrendering, he shoved himself up on his elbows so she could prop the pillows behind him. "I bet you always had to win at kick ball in third grade, too," he grumbled.

"Duck, duck, goose," she corrected. "But my real passion was Ping-Pong. I was a whiz at Ping-Pong."

"Ping-Pong?"

"Oh, yeah," she said, giving the hot broth a stir. "Table in the backyard, neighborhood championships, the whole nine yards. How 'bout you? You ever play?"

His smile faded. "That a trick question?"

"Not if you remember it." She watched the muscles in his jaw tighten as he stared out the window.

"I...remember how it's played, but...can't remember how I know. I can't remember doing it." Desperation shadowed his eyes as he looked back at her. "Put keys in my hand and I can drive a car, or bullets and I can load a gun, but I can't tell you how I know what I know."

She could have gone all day without the gun example. She offered him a spoonful of soup. "Eat."

"You don't need to feed me, for God's sake," he said.

"Fine." She handed him the bowl and watched him try to balance it with his injured arm. The silver teaspoon rattled against the side of the bowl and he spilled the contents before it ever reached his mouth.

He swore and tried again. She held her breath as she watched him begin to sweat with the effort to control the spoon. The results were the same. Angry with himself, he shoved the bowl at her and admitted defeat. For a man who she suspected didn't lose gracefully or often, capitulation was harder to swallow than that soup.

She fed him a spoonful and watched his eyes slide shut as he focused on getting it down. "I don't think you realize what your body has been through. You have to give yourself time, Jack. You were very sick."

He didn't reply, just stared sullenly at the bowl as she dipped up another spoonful.

"Patience was never one of my virtues, either," she admitted. "But I have learned over the years that it's required for healing."

"I don't have time for patience."

"You're safe here. No one knows where we are." Even as she said it, she knew that was a lie. Gil knew. But she wouldn't tell Jack that.

"You can't know that," he said. "They found me once. They can do it again."

He was right, of course. Jack and she were here on borrowed time. Whoever *they* were, their resources were well beyond hers to protect him—protect them, she amended.

"Do you remember anything? Anything specific?"

Jack slid his eyes shut. "No," he said, but that wasn't entirely true. Memories flitted through his mind—of the jungle, the sting of insects and the heavy weight of the gun in his hands. And there was the desert and something about a dog. But those memories might as well be shifting sand. He couldn't pin them to anything, or be sure that they were memories at all. How much danger had he put her in, coming here with her, and more importantly, how long could he stay before she understood that fact?

What choice did he have? He had the stamina of a newly hatched chick, and he wasn't going anywhere on his own in the next day or so. Not till he got his strength back.

He took another spoonful of soup from her, watching her when she wasn't looking. The sweet, soapy fragrance of lavender still lingered on her. She'd changed into one of her friend's silky shirts. Her hair, pulled back in a neat ponytail, was still damp from the shower she must've taken while he was asleep. He studied the color of her hair as she bent her head over the bowl. No dark roots. A natural blonde. Why didn't that surprise him? A no-nonsense, no frills woman like her didn't take time for things like that.

He smiled inwardly. Not that she needed any. Without a speck of makeup, Dr. Tess Gordon had a face that could knock a man on his butt with a simple smile. Those eyes of hers, mink-brown shot through with gold, were the kind a man could get lost in. And her mouth…

Well, he'd better not think about her mouth.

He held up his hand when she tried to feed him yet another spoonful. She was a damned fine doctor, but he couldn't stomach another mouthful of her soup.

"I'm tired," he said, sliding down on the pillow. His head felt too heavy to hold up any longer.

"Just one more thing, Jack," she said, putting the bowl down on the table beside the bed. "Do the names Joe or…Benedict mean anything to you?"

Jack frowned as something frizzled along his nerves. The second name meant nothing, but the first…Joe. It seemed to touch off something in the back of his mind, which promptly disappeared. He looked up at Tess for an explanation.

"You said those names when you were out of your head

with fever," she told him. "You called them out and said...well, some other things."

"What?" he demanded. That she knew more about him than he did made him feel even more helpless.

"It didn't make much sense, except that you seemed very angry with someone. You swore to kill him. But you were delirious. It could mean nothing."

"Yeah. Probably." Jack slid a look at the window, where a pine bough cast a shadow against the pane. His head ached and his body craved sleep. He couldn't sort it out now. His mind was a file cabinet whose contents had been thrown indiscriminately across a room. He couldn't retrieve anything, much less figure out where to look for it. He closed his eyes, deciding he'd think about who "Joe" was later. But before he could even finish the thought he was sound asleep.

Chapter 8

Long shadows spilled across the room by the time Jack woke again. His sleep had been dreamless and deep. The smell of food simmering in the other room drifted to him. Not the soup she'd fed him earlier. Something with more body to it. This time, surprisingly, the fragrant scent held a certain appeal.

He turned his head to listen for sounds in the house. He heard only silence. Was Tess asleep, too? Or maybe she'd gone out again.

Jack threw the covers off and eased himself up to a sitting position on the edge of the bed. The room swam for a minute and every aching muscle in his body protested the sudden movement. He stared down at the fading bruises across his ribs and touched the still-tender one that darkened the side of his face. It was healing, too, but not fast enough for him. He flexed his left hand and tried to lift his arm. The pain in his shoulder had faded to a dull ache, but he knew it would be days, maybe weeks before he'd have full use of his left arm again.

And his throat… Man, he thought, the Sahara had taken up residence there. He needed water. He got to his feet and made his way slowly to the bathroom, where he drank about a quart of water directly from the tap. His thirst slaked, he moved cautiously to explore the living room and find Tess.

What remained of a fire still glowed red in the fireplace. The smoky scent lingered in the air, reminding him of something. Some…memory. He knew that senses could trigger memory, like cinnamon and Christmas. Or pumpkin pie at Thanksgiving. He could remember those holidays, even recall the feelings those events evoked, but could not directly recall any details about them. Did he have a family? Did they gather together in rooms like this one to exchange Christmas gifts? Did they sing carols or string popcorn?

His gaze fell on a row of bookshelves against the far wall. A tapestry of books filled the shelves, from fiction to art and everything in between. His gaze drifted downward to the handful of framed pictures poised between two piles of art books. Moving forward, he lifted the one that caught his eye first.

Tess.

She and another woman—the dark-haired beauty who was in all the other photographs here—were standing on the slopes in ski clothes, laughing uproariously at something someone had said. Tess was pointing her pole at the camera with her nose wrinkled the way it did when she smiled. The cold air had put color in her cheeks.

He'd never heard her laugh, and wondered suddenly what it would sound like.

He put the picture down and picked up another—a group shot, with the brunette and Tess and two men. One of them, tall with dark brown cropped hair and a square jaw, had his arm possessively around Tess, whose head was resting against his shoulder. Jack searched the picture and found what he was looking for. A wedding ring on the man's left hand.

It staggered him. It hadn't occurred to him until that very moment that she could be married. That there was a Mr. Tess Gordon somewhere. How could he not have thought of it? He'd been so wrapped up in his own problems, he'd barely given a thought to hers. But she wore no ring, so maybe Mr. Gordon was past tense. He had to assume it or she wouldn't be here alone with him, would she?

He studied the picture. She looked different there with this man. He couldn't put his finger on it at first, but it came to him slowly. She looked…happy. It was something he didn't see in her eyes now. Then again, God knew what she'd risked for him, stealing him out of the hospital that way. Tess had good reason not to look happy.

Replacing the photo, he happened to glimpse something behind the stack of books. He reached out and his fingers closed around the ridged grip of a gun.

Jack smiled. So this was where she'd hidden it. He withdrew the weapon and studied it. It was a 9 mm, nickel-plated Heckler and Koch P7. An expensive gun, but one a woman could easily handle.

He blinked. How the hell did he know that? And how did he know that by pressing this button—

The clip ejected from the gun. Lifting it to eye level, he checked the load. Full. He hefted the weight in his hand. Good balance. He straightened his arm and peered down the sight. The motion felt as familiar as breathing to him.

Who the hell was he and what sort of a man had he been? Whoever was after him knew him better than he knew himself. The disadvantage was his, not to mention Tess's. The longer he stayed with her, the more danger he put her in. But he wasn't strong enough to leave just yet. Until then, he'd let her help him. And then he'd go.

The sound of footfalls on the porch jerked his attention to the door. Dammit! Someone was coming in. Instinctively, his hand tightened on the gun and he drew his left hand over the cocking mechanism. But through the shaded windows he saw a familiar shape pass by on the way to the door. Jack quickly slid the gun back into its hiding place and moved toward the kitchen.

The door thudded open and Tess, hidden behind an armload of wood, staggered into the room.

"Hi." Jack peeked around the corner with a guilty grin.

"Ohmigod!" she gasped. "You scared the hell out of me, Jack!" She slammed the door shut with her foot. "What are you doing out of bed?"

He shrugged. "I was thirsty."

She rolled her eyes. "You're supposed to be resting."

Jack couldn't help but notice that she'd thrown on a pair of old carpenter's jeans that were a hair too big for her. She'd cinched in the waist with a belt, which served only to emphasize the slenderness of that long stretch of legs beneath. "I *was* resting," he said. "And then I was thirsty. And you were—?"

"Replenishing the wood box. Obviously. You should have called me. You look terrible."

"Funny," he said, leaning his hip against the doorjamb. "I was just thinking the opposite about you."

Tess glanced up at him, ready to laugh, considering the worn flannel shirt and too-big jeans she had on. The impulse died as she took in the look in his eyes. His illness had done nothing to diminish the intensity in his sky-blue gaze or the utter maleness that oozed from every pore of his poster-boy body. "Are you...flirting with me?"

His gaze moved down her features one by one. "Flirting would imply untruth. And I meant what I said."

With an unconvinced smile, she began to unload the

wood into the box. "Maybe I should take your temperature again. I think your fever's up."

"Can't take the truth, Doc?" he asked with a slow grin.

"No, I'm just immune to one-liners," she replied lightly. "They give you a book of them in medical school and tell you to watch out for charming patients."

His face brightened. "Charming?"

She sized him up thoughtfully. "You do have a certain charm, Jack. It just won't work on me."

"Because you're married?"

She felt the blood rush away from her face. *"What?"*

The teasing expression had vanished from his. "Are you?"

She didn't answer for a long moment. "No."

He pushed away from the doorway and took a few steps toward her. "Divorced then?"

Tess tossed the last of her burden into the wood box and stood. "No."

She followed his glance to the handful of framed pictures nestled among Cara's book collection. Tess didn't have to ask which one he'd been looking at. Her chest tightened.

"Not that it's any of your business, but I was married once," she told him. "That…that's Adam. He died two years ago…. Anyway, you should go lie down. Do you need some help?"

"What, you're sending me off to bed? I'm not five years old, Tess. You can't get rid of me that easily." Jack's eyes had gone dark. "Look," he said, moving toward her even as she backed away. "I'm not trying to rattle any skeletons in your closet—"

"Then don't."

"—but it occurred to me as I looked at that picture of you that I've never seen you laugh. And I wondered who that guy was who'd wrestled one out of you."

"I don't talk about Adam, all right? With anyone. Not anymore."

"Why?" he persisted.

She twined her fingers together. "Because I chose to get on with my life. It was a choice. Do you understand?"

Jack frowned. "A choice to not talk about your dead husband? Was it a bad marriage?"

Tess rolled her eyes and braced her hands on the countertop with her back to Jack. "No."

"Did he hurt you?"

She heard the beginnings of anger in his voice. "No!" she answered, and for a moment she dared hope he'd finished the inquisition. He hadn't.

"Did you love him?"

"Yes," she said, staring out the kitchen window at the jay that had fluttered to the sill.

"Then I don't understand," he said flatly.

"Because," she said slowly, "I killed him." She turned back to Jack as he was still trying to regain a neutral expression. "How's that for a skeleton?"

For a change, Jack didn't say anything. He just stared at her.

"Don't you want to know how?"

"Are you trying to shock me now? Because if you are, you should know that I'm pretty much beyond that, considering what I've been through. Tell me what happened, Tess. Nobody's judging you here."

Damn him for being so kind, she thought, if not for forcing her to talk about it for the first time in so long. She twisted her fingers together, again inhaling the stale scent of the wood smoke lingering in the warm morning air.

"Adam was a cop," she began haltingly. "We were married for eight years. We got married young. He put me through medical school on a beat cop's salary. It was hard. We were both so busy we rarely saw each other."

Tess moved to the island and braced two hands there, staring at the wood to avoid looking at Jack. "When I moved into practice in the ER, he was offered a promotion—detective, robbery and homicide. We both wanted it. I thought he'd be safer there than dodging gang warfare bullets on the streets of L.A. He thought we'd see more of each other."

She started to pace. "Naturally, it didn't work out that way. We saw less and less of each other as our careers took off. Things started to get shaky. Talk of children all but stopped. But I think we both believed we'd have time to fix it later when things settled down. You know how it is? You think you're bulletproof, invincible—but you're not?"

Jack nodded silently, knowing only too well what she meant.

"One night, two years ago, we were short staffed at the hospital. It was, I don't know, flu season, and there was an hour when I was the only doctor on duty." She took a deep breath, leaning against the counter and folding her arms across her chest. "When they rolled him in, the staff immediately recognized him and called for backup. They tried to keep me away. But I knew as soon as I saw his partner who it was. And there was no one else. I had to do it. He'd taken a .38 in the chest—an inch or so lower than where the bullet caught you. He hadn't worn his Kevlar vest that night. He always hated that thing...." The rest choked in her throat and it was a moment before she could talk again.

"His lung was collapsed by the time he got to the hospital, and he'd lost an incredible amount of blood. And I... I couldn't save him. He was bleeding and bleeding and I tried to stop it. God, I..." Her eyes burned, but she didn't want to cry. "I couldn't stop his bleeding. He was dying right in my hands. And I couldn't do anything to *stop* it."

Suddenly, Jack was beside her, turning her and holding

her against him. She didn't even try to resist leaning into him.

"Shh" he murmured. "It wasn't your fault."

She shook her head. "If I'd done something different. If I'd—"

"You aren't God. It was his time. That's all."

"I don't accept that. I can't accept that. I failed him."

He leaned back and looked down at her. "Is that why you gave up medicine? Because you aren't perfect?"

His words stunned her, but deep inside she knew they were absolutely true. She had always expected perfection of herself. It wasn't that she hadn't lost patients. She had. Every doctor did. But losing Adam was different. "If I wasn't his wife, if I hadn't been so emotionally involved, if I'd thought more clearly, if I'd loved him better maybe I could've saved him. I don't know. I'll never know."

"*I* know," Jack assured her softly. "I know you did everything that could be done, because that's who you are. You saved *my* life. And God knows, you did it without a hospital. You didn't give up on me, and you didn't kill Adam. Whoever fired the bullet from that gun killed him."

Tess pressed her cheek against Jack's chest and held him, finally letting the tears come. Oh, how she needed someone to just hold her.... Why did she feel so safe here with this man who had the power to break her heart again?

Crazy. You're crazy, Tess. That's what. Crazy to think this could ever be for you again. It couldn't, and deep down, she knew it.

She pulled away, brushing her hair back out of her puffy eyes, and held up one palm when he tried to pull her back. "Why don't you go and lie down now? I'll fix you a bowl of soup."

Indecision held him there for a protracted moment. "Tess—"

She pressed two fingers against his lips. "Please." It

wasn't like her to beg, but she was doing just that. She needed a moment to gather herself back up again without him so close.

"Okay. How long has it been since *you've* eaten?"

She brushed a knuckle along her damp cheekbone. She couldn't remember.

"Bring in some for yourself when you come," he said. "I could use the company. And no more questions. Deal?"

A smile jerked at her lips. "Deal."

Jack refused her help this time, insisting on feeding himself. The mug made drinking the soup easier, and for a time they sat in companionable silence, eating. Finally, he glanced up at her over the rim of the cup. "I don't think I've actually thanked you."

She shrugged. "I just threw some precooked chicken and some rice—"

"I didn't mean about the soup, although it's actually good." Lowering the mug, he studied her. "I mean this." He glanced down at his shoulder. "I never thanked you for saving my life."

She dismissed it with a shake of her head. "You did all the work."

He shook his head. "Say, 'you're welcome,' Tess."

"You're welcome, Tess," she repeated, grinning in spite of herself.

He smiled back. "I'd be six feet under if you hadn't come along."

She couldn't think about that. Couldn't even contemplate it now that he'd become real and vital; not some stranger on her ER table, but a man who'd made her imagine what it would be like to live again.

She ran a finger over the rim of her mug, watching the steam rise. "You know, I practiced emergency medicine for a long time. I saw patients who were much better off than you die. Many of them. For no logical reason. I came to believe eventually that it was the strength of a patient's will to live that kept them alive.

"When you were sick, even then, I felt it from you— the burning need to live. You saved yourself, Jack. Whoever you are, whatever you did before, there's a reason you want—very much—to live."

He looked lost when she said it, as if she were talking about someone he hadn't met.

Before pondering the wisdom of it, she reached out and put her hand atop his. "It'll come back. Just give it time." She realized her mistake, but it was too late. His fingers curled around hers, sending a tingle up her arm.

"That's one thing I don't have. Why can't I remember? How can my whole life...go away?"

"It's probably just temporary." She wanted to comfort him, but didn't know how.

"*Probably?* You mean this could be permanent?" His eyes took on a deer-in-the-headlights quality. "You mean I could never remember my name or who I was before?"

She wished she could swallow back the word. "That's very unlikely."

He pulled his hand away. "Stop talking to me like a doctor. Give it to me straight. What are the odds I'm going to get my memory back?"

"I'd say the odds are in your favor. It's very unusual for amnesia patients to never regain what they've lost. Most often, after a temporal-lobe trauma like you've had, some memory loss is expected. The minutes or even hours surrounding the accident will often vanish, never to return. It's as if it never happened."

Jack's knuckles whitened around the bedsheet.

"Occasionally, for reasons we don't fully understand, a head injury will more profoundly damage memory. More, and perhaps *all* memories are erased. I can assure you, that's *very* rare. And I think because you seemed to have some memories while you were unconscious—''

''Memories?''

''The names Joe and Benedicto.''

''What if they weren't real, just dreams?''

''Do you remember anything about those dreams?''

He stared past her out the window. ''Fragments.''

She shook her head. ''Can you tell me?''

Running a hand down his face, he looked ready to jump out of his skin. ''You're not gonna like it.''

''Why not?''

''Because all of them involve guns.''

He was right. She didn't like it. She cleared her throat. ''How…exactly do you mean?''

''I mean I know things—about guns. I don't know *how* I know. I can load and unload a gun faster than you can say 'where do you come from?' And I'm not just talking about Glocks or Saturday night specials. I'm talking automatic, serious weaponry. I *know* them. I remember the weight of them in my hand.''

''Military?'' she suggested, watching him for a reaction.

His lips parted as he searched for a connection. ''A soldier?''

''Not a uniformed one, at least, but you might have been on leave, or maybe you've already mustered out.'' She reached out, took his left arm and turned it over so he could see the tattoo on the inside of his forearm. ''Does this ring any bells for you?''

Staring down at the blue marks on his skin, he began to sweat. He shook his head. ''I don't—''

''I knew a man once with a similar tattoo, Jack.'' It was a lie. A white lie, but a lie nevertheless. ''He was in the Gulf War.''

A muscle in Jack's jaw jumped as he stared at the tattoo.

''It makes perfect sense,'' she said, leaning toward him

again. "Look at you. You're in amazing condition. But you don't look like you got there at a gym. And if you were in the military you would know about guns."

"The Gulf War?" He shook his head. "I can't...it doesn't mean anything to me."

"Okay," she said softly. "Don't worry now. It was just a thought."

He couldn't stop staring at his arm. "How could I forget a whole war? How could my whole life just disappear this way? I was *somebody.* I had a goddamned *life.*"

She could only imagine how he must feel. No, she amended. No one could honestly imagine losing everything—every memory, every mental photograph. It was too awful to contemplate, and she realized she'd just piled his plate one helping too full.

He turned his face away so she couldn't see the frustration and doubt written there. It was her fault for pushing him so hard. She moved to sit on the bed beside him. "You're tired. Don't think about it now."

As if just remembering she was there, he returned his gaze to her. His emotions were naked on his face, laid bare by her. "What if I never remember?"

"Shh." Shaking her head, she brushed her fingers across the ink stain as if to erase the memory of the tattoo and all the loss that went behind it.

His eyes searched hers as if he were looking for his own soul. She'd been looked at by plenty of men in her time, but never with the singular intensity that Jack had in his eyes right now. "What if this—" he gestured at the room and at himself, as if he were a stranger in a foreign body "—is all I ever get?"

The possibility echoed with the finality of a drumbeat. "It won't be," she told him, praying it was true. "We'll figure it out. I promise." Instinctively, she reached out and touched his cheek. The dark stubble there prickled her palm, but before she could even think to move it, he covered her hand with his and leaned into the comfort of her touch.

The raw look in his eyes made her pulse stutter moments before he pulled her palm against his mouth and pressed a heart-stopping kiss there. The sensation coiled somewhere deep inside her. All she could do was stare at the way his dark lashes cast a crescent of shadow across the rugged contours of his cheekbones. And the way her hand seemed to fit there as if it were designed for it.

He looked up at her then, the need in his hooded eyes as ragged as the rhythm of the blood pumping through her veins. Lowering her hand, he waited for her to stop what was about to happen. Tess's lips fell open—denial poised there—but in the next instant, he changed his mind about asking permission.

She forgot to breathe as he pulled her toward him and slanted his mouth possessively against hers with the skill of a man who did this often and well. There was nothing gentle about this kiss. It was primal and hungry, and his fingers splayed against the back of her head as he dragged her closer. She was too stunned to fight him as he breached the seam of her mouth with his tongue and invaded. The small sound of need, she realized too late, had come from her own throat, and her hands, despite their all too obvious tremors, were clinging to his upper arms. She felt his whole body tighten in reaction to her surrender. His breath came in ragged, uneven bursts and his fingers dug into the back of her skull.

Dimly, through this haze, came the realization that this could not happen. He was her patient and she was...she was...oh, mercy...she was drowning. He deepened the kiss, slanting his mouth more firmly against hers and delving into her with his tongue. Panic crept past the haze of desire that coiled more tightly with each passing second.

She seemed to have no control over the tremors that tumbled through her.

She wrenched her head away, breaking the kiss. "Jack—"

Undeterred, he turned his attention to her jaw, then down her neck. "What?" His lips moved against her throat.

"Don't," she breathed, but her neck arched upward without her consent.

Effortlessly, he turned her head back to him so his mouth hovered just above hers. But his lips merely brushed hers as he spoke. His warm breath heated her already flushed skin.

"Don't what?" he whispered against her mouth. "Want you?"

She needed him to stop doing that. She couldn't think when he did that. "No. I can't—you aren't—"

He hesitated, his lips lingering over hers, his gaze searching her eyes for what she wasn't saying. When he found it, he eased back with a frown. "Are you…afraid of me?"

Yes. Oh, yes… "Let me go. Please."

His hesitation lasted only a moment—long enough for her to glimpse something more than disappointment in his eyes—before he did so. Tipping his head to one side, he didn't look at her, but stared hard at the rumpled sheets on the bed.

Tess scrambled to her feet, straightening her blouse and hair and backing toward the bedroom door. Her legs were shaking along with the rest of her. "That…that can never happen again."

"Why not?" His eyes were steady on her.

"Because," she said slowly, "it's not what you think it is. You're…confused."

He sat up straighter, looking anything but. "I may have lost track of my whole life, but I'm not confused about what just happened between us."

Crossing her arms across her chest, she tried to rid herself of the chill that had taken hold of her. "It's very common for patients in situations like this to think they feel something for their doctors. It's misplaced gratitude. Classic transference."

He sent her a sexy, indolent grin. "So, I guess that 'transference' thing must go both ways then, huh? I mean, I wasn't the only one doing the kissing."

She looked away. "You caught me off guard. Believe me, Jack, it's better if we just forget this ever happened."

His expression darkened and his slow, assessing gaze slid over her. "You always do that?"

"What?"

"Pull your professional ethics around you like a goddamned winter coat whenever you're threatened with a real emotion."

She winced as if he'd struck her. "And what emotion would that be? Lust?"

"God forbid you should allow yourself to enjoy a kiss from somebody other than your dead husband."

The blood fled from her face. "This has nothing to do with—"

"Maybe it's safer to hide behind a ghost than admit that a kiss from a man like me could turn you inside out, make you shake like you're shaking now."

She tightened her arms around her and swallowed hard, wanting to deny it all. But she was too busy trying to keep her teeth from chattering.

He slanted a shuttered look up at her. "Is it me you're afraid of, Tess? Or the fact that I made you feel something?"

His words hung in the air between them for the moment it took her to regain the power to move. Then she simply turned on her heel and walked out of the room. And she didn't stop moving until she'd put a mile between herself and the stranger in the cabin who threatened everything she knew to be true about herself.

Jack jerked the top two quilts off his overheated body and stared at the ceiling. If there had been something to hit, he would have knocked it across the room. As it was, he settled for pounding his fist against the pillow.

That kiss echoed across his mouth and sent a shaft of desire through his still-hard loins. How the hell had that happened? he asked himself. One minute he was looking at her, and the next he had her practically underneath him. He'd scared her. But, hell, it had come as something of a shock to him, too. Particularly the way she'd responded— as if she hadn't been touched in a very long time.

And she needed to be touched. That much was clear.

He swore silently, scrubbing a hand down his stubbled face. Who was he kidding? He was trouble, and she didn't need him trying to drag her any deeper into it. She hadn't gotten through medical school by being stupid. And apparently she'd learned the art of marshaling her needs better than he had. He had to admire the iron will it must have taken for her to walk away from what they'd both been feeling.

Well, so be it. He'd stay away from her and shove any ridiculous ideas about her out of his mind. Yeah, he thought, that and a cold shower oughta just about do it.

Jack jerked to a sitting position, unable to tolerate the inactivity that was leaching his strength. He had to get moving if he was going to get well. But even as he moved, the room took an odd turn and the flash of another room, in another time, spun before him.

The images lacked color and definition, but he could almost reach out and wrap his hand around the coat of the man standing in shadows before him, the one who spoke in low, edgy tones about a man named Ramon.

"*You got a problem with meeting him at nine?*" the shadowed man asked, apparently immune to the rhythmic sound of metal slapping metal.

"*No,*" he heard himself say. "*The only problem I've got is waiting that long.*" Like a camera, his gaze panned down to the 9 mm gun in his hands as he inserted and ejected the clip over and over again.

"*Don't worry. It'll all be over soon,*" said the shadowed man, turning toward him.

Then, like a blinking screen, the scene flicked off and eluded his every attempt to call it back.

Jack sat gripping the edge of the bed, breathing hard, staring at the rough log walls before him. The fleeting memory had merely teased his unwilling brain into daring to hope there was more. That same elusive something told him that whatever it was, it had been important enough to risk his life over. Some business he'd left undone. But what? What had he been involved in that had brought him to this?

Chapter 9

She couldn't sleep. Tess glanced over at the clock beside her bed: midnight. Another midnight in a long string of midnights. She hadn't slept well in years. But the reason for her insomnia this night was different from all the others. Tonight the reason was lying downstairs on his bed.

Well, they were a pair, weren't they? He with no memory, her with too many?

What had made her pull away? Why hadn't she just let him kiss her?

The honest answer was that his kiss had scared the hell out of her. Oh, she'd been kissed since Adam died. Her boss, Daniel, had kissed her that time he'd brought her home from a late night dinner he'd forced her to go to at Kiki Rader's house. But that kiss had been a simple meeting of the lips. It hadn't made her knees go weak, or stalled the air in her chest. It hadn't made her question her loyalty to Adam's memory or even wonder if she still owed it to him.

But Jack did. Jack did all that and more. And it terrified her.

Propping the pillow behind her, she leaned back, stared up at the darkness and wondered what had become of the Tess she used to be. The one who used to laugh. Had she lost that part of her that made her a woman?

And who was he to make her question herself like this? Wasn't her life just fine as it was? After all, she was functioning, wasn't she? All without a bit of help, thank you very much. And then Jack had to go and mess it all up.

She flicked the light switch on and reached for her purse. Taking out the cell phone, she punched in Gil's number and hoped he was awake.

A rough voice answered the phone on the first ring. "Hello?"

"Gil?"

A sigh reverberated from the other end of the line. "Well," he said impatiently, "there you are. It's not afternoon anymore, but at least it's not tomorrow yet. Oh, wait. Check that. It's 12:05. Morning, Tess."

"I know you're upset."

"I'm not upset. Do I sound upset?" His voice rose two decibels. "I'm worried as hell about you and you're gonna give me an ulcer!"

Her mouth went dry. "What's wrong?"

"Oh, nothing. Except for the goons I had on my tail all day. I managed, however, to ditch them once I located the numerous surveillance devices they'd tucked into my car, my squad-room phone and my home phone. They've been inside my house." He stopped and let that sink in for a minute. "Aside from that, my day was peachy. You were right. About all of it."

"Oh, Gil—" she shut her eyes "—I'm sorry. I've made such a mess of things."

"This isn't your fault, Tess, but whoever these guys are,

they're playing for keeps. And they're good. I can't help but think they wanted me to find those bugs. As a message. I was on my way to get you when I spotted them.''

"Gil! You promised you wouldn't—''

"I know what I promised. But you're in way over your head on this. And I'm not sure who they've got on me. Or what tags I've missed. I can't take the chance of trying to get to you or I'll lead them right there.'' He paused for a long moment. "Who *are* those guys?''

Who, indeed? Tess fell silent. If they had spied on Gil, what else did they already know about her? Did they know about Cara? This cabin?

"I called your Dr. Waltrip.''

Tess dragged her thoughts back to the conversation. "And?''

"He claims someone did call him into work that night on an emergency gunshot wound, but he was called not fifteen minutes later on his cell phone, canceling. Someone claiming to be the charge nurse said the patient had been transferred to another facility for insurance reasons.''

Tess smiled grimly. So they had covered almost all of their bases, but whatever information Waltrip had wouldn't hold up in any investigation without the rest of the pieces. It seemed that the whole night had been erased. But how and by whom?

"By the way,'' Gil said, breaking into her thoughts, "how's the patient?''

"Cranky,'' was all she said.

"He hasn't tried anything with you, has he?''

Gil sounded like an overprotective brother ready to jump to her defense at a moment's notice. He knew her the way a professional gambler knew what hands his opponents were holding by just looking at the way they were sitting at the table. "Tried anything? No,'' she lied. "I mean, he's practically an invalid.''

She thought briefly of the look in Jack's eyes when he'd trapped her against him, that predatory glint that had reminded her of nothing less than a hungry mountain cat. And she thought about the way he'd kissed her. That wouldn't go away.

"Don't get involved," Gil warned. "It would be a mistake."

"Involved?" Her attempt to infuse the word with innocence failed utterly.

"You know what I mean. You're caught in something bigger than the two of you. It's easy to lose perspective."

That's exactly what she'd told Jack. "Can I ask you something, Gil?"

He was silent a moment, as if trying to brace himself for what he knew was coming. "What?"

"Am I...do you think I seem...unapproachable? Cut off from my emotions?" She waited for him to reply, but when he hesitated, she pressed on. "I mean, since Adam died, am I so different?"

He seemed to choose his words carefully. "Of course you're different. You lost your husband. You've been hurt. It's natural that you'd take a step back for a while."

Her throat felt thick. "So I am, then."

A long pause stretched across the airwaves between them. Gil's voice, when he spoke, was roughened by emotion. "Is this about him?" About Jack, he meant.

She shook her head in the dark. "It's about me. About the me I seem to have lost. I don't know where I went, Gil."

"You're healing," he said gently. "That's nothing to be ashamed of." She could almost hear him rubbing his temples. "You're falling for this guy, aren't you?"

Gil's question hit her like a fist to the stomach, pushing the air from her lungs. "That's ridiculous. I don't even know his real name. Besides," she added, "Adam is—"

"—dead. He's dead, Tess."

Tess fell silent, waiting for Gil to take it back, to remind her that she owed her loyalty to his late partner, her husband. But he didn't.

"Be careful, darlin'," he said at last. "Be very, very careful. Because if he breaks your heart, I'll personally finish what those other guys started."

She wished, for a moment, that Gil was the man who made her feel light-headed. But it was Jack who did that, and there was nothing she could do about it. "Bye, Gil. I'll be in touch."

"I'm counting on it."

Tess didn't go back to his room again until morning. She was surprised to find him standing at the window staring out through the pines. He'd dressed, wearing his jeans, which she'd washed, and a men's white, button-down shirt she'd scrounged out of the back of Cara's closet. His feet were bare, sticking out under the worn hems of his jeans. The sight set something tumbling through her stomach. Setting down the tray of food beside his bed, she stood still until he turned around.

"You're up." Stating the obvious was becoming a habit. "I brought you some breakfast."

He glanced at the tray without replying.

"I'll, uh, leave you alone."

"Tess," he called after her.

She turned back with a questioning look.

"About last night— It was my fault. I shouldn't have pushed you. I was way out of line."

She shook her head. "But you were right."

A frown tugged at his brow. "What happened between you and your husband is none of my business."

Tess wrapped her hand around the pineapple finial at the end of the bedpost and fingered the carving there. "It's been nobody's business for a long time. A taboo topic. I thought if I didn't think about him, about what happened, that I could put it behind me and move on. But last night, I realized that it's had just the opposite effect.'' She looked up to find Jack watching her intently. ''You were right when you said it was easier for me to hide behind his ghost than to really feel anything. It's so much easier.''

Jack didn't say anything. He just watched her.

''And I haven't felt anything in a long time. Really *felt* it. Not until you.'' The admission shocked even her, and she half wished she could swallow it back down.

He stared at the floor. ''It shouldn't have happened, Tess.''

She knew he meant the kiss, but she was talking about so much more. ''No, you're right,'' she said quickly. ''You're absolutely right. And it won't. Ever again. But it made me realize how I've been using Adam's death to straight-arm the people who care about me. To hold them at bay. And, Adam doesn't deserve to be remembered that way.'' She looked up at him. ''You would have liked him.''

Jack wondered, considering that the man had stolen a piece of Tess that she might never reclaim. A piece of her heart he wanted to know. He shook off the thought. No, she was still in love with the guy. That was plain enough. And there wasn't enough room in what was left of her broken heart for a man with no name and no past. And no room in whatever fragments remained of his for a woman like her. But it didn't stop him from wondering about the man who'd gotten there first.

He lowered himself down on the bed, covering his aching shoulder with his hand, and against his better judgment said, ''Tell me about him.''

She hugged her arms to her chest. ''He was a good man. Kind. Ambitious. A little impatient…like you.''

Jack wasn't sure why, but he smiled at the comparison.

"He would take me fly-fishing. He loved to fish. Of course, I was abysmal at it. I couldn't throw the darned thing and I had the ungraceful tendency to fill my waders more often than I hooked a fish. But this one time, a few years ago, he had this brand-new, shiny fly rod he'd saved months for, and he couldn't wait to use it. He had it all set up with a handmade fly he'd taken hours tying." Tess laughed, remembering. A dimple appeared miraculously in her cheek.

Jack couldn't stop looking at her, wondering how he'd missed it, and thinking she was the prettiest thing he'd ever laid eyes on.

"Anyway," she continued, "he carefully baited mine, knowing I wouldn't catch anything because I never did. And then he cast out over the river and waded in."

She looked at Jack with a twinkle in her eye. "Well, naturally, not two minutes later, something hit my line like a Mack truck and nearly pulled me in. I got so excited, I screamed for him to help me, and he came lumbering over in his waders to my rescue. And he would've made it, too, if it hadn't been for that deep hole in the river bottom."

Laughing, Tess covered her mouth with her hands, remembering. "Oh, he was *mad,* and soaking wet. His prize pole went flying downstream, never to be seen again, and that fish that hit my line? History. Gone with my bait."

"No," Jack said, just wanting her to keep talking.

"Yes!" She shook her head. "And I couldn't stop laughing. Oh... He never forgave me for that darned pole. And from then on, I sat on the bank and watched him."

Still smiling, she looked at Jack, flushed by the memory. She sighed. "That felt good."

"What?" he asked softly. "To remember him?"

"To remember something other than that last day. Something good." But in the next instant she looked stricken. "Oh, Jack, that was mean of me. I'm sorry."

"What?"

"When you can't remember anything...I'm sorry."

She continued to amaze him. "Don't be ridiculous. Just because my memory's gone the way of the dinosaurs doesn't mean I can't enjoy yours. I like hearing you talk, watching you smile."

Color crept to her cheeks. "It's ironic, isn't it? You want so desperately to remember, and I wish I could forget."

"Not so ironic," he mused. "You know what they say? Opposites attract."

"Do they?" She smiled slowly. "Maybe we're not so opposite, after all."

The sound of a car on the gravel drive outside the window drew their attention.

"Oh, hell," Jack swore, pushing the curtains aside just as a khaki-uniformed sheriff stepped from the green-and-white patrol car sitting in Tess's driveway.

Chapter 10

"Let me handle this." Tess got to her feet, feeling panic creep up her throat.

Jack's eyes went wide and they scanned the room like a trapped cat. "*Handle* it?".

"I know him. It's Dan Kelso. Just take a deep breath.'

The loud knock on the door in the next room made them both jump.

Stay here, she mouthed, and walked to the living room

She opened the door as Dan was pulling his sunglasse off.

"Tess." His smile was genuine, and the lump in her throat eased a bit.

"Dan. What a surprise." Her own smile felt frozen, and she hoped he didn't notice the way her lips quivered. Swea gathered between her breasts as she eased past the door and forced him back onto the porch. Tandy, the golden retrieve from next door, bounded up the steps to Dan, wagging her tail.

He scratched the dog behind the ears. "Hiya, girl. Long time no see."

Tandy panted and sniffed at Tess's legs, then moved her attention to the door, ignoring them both.

Dan lifted his hat off and curled the brim in one hand. Tall as the door frame, he had the kind of boy-next-door looks—with his sandy-brown hair, hazel-green eyes and endless smile—that could turn a girl's head. He hadn't seen thirty-five yet, but he had small lines around his eyes from smiling. He'd been pursuing Tess for the last year with a quiet patience she couldn't quite comprehend.

"Ned mentioned that you were in town," he said in that slow drawl that betrayed his Texas roots.

She frowned, her mind blank as she scratched Tandy and kneed her away from the door. "Ned...?"

Dan grinned. "...Wilton? At the pharmacy?"

"Oh." She laughed. "*Ned.* He told you?"

"Yeah, he said you'd been in for some bandages and things, and I thought I'd just drop by and see if you were okay."

"Oh! That's so nice of you to worry about me, but I'm fine. Right as rain. It was nothing. I told him. Just a scratch from a fence. I fixed it right up."

The same famous smile that had gotten him elected spread across his mouth. Under different circumstances she might have welcomed his visit. But not now. Not with Jack inside the house.

"You up here for a vacation?"

Tandy whined and scratched at the door.

Tess laughed, and it sounded suspiciously like a bubble of hysteria. "Yeah. A vacation. You know what they say, all work and no play..." *Oh, that was original.* She took the dog by the collar and hauled her back to sit near her feet.

"Yeah, Cara said you'd been working way too hard last time I saw her."

"Oh," Tess said, "she worries too much about me. She's in Brazil, you know. She said I could use the cabin. Anytime. So, I'm just, um, using it."

"Good. Well, that was another reason I stopped by," he said, looking more serious.

Tess felt her smile slipping.

"You got a cat in there or something?" Dan asked with a laugh, watching Tandy.

"Uh, no. I don't know what her problem is. Just wants in, I think. You were saying?"

"Your promise," he reminded her.

She frowned, hauling back on Tandy's collar. "My p-promise?"

"That you'd have dinner with me the next time you came up. Remember?"

Her heart sank. Of course, she remembered. She'd only said it because he wouldn't stop asking her, and she'd decided that it wouldn't be so awful to spend an evening with a man like Dan. She could do a lot worse. But his timing could use some work.

"I did promise, didn't I?" she said, wincing. "It's just that I brought a lot of work up with me and I'm kind of behind on this deadline…"

His eyebrow went up in reprimand. "I thought this was a vacation."

She smiled. "Well, you know how it is. I can never get completely away from work. It kind of follows me around." Tandy growled and woofed. Tess pulled the dog to the step and pointed to the house next door. "Tandy, go home! Now!"

The retriever's ears drooped and she slunk disconsolately down the steps, glancing back as she plodded across the yard.

"Listen—about my invitation. You still have to eat," he said easily. "It's just dinner. What do you say? Tomorrow night at seven? There's a real nice little place that just opened down on Main. Dilly's. They're having a little thing for the Pioneer Days Festival. Good food." When she still hesitated, he added, "C'mon, Tess. It'll be fun. You could use a little fun, I think."

That phrase sounded vaguely familiar. She should have felt simple relief that he hadn't come about Jack. But what she felt wasn't relief. It was trepidation. His invitation was a minefield, strewn with more complications than she could navigate. But if she turned him down again, he'd be suspicious.

"Tomorrow at seven then," she said, forcing a smile.

Dan returned it in spades. "You won't be sorry, Tess."

Yes, she would. But she smiled anyway. "I'll look forward to it."

Dan slid his Stetson back on his head and skipped down the stairs. She watched until he waved, pulling out of her driveway, before she slid back inside the house. What she saw made her suck in a breath.

"*Jack!*" Her horrified gaze went from the gun he was holding, to his face, and back again. "What are you doing?"

He shoved the pistol back behind the books. "What does it look like?"

Her mouth opened and closed soundlessly. It took her a moment to realize that all the while she'd been talking to Dan, Jack had been standing there with the gun trained, ready to blow him off her porch. "And what were you going to do with it? *Shoot* him?"

"Just playing it safe, Tess. That's all. I wasn't going to shoot him."

"No?" She wasn't sure she believed him.

He didn't reply, simply prowled back to the bedroom.

She followed him. "Are you capable of shooting a man in cold blood, Jack?"

He slumped down on the bed and rubbed his temple. "Do you think I am?"

"I'm asking you."

He closed his eyes and draped one forearm over them. "I guess the fact that you are answers my question."

Anger vibrated through her. What if she'd been wrong about him? What if Gil was right? What if that APB belonged to him and he *had* murdered someone? "How dare you question my motives? You're the one who was holding a gun. And how did you find that gun? I hid it."

He lifted his forearm and sent her a look that said she should have known better. "What did Deputy Dan want?"

Tess ground her fingernails into her palms. "Sheriff," she almost spat. "And he wanted a date."

"A date?"

"Yes. He wants me to go out with him. Tomorrow night. For dinner."

"You turned him down." It wasn't a question but an assumption of fact.

"Actually," she said, strolling to the window, "I accepted."

Jack gaped at her.

"I had to. I had promised him that next time I came up I'd have dinner with him. I tried to get out of it, but he was persistent. If I'd flatly turned him down, it would have looked suspicious."

"Suspicious? Do you think he might be the least bit put out by the fact that you're harboring a fugitive under his nose?"

Tess folded her arms. "Only if you do something foolish again like point a gun at him. Otherwise, he won't even know you're here."

But I'll know you're with him. The thought made Jack

want to smack his forehead with an open palm. What was wrong with him? Was he actually jealous? The possibility was laughable. Jealous of what? Tess''s affections? The flush Deputy Dan had put on her face? Or was it simply the knowledge that nothing that started out this bad could ever be good?

Frustrated, Jack lurched off the bed. The sudden movement made him freeze. He grabbed his throbbing shoulder, bit back a curse and sat back down, cradling his arm against his chest. Jack wanted to lash out at something. Just when he thought he was getting his feet under him, the damned rug disappeared from beneath him again. He needed some control. He needed his damned life back!

Tess took a few steps toward him before stopping. "Are you—?"

He waved her off. "I'm fine! I'm *great*. My shoulder feels like an elephant sat on it, my memory has more holes than Swiss cheese and my doctor's getting cozy with the local law enforcement."

"It's only dinner," she argued gently.

Only dinner with a guy every woman's mother would kill to have sitting at her—

The thought was cut short by an image in his mind. Like a silent movie screen on the blink, a picture flashed of a dark-haired, beautiful woman he didn't recognize seated across the table from him. *"It's only dinner,"* she was saying, her tone curt and angry. *"Why did I imagine it'd be anything more?"* Her hostility was palpable as she deliberately put her fork down and threw her napkin on the table as she shoved herself to her feet. Then the picture vanished like a blip on a computer screen.

Only then did he realize how hard he was gripping the bedpost.

"What is it?" Tess was asking, moving toward him with a frown. "Jack?"

"I—I don't know." And he didn't. He had no idea who that woman was and why he'd thought of her. But his pulse raced with the possibilities.

"Are you remembering something?"

"Maybe. But I can't be sure."

Tess moved to kneel in front of him. "What was it? Can you tell me?"

Sweat had broken out on his brow. He likened the feeling to remembering a dream once you'd opened your eyes. The truth of it evaporated a little with each passing moment. That tentative connection with the woman in that picture was even now fading. But the feeling that his memory would eventually return was growing stronger. "It's nothing solid. Someone I must have known. A woman."

She arched one eyebrow. "Were there weapons involved?"

"Only if looks could kill." He liked it when Tess smiled that way, as if they were sharing news over the breakfast table. As if she'd known him forever.

"Who was she?"

"I don't know. I didn't get much. Just a flash."

Tess bit her lip pensively. "That's encouraging, don't you think? I mean, maybe it'll all start tumbling back now. Maybe this is just the first trickle in the broken dam."

If it were only that simple, he thought. He looked down at the tattoo on his forearm and wondered about it. He felt strongly that it was somehow connected with that memory of the woman, but how?

He looked up at Tess, who was still watching him intently, as if she believed she could understand him if she simply tried hard enough. He suspected that a woman like her operated on that theory with a fairly high success rate. He suspected, however, that with him she was headed for a fall. And not the sort he would prefer. No, if she stuck with him, he would undoubtedly take her down with him.

A silent clock was ticking in his head. Time was running out. For both of them.

Maybe a date with Deputy Dan was the best thing that could have happened to her. Who better to protect her from whoever was pursuing them than the local constable?

That thought naturally led to the next, inevitable one: when the time came, how could Jack actually let her go?

"You need to rest," she said, putting a hand on his good shoulder and pressing him back onto the bed. "You'll never get well driving yourself crazy like this. Close your eyes. I'm going out for a while to get some food. I want you to sleep while I'm gone. Got that?"

Jack frowned as she tucked a quilt around him. He hated that she was right. But being horizontal was like a Pavlov's cue for his body to sleep. Fatigue weighed on him like a heavy blanket. He despised being less than whole and hated even more that she knew it. But sleep was the only thing that would heal him now. And whatever it took to accomplish that, he would do.

"Hey, Tess?"

She turned on her way out the door. "Yeah?"

"I was just…" He wasn't sure why he'd called her back. Maybe it was to see the way the morning light fell across the soft contours of her cheek, or the way his saying her name out loud always seemed to catch her off guard. Maybe just to keep her with him for a few more minutes. Whatever the reason, he didn't regret it. Fixing the sight of her in what remained of his memory, he decided against diving into water that was black and uncharted and strictly off-limits. "Never mind," he said at last.

"What?" she prodded. "Tell me."

"It's dumb. I was just wondering if…if none of this had happened, if we'd just met like two regular people, would you have turned me down for dinner—if I'd asked?"

She studied the fabric of the quilt on his bed. "I probably

would've," she admitted, "but it would've been my mistake." She looked up at him through a sweep of lashes and smiled. "Go to sleep now."

She was gone before he could ask her to elaborate.

He closed his eyes with a sigh. Hell, he thought, thinking of the look she'd sent him. He could probably get Tess Gordon into bed with him. And he was damned sure he wouldn't disappoint her. But she wasn't the type of woman a man diddled, then walked away from. She was the kind of woman a man put down roots with. Just the kind a tumbleweed like him could never have.

Late afternoon sunlight slanted through the room by the time Jack opened his eyes again. Groggily, he pulled himself awake to the sound of pans clanking in the kitchen and the awareness that Tess had returned. For a few minutes he lay there, allowing himself to imagine her moving about in the kitchen preparing food for them. Somehow the whole day had slipped past him, but a quick inventory of his various aching parts told him the sleep had been well worth the time spent. He felt better. Considerably better. As if his gas tank had been topped off.

He sat up and gingerly rolled his left shoulder, surprised to find that it no longer moved like a rusted-out hinge. It was still sore, but the pain was manageable. He threw off the quilt and got up. That was when he made the mistake of looking in the mirror hanging over the pine dresser at the end of his bed. The image that stared back at him was a stranger who looked as if he'd dragged himself in off the mean streets of L.A. He needed a shower and a shave and a clean shirt, but he guessed it might be a few more days before Tess let him get his shoulder wet. Even more than cleanliness, he thought, dragging a hand through his hair and listening to his stomach growl, he needed food.

The scent of it drew him toward the kitchen, where Tess

had her back to the doorway, fussing over something at the sink. She didn't hear him padding barefoot into the room, and jumped when he touched her arm.

"Sorry," he said, staring at the handful of grapes still dripping with water in her hand. "Didn't mean to scare you. How long have you been back?"

"About two hours," she said, wrapping the fruit in a paper towel and setting it on the counter. "I didn't have the heart to wake you. You looked so peaceful. How do you feel?"

"Better. A lot better." He opened the refrigerator door and pulled out a jug of milk. Twisting off the top, he nearly drank straight from the bottle, but Tess intercepted with a glass.

"Hungry?" she asked dryly.

He smiled and downed the milk without coming up for air. "Mmm. Milk," he sighed, pointing at the empty glass, "was a great invention."

"Yes," she agreed gravely. "Bovines are masters of technology. Yogurt was theirs, too, you know."

"No!" he said, lifting his eyebrows and watching the playful expression steal over Tess's face. "They invented that?"

"Oh, yes. And ice cream. They had it first. Before all the lactose-intolerant herds began producing rank imitations." She wrinkled her nose. "But you know, the quality just isn't there."

Jack grinned. "You're a wealth of information, Doc."

"And you've gotten your appetite back."

"Apparently," he replied, popping some more grapes in his mouth. "What's for dinner?"

"It's a surprise."

Jack moved in the direction of the covered pan on the stove to peek.

"Ah-ah!" she warned, coming between him and the

stove. "It's not ready yet." As a matter of fact, I think you have just time enough for a hot shower."

He swiveled, sending her a disbelieving look. "A shower? Don't tease me, Tess."

She grinned. "I never tease about something that important. You could wait another day or so, but I don't think irrigating your wound will hurt. Just take care not to let the spray hit it directly. Do you think you're up to standing that long?"

"I'd sell my soul for it." Jack was close enough to smell the fragrance of soap on her and the alluring scent that belonged only to her. He couldn't pull his gaze from the way her teeth slid against her lower lip.

"It won't cost you that much."

His gaze moved to her eyes. "What?"

Color flushed her face. "The shower. You can have it for free."

"Oh," he said. "Right. The shower."

"Do you, uh, need any help getting the bandage off?"

"Thanks, but I can handle it," he said, moving toward the bathroom and closing the door behind him.

"Okay," she said a little uncertainly. "Towels are in the cabinet to the right of the sink, and if you get dizzy just call me."

Call her? Stripping off his jeans, he knew calling her could be damn near fatal. He wouldn't think about Tess standing on the other side of that door, waiting for him to get naked. Nor would he contemplate the rather explicit image he had in his mind of her joining him there. No, he decided, giving the shower faucet a vicious twist, he would just step into that steaming water and not think at all. That and ripping the hair off his chest beneath this adhesive tape was his best defense against the creeping suspicion that thinking was the least of his problems where Tess was concerned.

* * *

When he'd finished his shower and shave, he wrapped the towel around his hips and opened the bathroom door, half expecting to see Tess there waiting to catch him.

Instead, he heard her humming in the kitchen, rattling plates and silverware. Dinner smelled sumptuous and he was prepared to make a hog of himself. He couldn't remember ever feeling so hungry. Of course, he couldn't remember much of anything before three days ago, so he supposed that didn't count for much.

The table in the living room was half-set. She'd picked some wildflowers and shoved them artfully into an old blue, speckled coffeepot. He ignored the two glasses of wine and went for the ice water set at one of the places. He had yet to quench this thirst of his and couldn't seem to get enough water. Glancing down at the towel around his hips, he decided it wasn't the proper attire for dinner, and headed back to the bathroom for his pants.

Her purse lay on the couch, but that wasn't what caught his eye. It was the cell phone tucked inside, exposed by the open flap of her purse. What the hell? She hadn't told him she had a phone.

Jack glanced at the kitchen, then reached into Tess's purse. He picked up the phone and stared down at it. The power was off. He pushed the on button and the small green screen flashed with the message, "Missed call."

A bad feeling crawled up his neck. She'd told him no one knew where they were. Who had been trying to call her? And who had she been calling? He scrolled up to the messages and found one: "Call me back. Gil."

He pressed the talk button twice. The phone automatically dialed the last number Tess had dialed. He waited while the number connected. A machine answered.

"You've reached Detective Gil Castillano. I'm not here to take your call, but leave your name, a brief message and your phone number at the tone and I'll get back to you as soon as I can.''

Jack sat down hard. *Detective?* She'd been calling a *cop?*

Tess's timing couldn't have been worse. Looking happy and content, with hands full of plates and silverware, she hurried into the room. ''Oh, you're finished,'' she said, setting the dishes on the table. ''But you're not dressed. Dinner's ready. I just have to—''

Then she really looked at him. The expression on Jack's face erased the smile from hers. The phone in his hands made her go absolutely pale.

''Who's Gil?'' he said.

She swallowed hard. ''What are you doing going through my purse? And how did you know about Gil?''

He stood, holding on to the towel loosely hanging around his hips. Redialing Gil's phone number with the punch of a button, he watched Tess go pale. ''What are you doing calling cops? When were you going to tell me? When you turned me over to them? Or were you just going to surprise me?''

She had the nerve to look stricken. ''It isn't like that.''

''Really? What is it like? And what happened to 'we have to trust each other, Jack'? I guess that means me, right? I have to blindly trust you even when you—''

''Stop it and listen to me. I didn't betray you. If I had, do you think we'd still be alone here? Believe me, we wouldn't. If you'll just listen for a minute—''

''I'm all ears,'' he snapped, tossing the phone down roughly on the couch. ''Let's start with Gil.''

Tess's eyes strayed to the towel at his hips and back to his face again. ''Gil is a detective with the LAPD.''

''Correct me if I'm mistaken, but isn't that exactly who we've been trying to get away from?''

''He's with the Westside Division, not Santa Monica. He was Adam's partner and he's a very dear friend.''

Jack's eyebrows went up. "Exactly how dear?"

She shook her head. "Not like that," she said, sounding defensive. "He's probably the only thing that held me together through the last two years. I called him because he would have been worried about me. He's the only one who would have been worried about me."

Jack stood watching her, his body taut with anger as she went on.

"When I smuggled you out of the hospital, I was afraid. I didn't know who those men were who were chasing you and I didn't know what to do. I needed someone on the inside I could trust to help me. Help us. You have to believe me, Jack, I never betrayed you."

"So, this Gil...he knows where we are?"

She shook her head. "Yes, but I didn't tell him. He figured it out. But these people, the ones after you—us—put surveillance devices on his car, they've bugged his phone...."

He rolled his eyes. "Ah, hell—"

"They're watching him. He wouldn't do anything to put me in more danger."

Jack stalked to the window, pulled back the curtain and stared out through the thicket of pines that surrounded the cabin. "*More* being the operative word. If they've connected him to you, what about to Cara? This place?"

"There's nothing at my house to connect me to her except maybe my address book, but they'd have no reason to think I'm here. It would be a long shot at best. This cabin belonged to her parents, anyway, and is registered under their names."

"What else does Gil know? About me."

Tess wished he'd put something on besides that towel. And that he'd stop looking at her as if she'd suddenly grown horns. "There's a warrant out on a man fitting your description."

"A warrant?"

She hesitated, not wanting to tell him. "For murder."

He made a strangled sound. "God Almighty! Who am I supposed to have—"

"A drug smuggler named Ramon Saldovar."

His gaze whirled around the room, landing on a dozen different places as if he were seeking some kind of handhold. "A *drug smuggler?*"

She nodded.

With an oath, he hugged his bad arm to his chest and started pacing around the room. "I *killed* him?"

His words galvanized her, and she intercepted him. "Jack—"

But he wouldn't let her touch him. Jerking his arm away from her touch, he glared at her. *"Did I?"*

"We don't know that. I believe you've been set up. There's more. Sit down."

"No." He stalked past her with no real destination, stopping only for walls and furniture. "Why didn't you tell me this?"

Indeed. "You've been very sick."

"Dammit, Tess, no more lies! Not now!" A vein throbbed in his neck.

The room had grown uncomfortably warm and she dragged her gray sweater off and dropped it on the upholstered ottoman beside her knee. "I couldn't tell you before. I didn't...know if I could trust you."

A laugh that sounded more like a bark erupted from him. "And obviously you still don't." He grabbed up the phone and thrust it at her.

Her head was beginning to pound. "You think this is that simple?"

"Simple?" He said it with the inflection of a man who'd just been told the moon was blue.

Guilt gave way to the first stirrings of anger. "Are you

forgetting that I saved your life? That I was the one who stayed up forty-eight hours straight so you wouldn't die?''

A muscle in his jaw jumped, but he didn't say anything.

Her whole body was trembling and she couldn't stop it. ''I did what I had to do to save your life. And to save mine. Tell me, Jack, if the situation were reversed, what would you have done?''

He bowed his head, staring at the floor.

''You owe me at least the benefit of the doubt here.''

Jack heaved the cell phone onto the couch and followed it down. Shoving his hands through his still-damp hair, he shook his head slowly. ''You're right. I have no right to question your motives.''

''No more than I do yours.'' She stalked into the bathroom, came back with his jeans and threw them at him. ''Get dressed. I can't talk to you in that towel.''

Turning her back on him, she listened to the slide of stiff fabric as he dragged the jeans on and buttoned them. She needed a moment to gather her wits, to calm down.

''You can turn around now.''

Losing the towel had done nothing to diminish the distraction Jack's body provided, she mused with annoyance, except perhaps to remind her that he was as sexy in clothes as he was out of them. With his hair damp from his shower and his jaw freshly shaved, he hardly resembled the man she'd stumbled upon the other night on the road, or the one Gil was so convinced was a villain.

The outrage that had sparked in Jack's eyes only moments earlier had cooled to a smoldering disillusionment. Never had she been more acutely aware of how alone and lost he really was. The possibility that she, his only friend, had betrayed him too, had been an ugly blow, and not one that made her proud. She should have told him about Gil sooner. Why hadn't she, honestly?

Was it that she was, in truth, afraid of him? Or—and this

possibility seemed infinitely more unsettling—did she fear that once he did remember his past, he would no longer need her?

"You said there was more. What else, besides the fact that I'm allegedly a murderer and a drug smuggler, is there?"

"I told you I don't believe that."

"So you said." Jack studied her with the cool detachment of a man who had already gotten too close to the fire and wasn't about to make the same mistake again.

Tess sat down on the couch and motioned for him to join her. Reluctantly, he did.

"The night I brought you to the hospital? Those records have disappeared. There is no record of either of us being there. Or of any gunshot victim." The expression on his face, she thought, was chillingly familiar. She went on. "The nurse who was assigned to you? She left on an extended vacation the day after you were there, and the surgeon we called in to operate on you was called off the case before he even reached the hospital."

"So it's been erased like the rest of my life." He slumped against the cushions. "How is that possible?"

She shook her head. "Perhaps someone on the inside was paid to take care of it."

"The plot thickens," he said dryly.

Tess smiled weakly. "There's more. Gil thinks you were in the military. In the Gulf War. That tattoo on your arm is a Special Forces emblem. He thinks Navy SEALS. Ring any bells for you?"

Like an explosion of frigid water crashing over him came the image of a mass of bodies moving through sand and darkness beneath a tangle of razor wire, of his own voice shouting hoarsely over the din of explosions. "Disengage! Fall back!" And the cries of men under a darkening sky. And then it was gone.

Shaken, Jack felt the thud of his heart against the wall of his chest and the rush of his own blood in his ears. Bells? That had set off a damned cannonade!

"What is it?" Tess was asking past the ringing in his ears. "Did you remember something?"

"Yeah," he said shakily, rubbing the fading bruise on his temple. "Yeah." Clenching his jaw, he got up and paced to the window. "Flashes. Images. Nothing . solid. Nothing—" he turned back to her "—real."

She was beside him then, touching his arm, holding him there like a tethered balloon.

"It's real," she said. "You just can't hold the pieces together yet. Give it time."

"Time?" he growled. His hands were suddenly around her upper arms, his fingers digging into her flesh. "That's something neither one of us has the luxury of. I need it now. Do you understand that?"

"Yes."

Her voice sounded small and scared, and the look in her eyes warned him that he was inches from losing what small grip he retained on civility. Deliberately, he loosened his hands and turned away from her. She didn't move away. She just stood watching him.

"Look," she said slowly, "I understand that you're frustrated and angry, and you have every right to be. But, Jack—"

He slapped the window frame and turned back to her. "That's not even my name! That's some guy you invented. Jack doesn't exist. I'm not him. I'm not even *me!*"

She moved to his left, where he couldn't avoid her. "What should I call you then?" she asked in a tone that made him look at her. "Bob? Or maybe Jimbo? Or we could eliminate names altogether. If you wanted my attention, you could just, you know, wave. If I wanted yours, I could strip off all my clothes."

He angled a look at her. "*All* of your clothes? Go on. I'm warming to the idea."

"I suspected you would," she said, tipping her chin up, "despite the hypothetical nature of the suggestion."

"Hypothetical, huh?"

"Purely."

His gaze slid heatedly down the length of her and back up. "Too bad."

Her dimple appeared when she smiled that way. On the right side of her mouth. When she looked down at the floor, it disappeared.

"So my thinking is this," she said, as if she'd never brought up a suggestion that had heated his blood in the blink of an eye. "Your memory will come back when it's good and ready and no amount of angst is going to make it happen any faster. In fact, stress could actually slow down the process."

"Stress."

"Right. For example, you're taking a test, trying to remember some critical answer that just won't come, which naturally pops into your mind hours later when you're not even thinking about it. That happens because your mind is clearer, unfettered by stress."

His mind must have just cleared, because the idea of seeing her naked, stripped of everything but the look he saw in her eyes right now, had taken root there and in other parts of his body.

"So," she added, "that's why we're going out."

"Out?" Surely she was joking.

"Out. A change of scenery. You've got cabin fever, Jimbo. I'm busting us out of this joint for the evening. After we eat, of course."

"I don't know. Maybe it's not such a good idea to—"

"Either you're going to trust me or not, Jack. What's it going to be?"

Chapter 11

They left at dusk, when the rest of the mountain community was settling down to cozy fires and supper. The lake had emptied of its daily quotient of tourists and boats. The half-moon rose like a broken coin above the black water. Tess's paddle bisected its reflection as she steered Cara's ancient birch-bark canoe toward the center of the lake.

At the bow of the canoe, behind the small light they'd hung there as a precaution, Jack leaned against a pile of seat cushions with his back to the water, watching her.

"Shouldn't this be the other way around?" he asked with a frown. "Me doing the work, you enjoying the view?"

"We wouldn't get very far that way with your shoulder, would we? Besides, I don't mind," she said, switching sides with the paddle. "I do this all the time alone."

"Really?"

"I like it out here at night. Sometimes early in the morning when no one is up yet. It gives me a chance to think."

"Is that my cue to shut up?"

She laughed. "No. Tonight, we're here not to think. Deal?"

"Deal," he agreed. "So, while we're not pondering our prospects, are we heading somewhere in particular?"

She smiled. "You'll see."

"So we *are* going someplace."

"My favorite place in the world."

He lifted his eyebrows and settled back against the seat cushions and blankets. Overhead, the stars appeared against the indigo sky like so many scattered diamonds. Up here, no city lights dimmed the view. The expanse of sky seemed contained only by the ring of mountains hemming the lake. Here, Tess thought, one could almost forget the realities that existed beyond the boundaries of this dark water, and imagine a different sort of life.

She paddled another twenty minutes in silence, listening to the sound of her paddle sliding smoothly in and out of the water. At the far end of the lake, they could just make out the colored lanterns glowing on the shoreline for the Pioneer Days festivities. Distant music drifted across the water. Jack lay staring up at the sky, lost in his own private thoughts. Occasionally, she would glance up to find him watching her instead. It gave her a secret thrill to feel his gaze on her.

Something was shifting between them. She couldn't identify it, or even describe it, because she'd never felt anything like it before. Not even with Adam.

She could attribute it to circumstances. It would be easy enough to blame the awful situation for bringing them closer. But it was more than that. And about more than the decidedly carnal thoughts she'd been having about him since he'd kissed her.

No, there was something about Jack...his intelligence, his utter masculinity, his strength—and not just physical strength, but the inner strength that had helped him survive. He'd done that with uncommon grace, especially for a man stripped of every cover he'd ever used. His vulnerability wasn't a weakness. It only served to accentuate the power of the man he really was. The more they uncovered in him, the more certain she was that the real Jack wasn't so different from the one before her now. And that Jack was someone she wanted very much to know.

Was that crazy? she wondered. Anyone looking at this from the outside—Gil, for instance—would absolutely say yes. And maybe he'd be right. Jack was a loner, as restless as the wind. She'd been around long enough to smell it on a man. It was part of Jack's scent, as elementally him as the stunning blueness of his eyes. But the truth was, that mattered less to her today than it would have a week ago. She was tired of the control she'd wrapped around herself so tightly she had forgotten how to feel. Jack had changed all that, and suddenly, she hungered for more. Was that wrong—to want to feel again? Even if it was just for tonight? Tomorrow, the past that Jack had left behind on that road might just catch up with them. And then it would be too late to wonder about what-ifs.

The dark silhouette of the island had drawn into view. The feeling of relief that spread through her was like a knee-jerk reaction. Over the years, this place had acquired sanctuary status in her mind. Nothing could harm her here. Not here, with Jack.

As the bottom of the canoe scraped the sandy bottom of the shore, and his gaze took in the miniature island, he sat up straighter, but didn't say a word. That it took his breath away, as it had hers the first time she'd seen it, pleased her.

In the darkness, the silhouette of the island jutted out of the lake like an iceberg floating on the sea. Accidental. Out of place. From end to end it measured a mere hundred feet, with a width of half that. The sandy shore was scattered with smooth rocks and boulders, some wrapped in the roots of the hemlock and pines that crowded the small strip of land. A pair of birds roosting somewhere within burst from the trees in a flutter of wings and disappeared into the night sky, and crickets confined to this spot faded into silence at the sound of the boat's arrival. It was as if some painter had, as an afterthought to a seascape, taken up his brush and inserted a moment of perfection into the center of it.

"Like it?" she asked Jack as she climbed out of the boat and pulled it closer to shore in the ankle-deep water, tying it up to a thick root.

"It's...amazing." The awe in his voice, she knew, was genuine.

He joined her on the shore, and she reached for the blankets and basket she'd packed for the trip. "C'mon. We're not quite there yet."

He followed her along the slender path worn through the pines. The half-moon cast shadows across the path. They walked for less than a minute before they came to a clearing surrounded on three sides by trees and the fourth by water. Thick, luxurious grass carpeted the patch of meadow. Jack stopped at the tall, crumbling stone structure at the center and placed his hands against the mortared stones, still warm from the day's sun.

"What's this?" he asked.

"A lighthouse. Or at least it was once. But all anyone's ever called it is Jacob's Roost." She spread the blanket in the clearing and motioned for him to sit.

Jack lowered himself to the blanket with a grin. "Now there's a loaded answer. I take it there's a story behind it."

"A legend," she clarified with mock gravity, pulling the lid off the steaming thermos. "Every lake needs at least one." She handed him a cup of cocoa and poured one for herself. "Jacob was a Scandinavian immigrant who came here late in the last century. Legend has it that Jacob had come to seek his fortune and had left his love behind him to wait for him. Her name was Analisse.

"According to the legend, he made his fortune in lumber and sent for her. He'd arranged to meet her on this very island because he wanted to see her expression when she saw the mansion he'd built for her at the other end of the lake. But after coming halfway around the world, un-scathed, Analisse drowned in a boating accident on her way to meet Jacob. Broken-hearted and half-crazed with grief, he wouldn't leave this island. He built this tower, this light-house hoping that she was alive, that she would find her way to him somehow. One day, he simply disappeared.

"Some say Jacob drowned himself. But others believe he found her at last. Some claim to have seen them, stand-ing together at the edge of this island looking up at the stars."

Jack was gazing not at the stars, but at her when she finished. Stretching out on the blanket he crossed one ankle over the other and propped his right hand beneath his head. "You ever see them?"

She laughed. "Jacob and Analisse? No. But one night I thought I saw a light coming through these trees. It was probably just the moon."

He hadn't stopped looking at her, and Tess wrapped her arms around her knees, feeling exposed. She wasn't sure why she'd told Jack that story. Perhaps because tonight she felt a little lost, like Jacob. Or maybe it was simply because they both needed the distraction.

"So," he said, curling his hands around the insulated cup, "you see beacons meant for someone else and believe in happily ever after. What else should I know about you?"

Tess grinned. "Hmm. I hate turnips and tight spaces. I've never been part of a crowd. I have a relentless curiosity that has earned me equal amounts of trouble and success.

Oh, and I bake a mean apple pie.'' She shrugged. ''There. Now you know everything about me.''

He moaned, rolling onto his back at the thought. ''You left out your sadistic tendencies. Leave it to you to bring me out to a deserted island and tease me with visions of homemade apple pie.''

She stretched out beside him on the blanket. ''You like apple pie?''

The very male look he sent her left little doubt about his appetites.

Her heart fluttered oddly in her chest, like wings flapping against her lungs.

''You cold?'' he asked with a frown, dragging an extra blanket toward her.

''No, I...'' she began, but it was a lie. ''Yes.''

He drew a spare blanket over them and pulled her toward his good shoulder. ''C'mere, Tess. I don't bite.''

Reluctantly, she slid over to put her head on his shoulder.

''Unless the situation calls for it,'' he added.

She punched him and he laughed, wrapping his arm around her. Tucked comfortably next to him she felt inexplicably safe. Protected. That was almost funny. Imagine feeling safe with a man like Jack.

The crickets had begun their serenade again. She pointed up to the sky. ''See that star?''

He followed her fingertip and nodded.

''And the two beside it?'' Again, he nodded. ''I think that's Orion's belt. The big reddish-looking one is—''

''Betelgeuse,'' he finished. ''The red supergiant.''

She turned to stare at him.

''And Bellatrix—the smaller one, there. And the blurry ones below it? Orion's dagger.''

She sat up. ''Jack—''

''Orion, the hunter. Don't ask me how I know that. I just do. I know about the ascension and declination of stars. If you put me in the middle of nowhere, I could find my way back by their positions in the sky. If I knew where 'back' was."

"A Navy SEAL would know how to do that. Sailors navigate by the stars...."

"So do camel traders."

The picture made her laugh. "Somehow you don't look the part. No, I can see you in dress blues and spit-shined shoes."

"Nah, you've got me pegged all wrong. Turbans and caftans. That's definitely more 'me.' A bevy of women—"

"A harem?" she interjected dryly.

"Right, a harem at my beck and call. Dress blues and spit-shined shoes don't really hold much appeal compared to that. Sand, sun and fun. That's me."

"But seriously, Jack—"

He rolled toward her, stopping her thought midsentence. "I thought we weren't going to get serious tonight. And no talk about tomorrow?"

"Oh." She blinked at his sudden movement. "You're right. My fault. It—it won't happen again. I promise."

He leaned over her, smiling, close enough—if the light had been better—to count the freckles on her nose, but not far enough to miss the suddenly breathless look on her face as if she half expected him to kiss her.

The instant the thought materialized, he felt himself get hard.

All he had to do was lower his mouth to hers, taste her again the way he'd wanted to ever since the last time they'd kissed. One tilt of his head, one brush of his lips against hers...

Her lips parted and her tongue darted out to moisten them. The movement nearly undid him. Cursing silently, he rolled onto his back.

What was he thinking, letting those kinds of thoughts

rattle around in that empty can of his? She'd already told him she was off-limits. And even if she'd changed her mind, he knew better. However, he had the self-control of a flea where Tess was concerned—as evidenced by his lower regions—and all he needed was to act on the impulse to kiss her and it'd be all over.

The vaguest memory hovered on the edges of his mind of holding a woman this way before, but the punch of desire that settled in his gut seemed starkly unfamiliar. Had he ever wanted a woman the way he wanted Tess? And was this feeling that made him want to hold her forever just about sex, or was it something else altogether?

The first option appealed to him more; fewer complications and no big mystery. Tess was a beautiful woman; he was a man. Why should he muddle all that with emotions? Lust was maddeningly simple, and he was filled with it.

Heedless of that fact, or perhaps in spite of it, Tess rolled toward him again and tucked herself against his shoulder. Her fist rested on his rib cage, coiled there as if she were ready for a fight. "Who's afraid now, Jack?"

He set his teeth. "Leave it alone, Doc."

She shivered against him. "You're right—of course. I should. I should just ignore the feeling that something has changed."

Nothing has changed, he wanted to say, but he knew it was a blatant lie. Everything had changed—the way ice, unlocked by heat, turned to water. It's molecular structure was the same, but it became something else entirely.

The chilly night air carried the fragrance of pine and the sound of the lapping water against the shoreline. Overhead, the stars appeared in fistfuls against the black backdrop of sky.

"Do you believe in fate, Jack? That things are destined to be?"

"A strange question to ask a man with no past."

She looked utterly unrepentant. "But what put us on that road together at that very moment?"

"Bad timing?"

She laughed softly. "I mean, if I'd stayed at the lab that night, if Daniel hadn't sent me on vacation...if you hadn't been involved with those men...we never would have met."

"Probably not." His hand tightened unconsciously around her. "That would've been better for you."

"You think so?"

Her fingers, splayed against his ribs, sent quivers across his abdomen. Jack rolled his eyes. "Don't *you?* I mean, look what I've done to your life. I've torn it apart. Nothing's going to be the same for you, Tess. Maybe not even if we resolve this. If we ever do."

"Maybe I was meant to find you. Maybe it was our destiny."

"And maybe," he suggested dryly, "it was some huge cosmic mistake. And somebody up there is still scratching his head trying to figure out where he went wrong and how to untangle you from all this."

Her voice went soft. "And what if I said I don't want to be untangled?"

Jack sniffed. "Then I'd say you need a vacation. A nice long vacation on some island paradise—one with palm trees and natives and complete bed rest."

She made a sound of disagreement. "It's not as if I had nothing to do with it. You can't take all the blame. I could have driven away."

"And pigs can fly."

He felt her smile against his shoulder. "Nevertheless, here we are. Two strangers lying together under these stars. Doesn't it make you wonder why?"

"I don't know. I think it's just...serendipity. Luck. Good or bad. It happened and we have to make the best of it.

You saved my life, and now I'm going to try my damnedest to save yours. That's all. That's all there can ever be.''

"But what if it isn't?" The question loomed large between them, like the proverbial elephant in the living room.

"Trust me on this, Tess."

"I do. That's just it, Jack. That's why I'm asking you. What if it isn't?"

He didn't have an answer for that. If he dared to consider it...

"All these months, years really," she continued, "it's been easy for me to stay hidden, to run to research and away from all the things that terrified me. I've been running from myself and my own feelings. I never really stood still long enough to get my bearings. Not until..."

He frowned. "Until?"

"Not until I met you."

He exhaled sharply. "I'm no road map, darlin'. God knows..."

She rolled over onto her elbows and smiled at him. "I wasn't looking for a road map." She hesitated. "I guess I was just looking for a reason to 'be' again."

Jack's gaze traveled over her features one by one, cataloging them in his memory so he would never forget what she looked like right now. He brushed her hair back from her face, thinking that it had been worth getting shot for this. And simultaneously, wondering how to stop it.

Her eyes darkened and grew shiny. Then she leaned closer and brushed her lips over his once, twice. Mistake, he thought raggedly, but he hadn't the will to push her away. Instead, he breathed in the scent of her as she covered his mouth with her own in a kiss that no longer asked permission. A full-bodied, aching, damn-the-torpedoes kiss that would've knocked him on his butt if he hadn't already been there.

His hands were in her hair before he knew what had

happened, and he was dragging her closer. She tasted of chocolate and a little bit of heaven, and he couldn't get enough of her. He slanted his mouth against hers hungrily. God help him, he wanted her underneath him with her legs wrapped around his waist and her breasts bare and soft against his chest.

She made a sound against his mouth, a greedy, anxious sound that stirred his overheated blood like a poker of molten steel. He deepened the kiss, his tongue dancing with hers, exploring her mouth and the smooth edges of her teeth.

His hand slid downward of its own accord, skimming over the contours of her backside and up again until he'd reached her breast. Filling his palm with its weight, he felt the taut peak harden against his hand. "Ah, Tess..." he murmured.

She leaned into his caress. "Jack...oh, Jack..." she whispered against his ear.

Like a well too long dry, need rose up in him in a rush, scraping past all the well-considered arguments against this. As her lips tortured his jaw and neck, it filled him with a pounding urgency. And when her hand slid down his ribs, exploring the contours of his abdomen and the waistband of his jeans, he nearly lost it.

He pulled her cheek alongside his and held her close. "What're you doin' to me?"

"Kissing you," she breathed, sliding her open mouth down his neck, then moving up toward his ear again.

He shut his eyes as pleasure tingled down the length of him. He turned his head, denying her access, which brought his mouth back in line to hers. "You said—"

"I said a lot of things," she whispered against his mouth. "Forget what I said."

He dragged her face against his shoulder and held her

there. If he looked at her, he'd take her right here. Right now. "Think, Tess."

"I'm tired of thinking."

"Tomorrow you'll regret this."

"Will *you?*" Her question, stark and forthright, almost weakened his resolve.

"Dammit," he said, tilting his hips against hers. "I want you. More than air. Can you feel it?" She tightened her arms around him. "But there's no future in it."

Her lips pressed against his shoulder. "I told you, there is no future. It doesn't exist. Not tonight."

"Tess. What if I'm married? You said it yourself."

"Don't." It was her turn to warn now.

"And if I took you here like this, knowing that, what would it prove? Only that I am the bastard they say I am. If I made love to you, and left you in a day or two, not knowing—"

She lifted her eyes and searched his face. "Leave? You're leaving?"

"You know I have to."

"No, I don't! Jack—you just—you can't *leave!*"

"I won't until I make sure you're safe."

"Safe?" Shoving herself upright out of his arms, she threw the quilt off her. "Where is that going to be? Where can I be safe without you?"

Or I, without you, he thought. "Don't worry about that now. I'm not leaving yet."

"But soon. You are, aren't you? What about Gil? He's trying to help us. If we just give him time, he'll figure out how to—"

"Time we may not have, Tess."

At the far end of the lake, a burst of color exploded in the sky. Red-and-white streaks of light showered down over the hanging lanterns of the Pioneer Days Celebration. Fireworks. Perfect, he thought, sitting up beside Tess.

"Where will you go?" she asked.

"Back. To find out who tried to kill me and why."

"Then let me take you."

"No," he said too sharply. "I don't want you anywhere near—"

"But you wouldn't know them if you saw them. They could walk right up to you and...Jack, I saw them in the ER, those two men. I could find them again. I could help you."

He took her by the arms. "That's my problem. Not yours. Your job is to stay alive. When this is over—"

"You mean when they've killed you?" Her expression was angry and scared.

"I got you into this. I'm going to get you out."

"Then wait," she begged. "We'll go somewhere else. We'll keep moving so they can't find us."

"And then what? Change your name? Dye your hair? Pretend you're somebody else? Is that what you want, Tess? To be on the run from them from here on out?" She put her hands over her ears. He reached for her when she moved to get up, and pulled her back down. "Listen to me, Doc. It's the only way. Whatever went down back there, there's some business I've left undone. And I've got to finish it."

Tears were gone as she lifted her head. In their place was frustration. "I worked too damn hard to save your life to watch you throw it away as if it didn't mean anything. It means something to *me*, Jack. I don't want to see you die!"

He wrapped his arms around her, pulling her back against his chest. "I'm too damned stubborn to die. Don't you know that by now? But you were right. Let's not talk about tomorrow. Let's just...watch the fireworks together. Let me hold you. Nothing more."

He ached to kiss the fight out of her, but instead he held her like a trapped animal against him. If she could squirm out of his arms, he thought, to find a way to keep him here, she would. But a woman as smart as Tess would see the logic in his reasoning soon enough. A little time was all she needed. She had no business with a man whose history was as tangible as those colorful specks of gunpowder drifting down from the sky and vanishing into the dark. And a man like him had no right to dream of a future with a woman like her.

But that night, when he slept, he did dream of her—hot, erotic dreams of Tess's sweet, slick body wrapped around his and the heart-thudding rhythm of their passion. Dreams, he thought with resignation, that would be his only solace when he left her.

Chapter 12

Gil picked up the phone on the first ring. "Tess?"

"Sorry to disappoint'cha," the decidedly unfemale voice at the other end replied. "It's Ben."

Gil's colorful oath earned him a chuckle from across the phone line.

"Hey, don't hold back, pal. Tell me how ya really feel." Nearing fifty-five, with his last opportunity at sergeant gone, Ben Tepper was still one of the best cops Gil had ever known. There was no one he trusted more, which was why he'd sent him where he himself couldn't risk going.

"Sorry. I'm contemplating homicide," Gil retorted. "Not yours."

"That relieves my mind, considering it's only 9:00 a.m. What? She hasn't called yet?"

Gil growled a reply that needed no interpretation. "Well? What did you find?"

"Just what you thought. They ransacked her place."

Gil swore.

"Looks like yesterday, if fresh tracks around the house belong to the perps. I checked her automatic sprinklers. They went on yesterday, 7:00 a.m. These pricks took her place apart piece by piece. Beds. Couches. Drawers. Impossible to say if anything is missing. Except maybe..."

"Maybe what?" Gil dreaded the answer.

"Well, I don't know if it means anything, but I found an empty picture frame, glass broken on the floor near her mantel. Five-by-seven. Any idea what it was?"

Gil scanned his memory of her mantelpiece and the photographs he knew she kept there. He remembered pictures of Adam and her. Pictures of him and Adam. Pictures of vacations and—

"Dammit!"

"What?" Ben asked.

It took a moment for Gil to get control of his voice again. "Ben, will you do something else for me?"

"Name it, pal."

"Cover me with the captain. Tell him I'm taking a personal day. Maybe two." Gil shoved himself away from his desk and grabbed his jacket off the back of his chair.

"Where you goin'?"

He shifted the receiver to his other ear. "I would tell you, but then I'd have to kill you."

Ben laughed. "Yeah, well, I don't wanna know that bad."

He shoved one arm into his jacket and wrestled with the other. "And one more thing."

"Yeah?"

"I'm gonna transfer my calls here to you. If Tess calls, you tell her to get the hell out of there. But not a word to anyone about her, got that?"

"I do, my friend. You can count on me."

For most of the next day, they kept their distance. What had happened on the island had left them raw, their nerves scraped. It seemed easier to move in separate circles than to allow intersection again. It was too hard, Tess thought, pinning a T-shirt onto the clothesline behind the cabin, for both of them.

Last night she'd lain in bed, wide-awake, for hours, trying to think her way out of the situation. Over the years, her skill at rationalization had become something of an art. But nothing explained the feeling that her whole life before this moment had been mere shadowy preparation for this, and what she'd had with Adam paled in comparison.

Guilt stabbed at her with that thought as she reached into the wicker basket for another T-shirt to hang on the line. She'd loved Adam, and always would, she reminded herself, clipping a clothespin around the damp fabric. He had been so much a part of her life. They'd grown up together, been best friends, lovers. They had a history, for better or for worse. But somewhere along the line, she knew now, they'd lost it.

The affair he'd had with a young, beautiful female officer three years before his death had been the stake in the heart of their marriage. But the heart kept beating as if out of habit. She'd blamed herself for his affair, too, for her lack of attention. Had she been too busy to notice he was unhappy? Or, she wondered now, had their paths diverged long before that day, and neither of them noticed?

To his credit, even when they'd sought counseling together to try to repair the damage, Adam had taken the full blame for the affair. But while they'd survived it, they'd never fully recovered what they'd lost. No relationship survived neglect. And they had both neglected what had once been good about their marriage. By the time he died, they had made peace with it and with each other, and had settled into a comfortable routine that bordered on happiness.

But never, not in all the years of their marriage, had she

ever felt the kind of passion she felt with Jack. Lying in bed last night thinking of it, she felt wanton. She'd wanted to go to him, to tell him that he'd been wrong, give herself to him to prove it. But of course, she hadn't.

And now, as she cast a look back at the window of the house and saw him watching her, she wondered why she hadn't.

She slid a sheet from the basket and tucked one edge around the line. Was it because she believed what he'd said about there being no future for them? Or was it simply that she was too afraid he would send her away again?

Tess shut her eyes. What was happening to her? When had her life spun so wickedly out of control? The easy answer was also the obvious one: the night she'd first laid eyes on Jack. But the honest one was harder: it had spun out of her control long ago and only now was she recognizing how little she'd ever really had.

She pinched a clothespin around the sheet as the afternoon sun bore down on her. Lifting the last edge, she draped it around the coated line and clipped it in place. Maybe, she thought, she should go to him now. Tell him how she really felt. After all, she hadn't actually said the words—

A sound interrupted her thoughts and yanked her attention toward the wicker basket at her feet. It took her a moment to recognize the empty-gourd rattle of the snake that was coiled not two feet away from her leg, poised to strike.

Tess froze. Her thoughts slowed to a crawl, warnings flashing like neon road signs: *Rattlesnake! Oh God! Run!* But her feet felt mired in concrete and she couldn't force them to—

"Tess! *Don't—move!*"

Jack's shout came from somewhere behind her, far, far off. But she obeyed him because her body seemed not to be listening to her, anyway. The snake reared back, its rattle shaking ominously, its black, dead-looking eyes locked on hers.

Tess's lips moved as she screamed Jack's name, but no sound came out.

A moment later, the snake exploded and flipped in the air in slow motion. A gunshot rang in her ears. Tess staggered backward against the clothesline pole, jerking a look up to the porch to find Jack, arms outstretched, holding the still-smoking pistol, a good seventy-five feet away.

A tremor of disgust and relief worked through her as she looked back down at what was left of the snake. If Jack hadn't been watching her...

Heaving in a breath, Tess stumbled toward the house and Jack who, even as she watched, had a look on his face that frightened her almost as much as the snake. He appeared dazed. Disoriented.

"Jack?" she whispered. Then louder, "Jack?"

He lowered the gun and was moving toward her. His Adam's apple was working in his throat as if he were having trouble swallowing.

Reaching out, he grabbed her as she came near and held her tightly against him. "Are you all right?"

"Yes." She wrapped her arms around him so hard she was afraid she would hurt him. "Thank you," she whispered fervently.

With an oath, he pressed his cheek against her hair.

"How did you do it? *One shot,* Jack! From that distance with a pistol? When I think of how close I came to... God, if you'd missed—" His silence made her pull back, regarding the odd expression on his face. "That *was* luck," she said, "wasn't it?"

For the first time she noticed he was breathing hard and his face was covered with a fine sheen of sweat. "You're not feeling ill again, are you?"

He shook his head and moved away from her, scrubbing a hand across his mouth. "No," he answered distractedly. He took the steps of the porch two at a time until he spun around and sat down heavily on the wooden stoop, dragging both hands through his hair.

Silently, she moved to sit beside him. "Is it because I touched you? Are you angry with me? I'm sorry, I didn't think—"

"It wasn't luck."

He meant the shot. Of course, the shot. "It—it wasn't?"

Shaking his head, he didn't take his eyes off her. "No. The gun. When I fired the gun...I started...to remember."

Coldness shot through her like a flood of ice water. She thought she'd prepared herself for his memory to return. Now she wasn't so sure. "What?"

"A botched op. In a jungle. I thought it was a dream, but I know..." He stared at their hands. His were shaking. "Somewhere in Central America." Then, with more conviction, he stated, "Panama. An airstrip surrounded by jungle. It wasn't our specialty. Army Rangers take out airfields. But they sent us. Wick...Redbud—" his expression grew pained "—EZ...my friends." Jack squeezed his eyes shut, remembering. "Good men, all of them. All killed but me and three others." His glazed eyes met hers again. "SEALS. They were SEALS, Tess."

She tightened her fingers around his. Her relief and sadness were so sharp and so simultaneous she had no idea what to say. "I'm sorry, Jack," she murmured, but the words sounded banal and impersonal. The stark loss in his eyes was evidence enough that his memories were vicious. She wished them back into nonexistence. But like Pandora's box, the secrets were sneaking out and would not be repressed.

"What else?" she asked.

Jack exhaled sharply as another wave crashed over him,

pummeling him down and tumbling him over and over. The memories that had flicked by him in the past days like single frames of a film now sped by in a blur, flooding through the door that had slammed shut the day he'd been shot. But he couldn't filter the information. It was as if he was looking at someone else's life, yet he knew it belonged to him. Faces, names, rooms, landscapes...all swirled past him. Snatches of his life, all incomplete:

EZ, laughing over the rim of a brew, recounting a training exercise with a bunch of raw recruits... His own hands assembling an M-16 against a thirty-second clock... A Special op drop from a Huey over a black North Atlantic, and the bone-chilling misery of a twenty-foot sea. The BUD/S drill instructor, who would later become his friend, inches from his face, screaming until he'd lost hearing in his right ear: "Are you on a friggin' vacation, McClaine? Or just plain Stupid?"

McClaine. Jack's heart slammed against the wall of his chest. They called him Mac.

The pictures flashed again.

Standing up for Seth as his bride moved toward them through the crowded church. Seth! Oh, damn. Seth...in dress blues looking happy as hell. And her name. Her name was...Molly. Yes. Jack remembered now. Molly with the red hair and sprite's eyes. Molly, who'd been the one to finally talk Seth out of active, and steer him to Washington.

Jack's mother, with her blond hair slicked back and her face scarecrow thin, smiling up at him from her hospital bed. "Take care of him," she'd whispered hoarsely. "You're all he's got now."

Then, the house he grew up in. White and clapboard sided, with a climbing tree—a willow—in the yard. From there, high up, he could see the world. And below, the kid scrambled up to join him.

Jack lurched to his feet and stumbled down the steps, leaving Tess alone.

The Kid. Something blocked this memory. He couldn't slip past. The boy…

"Joe," he said aloud, his hands clenching into fists at his sides.

Tess was beside him then. "That was the name you called out when you were sick. Is it your name?"

He shook his head. "My brother's."

"You have a brother?" Her eyes went wide. "Oh, Jack! This is wonderful! You have family!"

Barricade, dead ahead. Piled high between him and what was on the other side.

"It's not Jack," he said slowly, turning to her. "My name's McClaine." It came to him then, just like that. "It's Ian. Ian McClaine." He blinked hard. "And there it is. My goddamned name. Just turn around and there it is."

"Ian," she repeated, testing it on her tongue. "Ian McClaine."

His feelings of anger mixed with relief were tempered by the fleeting panic he read in her expression. Gone almost as quickly as it came was a look that said she'd opened a present she didn't really want.

"Jack, that's—" She caught herself. "I mean…Ian. Oh, how am I ever going to get used to calling you that?" She regarded him with glassy eyes and then shook it off. "Do you remember…everything?"

He rubbed his temple. "No. Not everything." He cursed. "My past is rolling by me like a movie, but I'm only grabbing pieces of it. There are holes big enough to drive a tank through."

"Your family? Parents?"

Shaking his head, he moved away from her to stare out at the lake. "Gone. Dead, I think. It's just me and…"

"Joe, your brother," she finished for him.

He nodded, moving toward the water where it lapped against the shore. He hunkered down beside it and reached down to splash some against his face. Bracing his wrists against his thighs, he stared out at the sun glinting off the lake. What about Joe? The kid who'd followed him to the top of the willow, the one who'd shadowed his every move for most of his growing up years. *Think. Think.*

Tess knelt beside him, reaching for a water-smoothed stone on the shore. "It'll come. Don't try to force it."

He blew out a breath. "You speaking as a doctor?"

"As a friend."

The stone shifted back and forth between her slender hands. He wanted to grab them and hold them, drag Tess against him until his life came back to him. But he knew that as soon as it all did, he would have to let her go. Was he afraid to know for fear of losing her? Was she worried about the same thing?

He did take her hand then and she allowed it. "I'm a soldier, Tess. A lieutenant colonel. I train SEAL recruits. And when they need me I do ops. My specialty is sniper— marksman. I'm a damned good shot."

With a lift of her eyebrows, she glanced back at the wicker hamper. "You'd get no argument there from the snake."

One side of his mouth quirked in a smile, but it faded almost as quickly. "Which is why what happened to me makes no sense. What was I doing here when my life is back in Virginia?"

"Virginia?"

He looked at her without reply. "And what does Ramon Saldovar, a second-class drug dealer, have to do with me?"

"You don't remember getting shot?"

"No. Nothing. Why would someone be trying to kill me? That part's still a blank."

"What about…" She hesitated. He met her gaze evenly. "Is there a *Mrs.* McClaine?"

Jack blinked, searching the sandy surface below the water for the answer.

The scene from that restaurant flashed through his brain again, of the woman with her designer suit and a smile that could chill an iceberg. "Why did I imagine this would be anything more?" she'd asked, as if he'd disappointed her once again in a long string of disappointments. "I should've known. You've known about this dinner party with my parents' friends for months. And you knew how important it was to me. Well, I'm sick of hearing what the Navy needs from you! More than that, I'm sick that I've wasted all this time on you. On us. Because the 'other woman' in this relationship was never female, Ian. It was your job." As she pushed away from the table, shoving a packet of papers toward him, she sent him a scathing smile. "Don't bother to call me a cab. I can find my own. I've been doing it for years."

Exit Marcy Tolliver-Eastwick McClaine.

His wife.

Tess stared at her reflection in the mirror as she applied the second color of lipstick over the first. With a frown, she pursed her lips and berated herself for the hundredth time for agreeing to go out with Dan tonight. The timing couldn't have been worse. An hour ago, she'd called Dan's office to call off the date, but he was out and they wouldn't divulge his home number. Which left her exactly where she'd started.

She pressed her lips together, fluffed her hair and jerked away from the mirror in frustration. So she would go out and keep it short. Dinner and home. She'd plead a headache or something equally lame and he would bring her back. Two hours, tops. And he would see right through her ploy and wonder what he'd done to offend her. And she would hurt his feelings.

Tess sighed heavily as she moved toward the kitchen. It couldn't be helped, she told herself. And Jack—Ian—needed her, now that his memory was returning....

She glanced at her phone, lying on the countertop. She'd tried to cal Gil earlier, but after a series of clicks, she'd been somehow disconnected. The odd sound had troubled her and she'd decided not to try again until later.

She glanced out the window as she passed through the living room, to see Jack sitting on the back porch swing. Her throat tightened as she watched him stare off at the water, lost in thought. Was he planning his departure, she wondered? He still didn't remember what had happened to him. Pray God he would wait to go until he did remember.

He'd never answered her about a family—a wife, children. She'd braced herself for it, but if he knew, he'd kept it to himself. Did that mean that he had one and he simply didn't want her to know? Or could it mean that he just didn't remember? How could he not remember a wife, she wondered, when the rest of his life was coming back? And his brother...another mystery. That one seemed more troubling than the first to him. Had they had some sort of falling out? Was Jack all alone in the world?

Tess walked out onto the porch, surprised to find Tandy, the golden retriever from next door, with her massive head tucked under Jack's obliging palm, a look of pure pleasure on her face. Jack's expression flattened at the sight of Tess, and he got to his feet.

"Wow," he said, scanning her from head to foot. She'd traded her jeans for one of Cara's knee-length, clingy black skirts and a classic camel-colored, V-neck cashmere sweater that complemented her coloring. "You look beautiful, Tess."

"Thanks. I see you've found a friend."

Jack's mouth quirked with a smile as he scratched the dog's head. "Yeah. She came over and introduced herself. I guess she decided I wasn't so bad, after all."

"Good instincts," Tess said, smiling at him, appreciating the full perfection of his profile as he glanced at the dog.

"Yeah, well..." His voice drifted off. With a shrug he stared out over the water at the gathering pool of color the setting sun had painted on the lake. He picked up a stick and threw it down the beach for Tandy. The dog romped gleefully after it, stopping to sniff the shoreline.

She let her gaze fall to the rough planks of the decking. "I wish I didn't have to go."

"That makes two of us."

"I tried to cancel, but it was too late. He'd already left."

"Where's he taking you, this Deputy Dan?"

"A new place. Dilly's, I think he said. They're all kind of alike up here. Homey saloons full of good ol' boys and girls." She laughed nervously. "It's—it's only for a couple of hours. I'll be back home before you miss me." Home, she'd said, as if they were an old couple and she was just stepping out for a game of bingo.

The look in his eyes frightened her, and she suddenly thought that he might not be here when she got back.

"You asked about a wife," he said abruptly, making her forget what she'd been about to say. She regarded him silently, holding her breath.

"I was married," he stated, and her heart did a free fall. "Her name was Marcy. She divorced me two years ago. No children. No attachments."

Tess's lips parted with relief. That meant—

"Don't you want to know why she divorced me?"

The way he asked it, she wasn't sure she did. But he didn't wait for her to decide.

"The reason she divorced me was because I neglected her. The SEALS came first. Not her. We were just another statistic. Divorce rate among SEALS is almost twice the national average—''

''Jack—''

''It's Ian, Tess,'' he said, walking toward her. ''Lieutenant colonel. Career military.'' He held out his arms, palms up, as he approached. ''I've sacrificed everything for it. It's who I am.''

Like some dark archangel, wings spread and swooping down on her, he closed in. The perfection of him stole her breath even as it had that first night. The sheer power of him made her step back, not out of fear, but with a staggering sense of loss. Not some mythical warrior, but a man. A good and noble man she would never really know. Because he was leaving her.

He stopped inches from her, so close she could feel the heat radiating from him in the cool evening air. No part of them touched. And yet she felt the caress of his eyes as surely as if he were touching her.

''Career military? Is that all you can throw at me? Because, frankly, if you're trying to scare me off, it's a little late for that.''

Regarding her with the slow heat of a man in no hurry to leave, he let his eyes roam over her face, while his mouth lifted in a half smile. ''That's what I like about you, Tess. Your strength. You'll get through this.''

It was a mistake that he touched her then. She could see it almost as soon as he brushed a strand of hair from her eyes in a gesture so bittersweet, her eyes began to sting.

''By 'this,''' she said haltingly, ''you mean...your leaving?''

A low sound vibrated at the back of his throat. ''You're incredibly stubborn, you know.''

''Character defect,'' she managed to say in her own defense.

His gaze fell to her mouth. ''It's sexy as hell.''

"Blah, blah, blah…"

The challenge in her voice proved his undoing and he hauled her hard against him, dropping his mouth down against hers. Shock gave way to relief, which, with the quick thrust of his tongue, deteriorated into need. Past caring about how, or why, or if, she welcomed his kiss and wrapped her arms around the strong hard breadth of his back.

He lifted her against him then, backing her against the railing until there was nowhere else to go, trailing moist kisses down her throat. Her body turned liquid and melted into his. His teeth skimmed her skin with exquisite restraint, as if his real goal, left unchecked, was to devour her.

She dragged his mouth back to hers, hungry for the taste of him again and for the delicious friction of her breasts against the hard plane of his chest. He ground his hips against hers as his hand slid down her buttocks and up her bare thigh, lifting her skirt until he reached the high-cut leg of her panties.

Then—oh!—back down.

Tess gasped as his fingers brushed against her with an intimate caress.

"Ah, Doc, you make me crazy. I can't keep my hands off you."

"Oh, please," she breathed back, teasing the soft edge of his earlobe with her teeth and tugging his shirttail from the waistband of his jeans. "Don't try."

He smiled against her cheek and his fingers obligingly slipped past the silken barrier of her underwear. Tess's whole body jerked as he dipped into the dampness at the apex of her legs. With a gasp, she dropped her head back. He took full advantage, torturing the sensitive spot beneath her ear with the swirl of his tongue.

She took his face in her hands and pulled him back to her, searing his lips with a kiss. She needed him. Oh, she wanted him! But not for just tonight. She wasn't sure if she was strong enough for only that.

Dimly, they both heard the sound of the car's tires crunching gravel as it approached the cabin, and the clip-clip sound of Tandy's nails as she trotted to the far side of the deck to see who was coming. It took a moment to orient themselves, but with a jolt, she realized it was Dan driving up.

Tess clapped four fingers over her mouth. "Oh, no!" How could she have forgotten?

Jack glanced toward the sound of the car with hooded eyes, still breathing hard. Dragging one hand through the hair that had fallen in his eyes, he said, "You'd better go."

How could she go now, with Jack's kisses still on her swollen mouth and looking as if she'd just been ravished? Her pulse was still wild and the ache he'd tendered inside her, down low, still throbbed with wanting.

Tess dragged her hands through her hair in a vain attempt to smooth it out, then she cleared her throat. "I look—"

"Beautiful." He reached up and pressed a brief, tethered kiss against her lips and swallowed hard. "Go fix your lipstick, sweetheart, and answer the door."

She nodded silently, begging him with her eyes not to do anything foolish before she returned. Then, she turned and left him there on the porch with wind ruffling his hair, looking more handsome than she'd ever imagined.

With his hands gripping the back porch railing, Jack listened as the car left the driveway and headed for town, and tried to remember ever hearing a lonelier sound.

He stalked to the water's edge, picked up a stone and heaved it into the twilight over the black water. The lake swallowed it up, leaving behind a score of concentric ripples that flowed back toward him and did nothing to dispel the violence that roiled under his skin.

Unleashing a string of expletives, he stood glaring at the water, feeling ready to explode. And then he did the only logical thing a man in his situation could do. He stripped off his clothes and followed the rock in.

The cold mountain water hit him with the desired effect and he plunged under the surface and swam until he needed air. Invigorated, he surfaced with a gasp, the cold sluice of water clenching his overheated libido. His shoulder protested but Jack ignored it, pushing past the ache with a steady, unyielding stroke. Swimming came as naturally to him as breathing, and he supposed almost half of his adult years had been spent exploring his own limits in water.

When he'd gone far enough, exhausting both the need and the anger inside him, he floated on his back and stared up at the stars overhead, thinking of Tess. He could still feel her mouth on his lips and the sweet give of her body against his. He wanted her with a fierceness that had blindsided him. And he knew it was more than lust. She challenged him, made him feel alive. He needed her.

But all that was beside the point. He knew better than anyone that he couldn't have her. Not the way he wanted her. A woman like her was meant for the Dan Kelsos of the world. Safe, honorable, dependable men who came home at night for dinner and coached their kids in Little League. But the idea of Dan putting his hands on her tonight, kissing her maybe, was a bitter pill he couldn't quite stomach.

Rolling over, he swam toward shore slowly. Enough of his memory had returned to know that the feeling churning his gut right now was one he'd never known before. It bore little resemblance to his mockery of a marriage to a woman who, once gone, he could hardly recall missing. Marcy was as opposite to Tess as day was to night, and he wondered now what he'd ever seen in her.

It had been the idea of being married to a SEAL that had

appealed to her, he'd discovered, not only because it flew in the face of her wealthy parents' expectations for her, but—and this realization came only after two long years together—she enjoyed being seen on his arm. For a time, it thrilled her to be with a man whose life turned on a dime between the normalcy of their life together and the brutality of what he did for a living. It was, he supposed, fodder for her circle of friends to chew on when he was gone. It made her feel important somehow. He'd actually believed he could make her happy—even make up for the obvious disparity between them. He'd hauled himself up from the mining towns of West Virginia, where his family had spent generations sucking coal dust. He'd educated himself, and driven himself hard to get where he'd gotten. But he'd overstepped his bounds with Marcy Tolliver-Eastwick of the Philadelphia Toller-Eastwicks.

When all was said and done, the arrangement they'd settled for wasn't enough. Not for her. Not for him. The hollow feeling inside him had begun to chip away at him even at work. And while failure went utterly against his nature, he'd known before she did that he'd failed at marriage.

And now here was Tess, seeding hope inside him again. Hope for what? he mused with a note of self-disgust. No, whatever was generating the heat between them now, he told himself, it wasn't love. It was mutual need. When this whole thing was over, she would go back to her life and he to his.

He got back to shore to find the golden retriever sniffing his clothes. Tandy let out a whining yawn as he emerged from the water, and Jack reached out a dripping hand to give her a sympathetic pat. "I'm with you there, girl," he said, tugging on his jeans over his damp legs. "We're a couple of outsiders, you and me, huh? Outside, looking in. Maybe I should take you back with me instead. A water dog like you? You'd fit right into the Navy."

Tandy panted and raised her doggy eyebrows in expressive reply. Jack let out a soft huff of laughter, tangling his fingers in her coat. Even as he did, in his mind's eye he saw another dog in another time. Smaller than Tandy and wiry-gray, she leaped straight up for a Frisbee his brother had thrown:

"Look at that!" the twelve-year-old Joe had crowed, arms thrown wide. "Did you see her, Ian? She's gonna win. I know it. Have you ever seen a dog jump so high?"

"Never," he'd shouted back, caught up in his younger brother's unvarnished optimism.

"Fifty-dollar prize. It's mine," Joe told him without an ounce of doubt.

A wave of nausea rushed over Jack as he reached down for his T-shirt.

Joe, who'd shadowed him from the moment he could walk, who had grown into a hell of a man and followed Jack into the Navy, where he'd made a damned fine officer.

The crushing memory pressed on his chest and Jack knelt down, trying to catch his breath. He didn't want to remember the phone call he'd gotten in the middle of the night from L.A., where Joe had gone to be a cop after washing out of SEALS training. He'd made a name for himself in L.A. and found his place. Which was why the phone call in the middle of the night had nearly ripped the ground from under Jack.

Joe, dead. Suicide. Hanged himself, the LAPD captain's voice had announced, the way one might describe the brand of cereal he'd chosen to eat that morning for breakfast. But the other caller, who phoned later, described it as hinky circumstances. That was the word he'd used: *hinky.* As if there were anything *hinky* or even ordinary about his brother. And when they'd told him that Joe had been implicated in a crime—in a drug-smuggling payoff operation—Jack had laughed. Because it was as unimaginable that Joe could have been on the wrong side of the law as it was that he was actually dead.

Grief struck Jack with the force of a two-by-four squarely across the back, and he braced his hands on his knees. He'd never shaken the picture of it from his mind, and he hated that his memories of his brother, the kid he'd practically raised, were tainted by that ugly image. Damn whoever was responsible for making him go through losing Joe twice in one lifetime! The last of his family. He was alone in this world.

Jack's glassy eyes traveled over the dark water with a feeling of emptiness that frightened him. His reasons for coming here surged back to him, pushing away self-pity and every other emotion but vengeance. Suicide hadn't been in Joe's vocabulary, and he'd been helped onto that chair in that lonely room that night. They'd needed a fall guy, but Joe wouldn't fall. So he'd died—his good name dragged through the mud the men who'd murdered him had created.

Jack had come here to clear his brother's name.

The relief of that sent him down onto the hard surface of the pebble-strewn beach. He'd never wanted to believe what Tess had said they suspected him of. And now the truth came back to him. His path had already been drawn.

A low, foul oath slid from his mouth. He'd failed Joe the last time. They'd won. At least they thought they had, the bastards. Well, he thought, reining in the venomous feeling rising in his throat, they may have won the round, but they were far from beating him.

Grabbing up his shirt and leaving Tandy behind, he stalked into the house in search of Tess's phone. The search proved fruitless. She'd taken it with her, he decided, slumping down on the couch. The jingle of keys drew his gaze down to the cushions. A grim smile eased the hard line of his mouth.

"All right then," he muttered to himself, tossing the keys in his palm. "All right."

Chapter 13

Dilly's was crowded with celebrants, fresh from the sailboat regatta Tess had seen earlier today on the lake. It seemed that everyone knew Dan and said their hellos to him as he moved through the crowd.

The owner broke into a smile at the sight of them. "Sheriff! Over here. I have a special table for you!"

"Just Dan tonight, Oscar," Dan requested with a humble shrug. "Not on duty."

"Phooey!" Oscar said, turning to Tess. "He's the best darned sheriff we've ever had around here. Only the best table for you two."

Dan introduced her. Oscar bowed in a low humorous sweep, then waggled his eyebrows meaningfully at Dan. "Very nice."

Dan sent her a helpless look as they were led to a small table far enough away from the country band that they could hear each other talk. He pulled out her chair for her, something she'd forgotten men do, and sat across from her. "You look great tonight, Tess."

She smiled, tucking her hair behind her ear. "So do you." Out of uniform—the first time she'd seen him that way since she'd met him—Dan had worn a pair of dark linen slacks and a handsome gray-green shirt that matched his eyes. The tie had been a nice touch, too, but as he ran his finger around the neckline, she guessed he'd worn it for her.

Regarding her for a long moment across the table, Dan leaned toward her. "I'm really glad you came."

"Oh," she said, scrambling for a response. "Me, too."

"It's okay if it's not the truth," he said with a half smile, reading her mind. "I figure I'm ahead of the game just getting you out of that cabin. You hungry?"

She could only smile. "Starved, actually."

"Good. Well, that's a good start, anyway."

He has a nice face, she thought, regarding him as he brought the menu up to browse it. Kind yet strong. A complex mixture of openness and mystery. He'd been sheriff here for almost two years, deputy sheriff before that. And yet no woman—and there had been plenty of volunteers—had landed him yet. Tess had always assumed that his interest in her lay in the fact that she played harder to get than most. And that his persistence could be attributed to the possibility that the chase was more interesting to him.

But that assumption was unfair. And even as she studied him now, with his dark lashes casting crescents of shadow across his tanned, handsome cheeks, she couldn't help but compare him to another man, one infinitely more dangerous.

"Wine okay?" he asked over the sound of the music.

"Wine sounds good."

He flagged down a waiter and ordered a bottle of chardonnay. "So, you're working too hard up here on your vacation. What exactly are you working on?"

Survival, she thought, but she said, "It's not all that interesting. Just putting together some research I'm doing for a paper I'm hoping to publish.'' That much was almost true. It was what she'd been working on in her spare time before this whole thing started.

''Impressive.''

She shook her head dismissingly. ''A necessary evil. Funding never lasts long enough.''

The waiter brought the wine and poured two glasses. Dan lifted his and chinked it with hers. ''Here's to publication and whatever else makes you happy.''

''Back at you.'' Tess took a sip of her wine. Happiness. What a concept. It had been so long since she'd felt it, she'd feared she wouldn't even recognize it if it ever happened to cross her path again. Tonight, with Jack, she'd realized she'd been wrong about that. Jack made her happy, and she had to find a way to convince him that she could do the same for him.

''So,'' she said, searching for a topic. ''What makes you happy, Dan?''

''Lots of things. I'm easy,'' he said. ''I like my job, my life, sitting down to dinner with a beautiful woman.''

Tess toyed with her wineglass. ''I hear there's a long line just waiting to oblige you.''

He actually blushed. ''Don't believe everything you hear. Besides, there's only one beautiful woman I'm interested in, and she's sitting across from me.''

Swirling the contents of her glass, she studied it. ''My life is complicated, Dan.''

He nodded, sipping his wine. ''How complicated is it?''

She wrinkled her nose. ''Pretty complicated right now.''

''You in love with him?'' The band had stopped playing the second before Dan asked the question, and a few heads turned at the table beside them. He looked sheepishly up at her, waiting for an answer.

Of course he knew it was another man. But the question

stalled her pulse for a moment. In love with Jack? She'd hardly dared to contemplate it. Was she? She'd been in love once. But this felt…stronger. As if she'd slid into the right place at last, found something she hadn't known was lost. "Maybe," she told Dan, taking in the disappointment in his expression. "I'm sorry, Dan."

He shrugged good-naturedly. "So, let's just have a nice dinner, as friends. What d'ya say?"

She'd never liked Dan more than she did at this moment. A woman would have to be crazy to pass up a guy like him. Strong, handsome, dependable—safe. He was exactly the sort of man any woman would want. Anyone but her.

No, she had to go for a man who lived for trouble, who thrived on adrenaline rushes and risked his life for a living—an ironic turn of phrase, she thought. The heart, she'd learned, was not ruled by logic, and her feelings for the man she'd left back at the cabin couldn't be defined by anything so simple as that.

She lifted her glass and touched to Dan's. "Here's to friendship."

Jack pulled Tess's car up beside the phone booth outside the pharmacy. A light illuminated the old-fashioned glass booth, and he pulled the door closed behind him, shutting out the sounds of foot traffic on the crowded street. He made one quick phone call to a number he'd torn out of the phone book, then punched in a long-distance number on the keypad. He shoved a handful of change he'd scrounged at the cabin into the coin slot.

The phone rang and a man answered. "Tanner."

"Hey, PB, it's Ian." PB—short for Polar Bear—was the name earned by the man on the other end of the line for enduring the icy waters off the coast of Greenland the longest without succumbing.

"*Mac?*" Seth replied incredulously, then sighed in relief.

"Oh, *man*. Where the hell are you? Are you all right? Sarah and I have been worried sick about you. I called three days ago and they said you'd taken some personal leave. But you were supposed to check in four days ago at commanding and nobody's heard from you. They know as well as I do you'd never go AWOL of your own free will."

It was good, amazingly good, to hear Seth's voice again. "I, uh, ran into a little trouble."

There was a long pause. "How bad?"

"Bad enough." He shifted the phone to his other ear, turning from a couple passing on the street. "But I'm still standing."

"Where the hell are you?"

"California."

"California?" He could hear the gears in Seth's brain grinding. "Is this about Joe?"

"They killed him, Seth. Murdered him in cold blood and set him up to take the fall. I'm next on the menu."

Seth's curse was low and foul. "I'm on the next plane. Just tell me where and when."

Jack's throat thickened with gratitude that he hadn't had to ask. He heard Sarah in the background asking who was on the phone. Seth told her.

"Ian?" he said into the phone. "Sarah sends her love."

"Back," he said, running his thumb along the edge of the pay phone. "Will she be okay with this? I wouldn't ask but I don't know who else to—"

"Forget about it. She's got another month yet before the baby. I've got some personal time coming. I'll catch a flight first thing in the morning out of Dulles. What do you need?"

He told him, and when he was finished there was silence on the other end of the line for a long beat.

"Christ, Ian," Seth said softly. "You can't go in alone."

"It's not me I'm worried about. Will you just do what I ask?"

"You're crazy, you know that?"

A foregone conclusion. "That's why ya love me, right?"

"Get outta here…" He laughed.

"Thanks, pal. And thank Sarah for me, too."

"Hey, Ian?"

"Yeah?"

The humor had leached out of his voice. "Give the bastards one for me."

He dipped his head and rubbed his aching shoulder. "It'll be my pleasure."

Tess and Dan had filled more than an hour talking about their lives and about inconsequential things before he'd managed to drag her out onto the dance floor. The girl singer's voice had a sexy, breathy quality to it as she crooned a bluesy version of an old Hank William's song, "I'm So Lonesome, I Could Cry." But even as Dan's hands tightened around hers, her mind was on Jack. She couldn't shake the feeling that something was going to happen, or help wondering if he would even be there when she got back.

The thought sent a chill down her. Jack said he wouldn't leave until he knew she was safe. On the other hand, she thought with a surge of panic, he may have decided that he couldn't leave her in any better hands than Dan Kelso, the town's sheriff. But rocking with him there on the dance floor with her eyes closed, she wished it was Jack's shoulder she was leaning on, not Dan's.

He turned them past a handful of couples and eased through the crowd, swaying with the music. She didn't care where they were going. But she wasn't prepared for what she saw when she lifted her eyes to the row of people sitting at the old-fashioned oak bar right in front of her.

Half-hidden by the people milling there, sitting alone on a bar stool as if she'd conjured him with her thoughts, was *Jack!*

Tess gasped audibly.

Dan flinched and pulled back to look at her. "Sorry, did I step on your foot?"

She felt as if she were on an elevator that had just dropped seven floors. "No," she told Dan, unable to pull her gaze from the dark, forbidding figure at the bar.

Dan pulled her back against him, satisfied with her answer.

Jack's piercing gaze followed her every movement. It was no trick of lighting that the dark shadow that lingered on his bruised cheek lent a ruggedness to his breathless good looks. But the predatory intensity of his stare sent a tingle down her spine, almost as if he were touching her.

Dazedly, she wondered what he was doing here and how he'd managed it. Oh, her car, came the next thought. She'd left her keys at home. Never let it be said that this man wasn't resourceful. But what was he doing, risking being seen? And by Dan of all people.

Had he come to say goodbye? The possibility almost made her knees give way.

At the bar, Jack lifted a glass of what looked like water to his mouth and emptied it in one long drink, all the while watching her move with Dan. He dragged the back of his hand across his mouth deliberately, but the slow, possessive narrowing of those hooded blue eyes was the only indication that he knew she'd seen him.

The erotic memory of their encounter on the back porch tonight tumbled through her as if she'd stored it somewhere in her cells. She shivered at the physical sensation of it and wantonly imagined where his hands would touch her if he could.

Dan moved her through the crowd as the singer crooned

her smoky number and the pedal-steel guitar wailed along with her. She tried to keep Jack in sight. The crowds seemed to recede, leaving only the two of them, their heated stares meeting across the dance floor. She saw the muscles in Jack's jaw work as he put the glass down, crumbling the cocktail napkin in his fist as if the action held him in his seat instead of pushing past a dozen people to steal her away from Dan.

She blinked heavily, keeping her eyes on him as they moved. *Don't go,* she told him silently. *Wait for me, Jack.*

But he got slowly to his feet as Dan guided them in the other direction. A half-dozen couples blocked her view of the bar. She'd lost sight of him and half expected to see him standing over Dan's shoulder, cutting in for a dance.

But when she looked again, he was gone. Vanished. Tess's heart sank.

Her eyes were burning as the music ended and an easy applause broke out for the band. Dan pulled back and smiled down at her. Feeling flushed and disoriented, she forced a smile back up at him.

He brushed the tip of his finger against her nose good-naturedly. "You are a million miles away."

She dropped her gaze to the floor. "I'm...I'm sorry. You're a wonderful dancer, Dan."

"The pleasure was all mine, Tess." A wistfulness edged the smile he sent her as the band started a new song. "C'mon. I'll take you home now."

It was close to ten when Dan's car pulled up in front of the cabin. He went around the vehicle, opened her door for her and escorted her up the walk.

Tess glanced at the house, noticing how dark it was. She'd left a few lights on when she'd gone. Her car was parked in the drive again, but she had already decided that

Jack would probably bring it back for her, and find another way off this mountain.

Beside her, Dan slid his hands in the pockets of his slacks as they reached the door. She turned to him with a smile. "Thank you for a lovely evening, Dan. I really enjoyed it."

"So did I." He studied her face in the dim light of the lamp, looking as comfortable in his skin as any man she'd ever known. "I've never made it a secret that I'm interested in you, Tess. I like you." He shrugged. "My timing's off. But just so you know, if things don't work out with you and... Well, I guess what I'm trying to say is, don't be a stranger." He extended a hand to her in lieu of a kiss. "G'night."

She gave him a kiss on the cheek. "Night."

She watched until the taillights of his car disappeared around the bend in the road. She lingered at the door, afraid to go inside, not wanting to know if Jack had left. But the faint sound of music coming from inside the house made her heart suddenly race.

It was dark inside. Utterly dark. She knew the way, though, as she dropped her keys on the counter and moved toward the sound of the stereo. Its green power light glimmered like a little beacon, silhouetting the figure sitting there alone in the dark in the overstuffed chair.

"Jack?"

Slowly, the figure moved, got to his feet. Relief bled through her. She would know him anywhere, the way he moved and held himself. The scent that belonged to him.

"Jack." This time it wasn't a question but an answered prayer.

He opened his arms and she found her way into them, pressing her face against his shoulder as he held her tightly to him.

He kissed her hair.

"I thought you'd gone."

His fingers curled against her skull. "I told you I wouldn't leave until you were safe."

"When I saw you there tonight, I thought you'd come to say goodbye."

He took her face between his hands and dropped his mouth on hers in a hard, answering kiss, meant to say what he could never, *would* never say. Tess surrendered to it, leaning into his embrace, the slick glide of their mouths against each other feeling as natural as breathing. The erotic tide rushed back, stealing the strength from her legs and flooding her senses as Billie Holiday's voice filled the darkness behind them with a throaty, soulful sound.

"I came because I couldn't stay away," he said against her mouth. "When I saw you there, dancing with him, I wanted…"

She searched his face in the darkness. The clash of will and need met there in the deep furrow between his brows and in the masculine hollows of his cheeks.

"I wanted to drag you away from him and dance with you there as if nobody cared who we were, and we belonged together."

"I wanted it, too," she told him. "Dance with me now, Jack. Hold me," she said, even though he already was. She laid her cheek against his shoulder, molding her body to the hollows and contours of his. Designed to fit together like two pieces of a puzzle, they clung to each other, moving in slow, carnal revolutions around the darkened room.

"Do you mind terribly if I just call you Jack?" she asked softly. "I can't get used to Ian. And by the time I do—"

"Jack's good," he said against her hair, cutting off what she'd been about to say.

The scent of him—fresh air and his own brand of musky maleness—played havoc with her senses, while the feel of his hands sliding languorously across her spine—as if the movement of their hips wasn't enough—made her pulse grow thick and heavy.

How could she have ever thought him wrong for her? she wondered, when every atom of her being remembered this closeness with a sense of déjà vu that bordered on eerie. This man who had stumbled into her life with all the grace of a wrecking ball had reawakened her from the kind of deadness she'd sought refuge in for so long. She knew he was meant for her. He was a gift she wasn't prepared to give back. And she would fight to keep him.

But even as she vowed it, she forgot to think as Jack's hands strayed to the curve of her buttocks and pulled her closer against the hard ridge of his desire. His mouth dropped against her ear and he breathed a handful of words about where he wanted to touch her even as his fingers slid beneath the soft cashmere of her sweater.

Tess inhaled sharply at the possessive pressure of his palm against the hardening nub at the tip of her breast. An involuntary shudder raced through her as his tongue teased the inside of her ear, then abruptly moved down to take the place of his palm. He licked her nipple in small, maddening circles until she squirmed against him, craving nearness. Then, with a sound of pleasure, he took it into his mouth and sucked until her breast felt heavy and full as the rest of her.

"Did I tell you how beautiful you are?" he whispered against her damp skin. "I've dreamed about you," he said, sliding his hand across her belly and down her thigh. His voice was shaky. Barely leashed. "Hot, erotic dreams, but even they didn't compare to this. To how you feel. To how you look right now."

Tess's hands wandered along his back, across the muscled contours of his shoulders and the twin ridges along his spine. "Jack—oh, Jack—"

"This is crazy."

"Yes," she murmured, placing moist kisses across his brow and down his cheek. "That's how you make me feel."

"I shouldn't…" he began, sliding his mouth against her neck in a helpless contradiction of need and common sense.

"Oh, you should. You absolutely should," she breathed. "Don't bring logic into this. There isn't any to what's happened with us. This is just—"

He silenced whatever she'd been about to say with his mouth, grinding a kiss there that left them both breathless and frantic for more. Then half carrying, half dragging her, he moved her backward until they collided against the log wall, his mouth still locked with hers. Control was slipping away and in its place was raw need.

His fingers shook as he tugged her sweater up over her head and sent the silken slip of fabric covering her breasts to the floor after it.

With both hands, he cupped her breasts, testing their weight. Admiring the perfection of her. She took his breath away. He'd imagined her naked, but hadn't reckoned on the creamy paleness of her skin or the dusky perfection of the nipple reaching up to him like a flower toward the sun.

There was a buzzing in his ears as he slid his hands downward to her waist, taking in the lean curve of her belly. He ground his hips against hers as she fumbled with the buttons of his shirt. He was afraid to let her touch him. Afraid that once she did he would lose control. It had been too long since he'd been with a woman. Any woman. He wanted this to be right, as wrong as it was. He wanted…oh, damn, he needed—

Her hands slid past his opened shirt and followed the planes of his chest, carefully avoiding his unbandaged, healing wound. Her eyes met his in silent concern and he kissed away her fears. The ache in his shoulder couldn't compare to the one in his loins.

A shudder tumbled through him as her thumbs found the flat disks of his nipples, and she caressed them the way he had hers. Then, before she could move farther down and risk pushing him beyond control, he took her by the wrists and brought her hands up to his mouth, pressing a lingering kiss in each before he drew her fully against him and wrapped her in his arms again. The friction of his chest against the softness of her breasts was almost more than he could bear.

"I want to touch you everywhere," he murmured, bending down to ease his lips against her belly and the soft underside of her breast. "Here." His teeth skimmed the slight indentation at her waist, nipping and tasting her. "And here."

Her fingers curled against the back of his head as he dipped lower, pressing kisses through the fabric of her skirt until he was on his knees before her and his hand was under her skirt, dragging the silk fabric of her panties down her long legs. He slid his hands up the sides of her hips, pulling her toward him.

Tess gasped as his fingers moved between her legs, and she threw her arms out against the wall to keep from falling. What he was doing to her stole the rigidness from her bones, and she swayed against his touch. All the while he watched her face, enjoying the expression of dazed pleasure there. And when he'd finished torturing her, he pulled her down to him there on the floor, shoving aside the basket of magazines and scattering them across the floor.

Tess felt drugged and dizzy with need as Jack stripped off his clothes and tossed them aside. She'd seen him before, of course. All of him. But not this way. Not with the raw hunger and the full, masculine essence burning in those eyes of his that made her want to melt into him. Crawl inside him and let him know her.

And then he was inside her, filling her, and they moved

with the graceless poetry of lovers, a slick, groping reunion of souls and sweet discovering. Every stroke, every sigh, every moaning endearment dragged her upward to the precipice they sought together. Climbing, climbing, she opened her eyes and found him watching her, his jaw clenched with a fierceness of will, his focus entirely on the rising swell between them.

A warrior, she thought. Her warrior. And then there was no more thinking.

She felt herself lifting off, tethered to earth only by his touch and the sweet, urgent tension strung between them like a bowstring ready to snap. Lifting, lifting…her body shifted, changed, transmuted into something else as she heard herself cry out his name, begging him to defy the laws of gravity with her. Then the ground fell from under her and she tumbled over the edge the way a bird tumbled out of a nest for the first time, only to be transported by the current of air beneath its wings. Weightless and free.

Jack followed close behind, spilling into her the weight of his need. And they forgot where they were and what they'd been and only remembered this moment between them. This incredible rushing tug of feeling that transported them above it all. And she heard his gasping prayer as he tucked himself around her, sweat slicked and sated and part of her.

She held him and he held her back, locked together by what they'd become. Their breathing slowed, but for long minutes they didn't—couldn't—speak, afraid to break the fragileness.

Tess felt tears running out of the corners of her eyes and spilling into her ears. He lifted his head from her shoulder. "Are you crying, cupcake?" She shook her head. "Yes, you are," he said, dragging his index finger along her cheek with a frown. "Geez, did I hurt you?"

"No. God, no. I'm not crying. Okay, maybe I am. But

only because...'' She closed her eyes squeezing more tears from them. "It's never been like that for me before, Jack.''

The intensity of his stare didn't change. "Me either. Never.'' He dropped a small kiss on her lips.

She gave a teary laugh. "I choose to believe that, even though it comes from a man who's only just remembered his own name.''

His mouth curved into a smile. "Some things a man never forgets.''

She smoothed the damp hair off his forehead. "Will tonight be one of those things?'' she asked, even though she wanted to swallow the question as soon as it was out.

He kissed her again in reply, this time with a lingering heat that only moments ago had spun them both out of control. "I'll always remember tonight.'' He dragged a finger down the side of her face, the seriousness edging back to his own. "Even though I never meant for it to go this far.''

"And I never meant to find you on that road. But I don't regret it.''

"This is different,'' he said, pressing his lips to her shoulder, then rolling off her. His sudden withdrawal left her feeling bereft. "Maybe you will this. I mean, damn, I ravished you right here on the floor. I couldn't even wait to get you into a proper bed.''

"Um-hmm,'' she murmured lazily, rolling over toward him there on the soft rug. She drew little circles in the hair on his chest with her fingertip. "There was nothing proper about what just happened, Jack. And as far as the bed goes, well, beds are fine for sleeping, but when it comes to ravishing, I'd take the floor anytime.''

He dragged her across his chest and regarded her with a subtle lift of his brows. "You would?''

"Absolutely.''

"I can think of a few alternatives. Just off the top of my head."

"*Can* you?"

"Umm-hmm." He brushed the curtain of hair from her eyes.

"For instance?"

A slow, heated smile lifted one corner of his mouth.

Minutes later, as they stood together under the steamy onslaught of the shower, Tess came to understand more fully the definition of "ravishment" as Jack took full advantage of the situation and her. And while the hot, soapy water sluiced down their bodies, and she succumbed to an erotic sensuality she'd only dreamed of, she redefined the word for him as well.

And for Jack, who had to remind himself to keep one foot in this world, the journey was only made more bittersweet with the knowledge that Tess, like so many other things in his life, was a temporary gift, and that sooner rather than later, he would have to give her up, too. But just for tonight, he would pretend that she belonged to him.

Chapter 14

The room was dark when Tess woke. She had no idea what time it was except that it was hours yet till morning. She wasn't quite sure what had awakened her except the sense that Jack was no longer beside her in the bed. Blinking in the darkness, she found him standing near the window, silhouetted by moonlight.

He took her breath away, even in the dark. The perfection of him startled her. Lost in thought, he didn't hear her slide out of bed. He jumped a little as she slipped her arms around his waist, then he covered her hands with his. His skin was warm, despite the chill in the air, as if he was impervious to the cold.

"Penny for your thoughts," she whispered, hugging him.

He didn't answer right away and she prayed it wasn't her he was contemplating. Because his silence felt foreboding.

"You should be sleeping."

"So should you," she replied, though there were always other possibilities.

His hands tightened around hers and she felt his chest expand with a sigh. "I've slept more in the last week than I probably have in ten years."

"Why don't you sleep?"

He shrugged. "Training, I suppose. Becomes a habit, even when you're not on duty. You learn to sleep with one eye open. Or you die."

What she still didn't know about him frightened her. "Are your memories getting clearer? Is that what you were thinking about just now?"

"Yes." He took her by the shoulders and led her back to the bed. "It's cold. Get under the covers."

"Only if you do."

He obliged, but she sensed he had other things on his mind now. Tess tucked her head against his shoulder and wrapped herself around him, listening to the steady thud of his heart.

"We're leaving today."

Something inside her went cold. Not today. Not yet.

"I've made arrangements for you," he said.

"Arrangements?" she echoed stiffly.

"I told you I'd make sure you were safe before I—"

"Safe? How marvelous. Do I get five-star accommodations? Two padlocks for the door? Oh, I hope you didn't forget the flowers, Jack. You know I require a large bouquet of—"

"Tess—"

"—roses with every *accommodation* and everything just…" The lump in her throat effectively silenced the rest. She rolled off him and slumped against her pillow.

"Tess, listen…" His hand hesitated above her shoulder for a moment before he thought better of touching her. "I haven't told you everything."

Obviously. She knew better, but she felt idiotic. As if she'd blindly believed that this night could change anything. But that had never been her purpose. No, she'd known this moment was coming, but now that it was here, she couldn't help feeling like a fool.

His voice behind her was soft and apologetic. "It's the only way, cupcake."

"Don't call me that. Don't use that name on me when you're leaving."

He slid downward, abandoning his decision not to touch her, and spooning himself around her. "All right. I won't. But we both knew this was going to happen."

"Yes. We both knew." She sighed heavily, loving the feeling of his hands on her but making no move to enfold them. "That doesn't make it any easier."

"Nothing about us has been easy. Why should this?"

She would have laughed if she didn't want so badly to cry. "What haven't you told me?"

"I finally remembered why I came to L.A. I came to find out who murdered my brother."

Tess squeezed her eyes shut. Her fingers closed over his and she half rolled toward him. "Oh, Jack. I'm—sorry."

For a long minute he was silent, holding her. Finally, he spoke. "I missed his funeral. I was out of the country when the call came and didn't find out until it was too late. His wife phoned me. They called it suicide, but we both knew they were lying through their damned teeth. The sons of bitches murdered him and then tried to destroy his good name."

"Who murdered him?"

"L.A.'s finest. His brothers in blue." Sarcasm twisted Jack's mouth. "They said he was a dirty cop. But anyone who knew him knew otherwise. Joe would've climbed into hell for the men under him in the Navy. He won a citation for bravery under fire saving two of his coworkers in a botched shakedown last year. Joe was expecting his first child this Christmas, Tess. He never would have done what they claimed, and I had proof. That's what took me up to that canyon the night you found me. I was trying to clear his name.''

Tess felt as if some great weight had been lifted off her. Relief so acute tumbled through her—relief that he wasn't what Gil had thought—that she almost yelled, ''I knew it!'' Not a drug deal gone sour, not a hit of some ruthless trafficker, but vindication. She pulled him against her.

He tightened his arms around her and didn't say a word. They held each other like that for a full minute before she lifted her hand to his face. ''What kind of proof did you have, Jack?''

Jack rolled onto his back, taking her with him and tucking her against his shoulder. ''To tell you that, I have to start where it began, two weeks ago. I'd been out of the country on training ops. We'd been out of touch with communications for three days when I finally got word of Joe's death. They helicoptered me out to a ship anchored fifty miles from our position, but by the time I got home, Joe was already in the ground. I was scheduled to fly out here to see his wife the next day. But then I opened my mail. In it, I found a package from Joe.''

Tess propped her cheek on the heel of her hand, listening.

''Inside was a floppy disk, complete with audio and video tracks, physical evidence he'd gathered against the sons of bitches who killed him. But he hadn't uncovered the top dog yet. He knew they might try to kill him if they learned he was on to them. In case that happened, he sent me the floppy and asked me to protect Jule, his wife. She didn't need any disk to tell her Joe had been murdered. She knew.''

''How?''

''First of all, she knew him. Knew how impossible it was that he would do that. He had a kid on the way, Tess.

Jule's due in December. He would never have missed that. But the other clues were more tangible. The note he left—he addressed it to 'Julia.' Other people called her that, but he never did. He always called her Jule. It was like a touchstone for them. He used to joke about how on a cop's salary she was the only jewel he could afford, but he told me once that even though he couldn't buy her the things he knew she deserved, every time he called her that, she'd know how he felt about her.'' He stared at the moonlight spilling through the window.

''What else?'' she asked gently.

''His handwriting looked wrong, as if he'd intentionally tried to change it to signal that he'd done it under duress. And he'd signed it 'Joey.' If nothing else should have alerted us, this would have. He hated that name from the time we were kids. He was always Joe. Just Joe. And the house—Jule thought it had been gone through professionally. Even though everything looked neat, some things were out of order, as if someone had searched the place.''

''But didn't Jule tell the police that? Didn't they investigate?''

''Of course. It's departmental procedure. What they turned up only painted a blacker picture of him. Unaccounted-for deposits in his bank accounts, calls that came in at all hours of the night that ended in wild-goose chases, but conveniently placed him without an alibi for that sliver of time. There were witnesses in the department who claimed he'd been distracted—which the internal shrinks read as 'despondent.' And the argument against the note's authenticity, considering all the other evidence stacked against him, was that he wasn't thinking clearly. 'Obviously,' they said, 'he wouldn't have killed himself otherwise.''' Jack gave a humorless laugh. ''Kind of a lose-lose situation, wouldn't you say?''

''How did they explain it then?''

"It was their theory that he'd killed himself because he couldn't live with the shame of what he'd done, or put his wife through it. The IA investigation concluded he was on the take in a drug scam. He was working narcotics, so it was relatively easy to set him up. And when his wife was out of town one weekend, it was a simple matter to make it look like suicide. A turned over chair. A scrawled note. Which takes us back to where I came in."

"Go on," Tess said, watching the intensity in his face harden in the moonlight.

Jack scraped his fingers against his skull, shoving his hair back. "After I found the floppy, I called Jule and told her to call me back from a nearby pay phone in case her phone had been bugged. When she did, I told her to get the hell out of town. She was to stay in the location we decided on, and if she didn't hear from me in two weeks, she was to go and retrieve the copy of the floppy I'd left in a safe place back in Virginia, and give it to my friend Seth Tanner. Naturally, she argued. Tried to talk me out of doing it alone."

"Hmm. Sounds vaguely familiar."

Jack smiled. "It didn't matter. She couldn't have helped me."

"How long has it been?" she asked.

"Twelve days," he said. "I would've had this whole thing wrapped up if they hadn't found out who I was."

"So you came to L.A. and what? Did some investigating on your own?"

"I knew no one knew me here. I'd missed the funeral. No one out here had ever met me. So I decided to do some snooping around. I knew the minor players—Saldovar, Detectives Lyle MacAvoy and Eddie Rodriguez."

Tess sat up. "Wait. The two at the hospital who wanted you dead—their names were Bruener and Rivera."

"The ID they flashed at you was fake, even though

MacAvoy and Rodriguez were the genuine article. The real Bruener and Rivera work narcotics in the Westside, and as far as I can tell, have no knowledge of this operation. MacAvoy and Rodriguez use those badges sparingly and only in situations where they themselves shouldn't be seen. Until Joe, no one had caught them, and their alibis had been airtight. Witnesses put them twenty miles away from any crime.''

''Which explains why Bruener and Rivera had no record of answering any calls at the hospital that night.''

''That's right.''

Tess fell back against the pillow, staring at the dark ceiling. ''So MacAvoy and Rodriguez were involved in what? Drugs?''

''Money. Lots of money. Drugs was just a means to that goal. They used Saldovar, once they caught on to his chop-shop operation and discovered he was smuggling laundered money from a Mexican crime family from California into Mexico in exchange for huge shipments of heroin, which the family would, in turn, resell here. Saldovar, seeing his opportunity to skim his share of the operation, used MacAvoy and Rodriguez to sneak shipments past customs, and they would take their cut. It amounted to millions. But they weren't the only ones reaping the benefits of Saldovar's disloyalty. Joe discovered that there was someone higher up that the two detectives were answering to. Someone who not only wanted the money, but whose career hinged on turning off the flow of heroin into Southern California.''

''But they were shipping heroin *into* the country.''

''Exactly. Which made timely drug busts a more exacting science. So while one hand was raking in the money, the other was slapping the wrist of the drug cartels. At least, it was the appearance of that. In truth, it's bigger than anyone knew. It was a cushy arrangement protected by none other than a small contingent of boys in blue.''

"Who was this man?" she asked.

"I don't know. I never found out." Jack rolled toward her and propped his head on his hand. "The day I was shot, I had set up a preliminary look-see meeting with Saldovar at a café in Santa Monica, to discuss the terms of a considerable drug buy I was in the market to make. I'd sprinkled a few familiar names around, and some rather seedy credentials. Saldovar was biting. I'd learned that a ship called the *Benedictus* was coming into San Pedro on the twenty-fifth."

"*August* twenty-fifth?"

He nodded.

She sat up. "That's today, Jack. The twenty-fifth is today."

Jack cursed softly.

"What's going to happen tonight?"

He ground his teeth together, staring straight up at the ceiling. "It may have fallen apart after what happened to Saldovar."

"What happened?"

"That day when I met him? I knew he was discontent with his relationship with the detectives and that they'd been putting pressure on him to step up the operation. I figured if I could win my way into Saldovar's confidence, he could give me the name of the man on top.

"It was my bad luck that his south-of-the-border compatriots chose that day to off him for skimming money from them. MacAvoy and Rodriguez, who had already seen my photograph in naval archives, caught sight of me there and put two and two together. They muscled me into a car with a little encouragement from a snub-nosed .38 upside my head."

"And they took you up to the canyon?"

He nodded with a sigh. "They'd already decided I had the floppy, and did their best to beat its location out of me. They forgot they were dealing with someone who'd been trained to resist that particular brand of persuasion and others they'd never dreamed of. I knew all I had to do was bide my time until that hothead, Rodriguez, who was waving his gun around like an American flag on the Fourth of July, did something seriously stupid. It didn't take long.

"I was on the ground feigning unconsciousness and Rodriguez was arguing with MacAvoy about whether he should kill me, and about the whereabouts of the lost floppy. Rodriguez walked close to me, pointing the gun at my head. What happened next is a little fuzzy, but I remember grabbing his leg and yanking him down. Then I rolled to my feet, with MacAvoy still trying to wrestle his gun from his holster. My only chance was to go over the edge, and I headed for it. But Rodriguez recovered the gun and shot me as I turned to slide down the cliff." He rubbed his temple with two fingers. "I don't really remember anything after that. Until you found me."

Tess shivered and slipped her arms around him, pulling him close. The thought that these two men were still out there, hunting him, sent a chill throughout her being. "Where is the floppy now?"

"Somewhere safe."

"We have to call Gil." She could feel Jack tense even as the words came out.

"*No.*"

"Why not? He can help us. I trust him with my life, Jack. He's known about you all week. He hasn't sent the troops in here after you. I asked him not to. He knows the situation better than anyone."

"Did you tell him where we were, Tess?" Jack asked pointedly.

"No. But he knows. He guessed."

"Are you sure?"

"Yes. Jack, he knows that this whole thing stinks. And he knows there are dirty cops involved. He's on our side." She took his hand in hers. "You have to trust somebody sometime."

"I trust you."

"But you won't let me help you."

"Gil doesn't know who's at the top any more than I do. Are you willing to set Gil up as the next victim? Because that's what you'd be doing."

She swallowed hard. "Gil's careful. Let him help you. You can't do this alone."

Jack turned his head away from her, looking at the pale edges of dawn that had leaked into the sky. "I'm not going to need a partner. Not for what I've got in mind. But if I do, I'll call him. Deal?"

It wasn't what she wanted, not by half, but she knew she'd have to settle for the crumbs he'd thrown her. He was as fiercely independent as any man she'd ever known, but probably ten times as capable. He wouldn't be caught off guard a second time with them, she thought. This time, he would go in armed with a plan. She would do what she had to do, just as he would, she decided, skimming her hands along the warm contours of his taut abdomen.

"Then let's not waste what time we have left," she told him, trailing her fingers downward until she met with the evidence that his thinking was running along similar lines. He inhaled sharply as she touched him there. "Make love to me, Jack. I want to feel you inside me again."

Jack slid his hand up to caress her breast in wordless consent, then dropped his mouth onto hers in a slow, deep kiss that said everything he couldn't. Slowly, they stoked the fires that had banked in the cool, dark hours of the morning. He loved the feel of her against him, flesh to flesh, the small perfection of her body as it fit snugly against his.

And as he tasted the sweetness of her skin and felt it quiver deliciously at his touch, he tried not to think about his life without her. He pushed that thought from his mind, knowing that even if he survived the next day or so, what had happened here with her had been like a miracle. Something out of time and place that couldn't be repeated.

His life was hard by necessity, dictated by forces beyond his control. It was all he knew and he was damned good at it. But he could never again ask a woman to share it. And Tess—who'd dedicated herself to saving lives, not taking them—needed a man who would come home for dinner and hold her every night like this, safe in his arms.

But for a few more hours she was his, and he wasn't a man to squander such a gift. As he tortured her with his mouth, leaving damp trails along her shivering skin, he felt her fingernails against his back, urging him on. She squirmed against him, and he pulled her roughly beneath him and nudged her long, sexy legs apart with his thighs. "Ah, Tess, you make me crazy," he murmured against the hollow at the base of her throat.

"Oh, Jack!" She sighed against his ear, fueling the thundering roar there as he slid into her.

They moved in an ancient rhythm, a desperate, hungry fusion of wills that tried to hold at bay the inevitability of the future. And when, at last, that furnacelike heat had been exhausted, and they'd fallen into each other's arms, spent and sated, Jack held her as if the morning would never come, and he wasn't about to lose the best thing that had ever happened to him.

When she woke the next time, it was with a startled gasp that had her shoving herself straight up in bed, wondering if she'd been dreaming. Early morning light spilled through the window and one glance at the empty bed beside her answered her questions.

Jack was gone.

The sleep cleared from her brain in an instant. Okay, she told herself. Stay calm. He's probably just gone to make coffee. But she heard nothing in the outer rooms. No sound at all.

She looked at the empty spot on the floor where he'd dumped his clothes last night as they'd moved their love-making into the bedroom, and she tried to remain calm.

Throwing the covers aside, she got up and pulled on her own clothes. Barefoot, she padded out of the bedroom and into the dimly lit hallway that led past the bathroom. She saw no sign of Jack, and her first instinct was to check if he'd taken her car.

Had he called Dan Kelso and told him to watch her? Jack had never been specific about exactly how he intended to protect her. She got mad all over again. Damn him for being chickenhearted enough to sneak out in the early hours of the morning after loving her the way he had! And damn her for still wanting him.

She hadn't moved two steps into the living room when someone slapped a hand over her mouth from behind and dragged her back hard against the wall.

Chapter 15

Every survival instinct kicked past Tess's shock, and she pawed wildly at the hands over her mouth as strong arms dragged her down toward the floor.

"Quiet, Doc!" a voice whispered urgently in her ear. "It's—" he grunted as her elbow connected with his ribs "—me!"

He cinched her against him, holding her as his words sank in.

She gasped. Jack?

He moved slightly so she could see him. The fierce look he sent her was meant to silence her as he swung the gun he was holding into her line of vision.

"What the hell are you—" She mumbled unintelligibly against the palm he'd flattened against her mouth, until Jack glanced pointedly at the door. Tess followed his glance.

And stopped breathing.

The shadow of a man moved past the drawn window shade toward the kitchen door.

Jack removed his hand gingerly and Tess whispered, "Who is it?"

He shook his head and signaled for her to be quiet and get down behind the sofa. His expression brooked no argument. Terrified, she watched him steal across the living room in a low crouch and disappear through the kitchen doorway.

Tess huddled beside the sofa, listening to the sound of footsteps on the porch and dismissing the notion that whoever it was could be someone they knew. Dan Kelso wouldn't be sneaking around her porch at seven in the morning, nor would anyone else she knew. No, whoever was outside meant to break in, she decided, pulling a heavy candlestick off the end table and removing the candle.

But how had they found them? No one knew where they were except Gil. No one could have possibly figured out that they'd come here unless—

The metallic rasp of a lock being jimmied came from the kitchen. Almost simultaneously, Tess's attention was pulled to a window on the other side of the house, and the deck off the lake, as a second man, dressed entirely in black, jiggled the lock on the French doors.

Oh, no! Tess's jaw went slack as she watched the metal handle move up and down, and she scooted farther into the shadow of the sofa. Her hands tightened around the candlestick and she mouthed Jack's name.

In the kitchen, Jack stood flattened against the wall near the door, his gun poised near his cheek, watching the lock slide back. It surprised him that they'd taken such a direct approach. He'd expected more from them. The door edged open, pushed by the man's glove-covered hand.

Wait, Jack counseled himself. *Wait.*

He sized up his opponent the instant he cleared the door. Six foot one and a good fifty pounds heavier than Jack, he wore dark clothing, including a baseball cap that covered his balding head and partially obstructed his peripheral vision enough for Jack to get the drop on him.

"Freeze," he ordered, placing the barrel of the gun firmly behind the man's ear.

The intruder swore under his breath and obeyed, with his hands raised in the air.

"That's right," Jack said through gritted teeth. "Give me your gun." He reached out and snatched the silencer-clad semiautomatic from the man's hand and slid it across the floor to the other side of the kitchen.

"On the floor!" he growled. "Now!"

"Hey, don't shoot—"

"Do it!" he ordered.

The man dropped down heavily on one knee, but Jack had enough experience in hand-to-hand combat to recognize the coiled readiness waiting for an opportunity to unfurl. Jack shoved the man down the rest of the way with a well-placed foot in the back. The intruder grunted as he flattened against the floor. Holding the pistol with both hands, Jack aimed it at the dark, straight hair just behind his ear.

"Don't think I won't do it," he warned, adrenaline pumping through his blood.

"Hey—" The man held his palms above the floor. "Easy—"

Jack pressed the gun harder against his skull. "Who sent you?"

The man, whom Jack didn't recognize, began to sweat. "You don't really expect me to—"

He moved the gun under the man's chin. "I'm afraid I do." From the other room, he heard Tess's voice.

"Jack?"

"I'm okay, Tess," he called, not taking his eyes off his prisoner. "Stay where you are." Turning his attention back to the man, he said, "Where I come from, we don't think twice about ridding the world of little pissants like you. So if you'd rather not see your brains splattered all over this nice kitchen floor, you'll tell me who—"

"*Jack?*" There was a note of urgency in her voice this time that made him look up.

The sound of shattering glass coincided with Tess screaming his name one last time. Almost at the same instant, the man on the floor rolled sideways, shoving Jack's gun out of his hand and throwing him off balance into the kitchen island beside him. Jack swore foully, simultaneously realizing that he had made a calculated error by taking his eyes off his opponent and that a second man had just entered the fray—and was after Tess.

There was no time to think. Only react. Jack flung himself at the man, who was still getting to his feet, and pummeled him with a fist across the cheek. Pain sizzled up his arm as flesh met bone, and Jack heard a hiss of pain, but the man staggered to his feet and whirled on him in a football tackle, low and around the knees. They went down, sprawling across the kitchen floor with a loud thud, then crashed into a bank of cupboards. Jack's shoulder took the brunt of his impact and he grunted in pain. Two solid punches landed against Jack's ribs. He gasped for air as the man took advantage, rolling him onto his back. He took two more punches to the face before wrestling the bastard off him. The man's head connected with the floor with a hard crack. Jack heard Tess scream as he looked wildly for the gun he'd kicked away.

Spotting it, he crawled off the man and dove for it, but an instant later felt his opponent's weight land on him with crushing accuracy. The man fought dirty, like a street fighter. Jack shoved an elbow into his ribs and rolled out from under him. The other man fell close to the gun and started crawling toward it. Jack kicked it out of his reach and drove another well-placed blow into his groin.

The man in black crumpled in half, gasping for air. Jack's hand closed around the grip of the gun. He swung the butt hard against the folded man's cheek with a sickening sound, then spun around, heading for the other room.

"Jack!" Tess was swinging helplessly against the man who was dragging her out the open French doors. Her captor grinned at Jack as he pressed a gun against her throat.

Jack didn't even contemplate what he did next. He swung the semiautomatic up and popped off a silent round. Surprise blossomed on the man's face as a small dark hole bloomed red above his temple. Then his eyes rolled back in his head and he dropped to the floor.

Tess stood in frozen horror, her hands over her mouth. *"Ohmigod, ohmigod."*

Jack rushed over to her and pulled her against him, moving her away from the body at her feet. "It's okay now, shh, it's over."

"You *k-killed* him," she said, and he nodded. "Right next to me. You killed him."

He nodded again, knowing what she was thinking. If he'd missed… But that possibility had never even occurred to him. He'd simply trusted the skill he'd spent a lifetime honing.

She pulled back and looked at him. "Oh, Jack, your face!"

His lip felt busted and he could feel the dampness of blood trickling from a cut on his cheek. But it was a small price to pay to have Tess in his arms. Alive. "It's nothing. Are you hurt?"

She looked down at her shaking hands. "No. Just bruised, I think. He was going to take me, Jack. Where was he going to take me?"

"I don't know." He let go of her and walked over to the dead man. Lifting the edge of his coat, he rifled his pockets for ID. He opened a wallet. "Toller Cruz," Jack said aloud. "Civilian ID. Could be fake, though." He rifled a little more until his hand hit something hard-edged in his inside pocket. He pulled it out, swore and looked up at Tess. "Recognize this?"

Tess went pale as he handed her the photograph of her and Adam, Cara and some other man standing in front of this very cabin. A sick expression crept to her face. "They found us from this picture?"

"Probably a scouting party," Jack said. "You know? Like a beehive? The queen sends her worker bees out to scout for flowers? Well, these two struck gold. They're probably looking at all the mountain communities within a certain radius of L.A. And we've gotta get out of here before they're missed."

"But what about…?" She sent a horrified look at the man on the floor.

"We'll call your friend Dan from the road and tell him what happened. I'll tie up the other one and leave him for Dan to deal with."

Tess blinked hard, trying to get her mind around what had just happened. She watched Jack wipe blood off his battered cheek with his fist and head back to the kitchen. The sickening sound of that bullet striking bone still echoed in her ears. She'd watched men die before, even in her hands. But never a man who wanted her dead as well. She couldn't stop shaking. Outside, in the distance, she heard an engine roar to life and the grinding sound of tires against gravel.

"God*dammit!*" Jack roared from the other room. A string of unrepeatable expletives followed and Jack appeared at the doorway. "He's gone! The son of a bitch got away!"

Tess could only stare at him as the implications dawned on her.

"I hit him hard. Dammit! I should have shot him!" Jack punched the air in frustration, then scowled at her. "Get your things. We're outta here." When she didn't move, he barked, *"Now!"*

The Travelin' Style Motel, a desert oasis of fifties-era bungalows tied loosely together by a meandering, Astro Turf putting green and a lozenge-shaped pool, sat tucked beneath a shady canopy of date palms off I-10. There were sixty-seven date palms swaying in the hot August breeze. Sixty-eight if you counted the dead one standing frondless and naked over the seventeenth hole. Tess had counted them twice since Jack had gone into the office to rent a room five minutes ago.

She stared now at the unripe fruit hanging in heavy clumps from the thickets of green that graced the tops of the forty-foot trees. The roadside date stands would soon be brimming with the dried fruit, she mused absently. The children splashing in the pool would be going back to school. And their mothers would heave a sigh of relief. The sun would set and the moon would rise, she thought. The world would go on, but it would never be quite the same after this morning.

Tess glanced up past the palms at the sky—a cloudless, cerulean blue, the perfect counterpoint to a perfectly awful day.

Forget the fact that she'd left a dead body back at Cara's cabin. Dismiss the disillusionment in Dan Kelso's voice when she'd called him from the road to tell him she'd left a dead body behind and that she'd lied to him about her reasons for being there—to which he'd kindly reminded her that leaving the scene of a crime, self-defense or no, was in fact a crime. Even overlook the very real possibility that by the end of this day, they'd find her and kill her, effectively ending any speculation on the irreparable damage she'd done to her career.

No, the worst part of the day was watching that office door, waiting for Jack to walk through it. Because once he did, once he had that key in his hand, he would tuck her in one of these awful bungalows and leave her, she knew. And she would likely never see him again.

The office door opened and Jack walked out, all loose-limbed grace and determination, looking like he'd stepped off the set of a road warrior movie. Tess's gaze fell to his hand and the shiny piece of metal catching the glint of the sun. Something twisted painfully in her chest.

Jack slid into the car beside her and sighed heavily. "All set."

"Wait, don't tell me," she said dryly, staring out at the putting green. "I have a fairway-view room."

He grinned. "Only the best for you, Doc."

He turned the key and they drove around to a small bungalow with the lofty name Augusta, for the famous Georgia golf course. All the other rooms had similar appellations: Pebble Beach, Saint Andrews and Riviera, lettered on cut-out wood flags.

Inside, the room, while clean, didn't disappoint. The cheesy decor, complete with rust-colored carpeting and plaid-upholstered furniture, looked as if it hadn't been redecorated since the seventies.

"Nice," Tess murmured, flopping down on the bed and testing the boardlike mattress. "Really nice."

"It's safe. That's the important thing right now," Jack said. "No one will look here."

"Did I mention that I despise golf?"

A smile eased the tension on Jack's lips. "No."

"Ah, well. One more thing you didn't know about me and wish you still didn't." She smoothed her hand across the putting-green-colored bedspread. "I mean, here's a game where otherwise intelligent people spend a whole day chasing after a small white ball that they've just knocked to kingdom come for the purpose of sinking it into a hole strategically placed to resist their every attempt."

"Ooh, stop," he said, sitting on the bed beside her. "You're getting me all hot just talking about it."

Tess laughed. "Am I?" She rose up and pressed her mouth lightly against his, teasing his lips with a flick of her tongue.

"Mmm..." He sighed against her mouth. "I think you're trying to distract me."

"That would be correct."

He kissed her deeply, with the slow thoroughness of a man at peace with who he was, a man who had nothing to prove. She savored the taste of him, the feel of his weight against her hips and her breasts, and tried to memorize the sensations. Because also in his kiss, so tender and so resolute, was the taste of goodbye.

Indeed, it was he who broke the contact first, pressing small kisses across her face. Finally he just held her—tightly, as if he didn't want to let her go. Oh! How she wished he wouldn't!

Tears gathered behind her eyes. She could feel the steady thump of his heart against her breast and her own answering in kind. What had happened to her that she couldn't imagine never feeling this amazing sensation again? What had happened to the girl who'd settled for dinner alone in commissaries and reading the Sunday paper from cover to cover on her solitary patio? Where had the notion of never falling in love again gone? She'd fallen madly, helplessly, disastrously in love with Jack. And now he was leaving. She curled her arms tighter around him.

"We have to talk, Tess."

"I don't want to talk."

He kissed her cheek with tenderness. "I know. But I have to go. You know I do."

"No, *you* said that, I didn't. *I* say you call it in. Let them handle this."

He untangled himself from her and sat up. "It's personal, Tess. I can't do that."

She sat up beside him. "Personal? I'll tell you what's personal. This is personal. You and me is personal. That? That's revenge. Pure and unvarnished."

"Maybe. But I won't risk leaving this thing to someone else to finish. They killed my brother and almost killed me. My brother's reputation hangs on what I do here. My sister-in-law's future hangs there, too. I won't leave it alone. I can't."

"Is it your macho Navy SEAL image that makes you believe you're superhuman, Jack? Is it worth dying over? Because this time they may just succeed in killing you." She shoved herself to her feet and stalked over to the venetian-blind-covered window.

He followed and put his hands on her upper arms from behind. "Listen to me, Tess. I'm not naive. I know the odds here. I have no choice. Not as I see it.

"What we've had," he continued, tucking his arms around her, "has been, well—amazing. I never imagined I'd..." He stopped, pulling her hard against his chest. "But I'm gonna say this for your own good and I want you to listen to me. You deserve better than I can ever give you. When this is over, I want you to forget me, Tess."

"What?" She blinked up at him in hollow shock. *"What?"*

"I mean it. No matter what the outcome. Let it go."

"Let it go?" she echoed incredulously. "Which part of it do I let go of, exactly? The fact that I love you? The fact that you make me feel whole again, like a piece of me has been missing all these years and now it's not? Should I let that go? Or maybe I should pretend that none of this ever happened. That some proud, stubborn stranger didn't find me on a lonely road one night and change the way I looked at my life. Or maybe that when that stranger held me in his arms, made love to me, he made me believe that he cared about me. Which part should I forget, Jack?''

He released her and walked to the bed, where he'd left the keys to her car. They jangled like broken pieces of glass as he picked them up. ''I called a friend of mine last night, Seth Tanner, to come and watch over you until this is finished. He's flying into Ontario Airport from D.C. and should be here by two.''

''Jack—?''

''I don't want you to leave this room. Understand? Not until Seth comes. Don't open this door to anyone else. He'll take care of whatever you need. Money. Food…''

''*Jack!* Please let me come with you.''

''Don't use the phone and don't use your credit cards. They can be traced in a matter of minutes.'' He moved toward the door and stopped with his hand on the handle. ''I know you think I'm what you want right now, Tess, but when you get a little distance, you'll see I'm right. You deserve so much more than I can give you. You deserve the best. Don't settle for less than that.''

He opened the door and Tess felt a desperate fist clench her throat. ''Was it just about sex then?'' Her voice was hollow and shaking. ''Is that all it was for you, Jack?''

His head jerked as if she'd struck him. Then, without so much as a goodbye, he walked out the door and shut it firmly behind him.

Curled in the plaid chair near the Formica-veneered table, Tess rocked numbly back and forth, listening to the tick of the bedside clock. She lifted the overused tissue to her nose and dabbed it, trying desperately to stop crying.

She couldn't do this, she told herself. This wasn't like her. She handled crises. She'd been trained to rise above them.

Tears flowed again and she dropped her face into her palms. But this wasn't just another crisis. This was Jack. And despite every hurtful thing he'd said, she knew he was wrong. He wouldn't be able to forget her any more than she would him.

Nonetheless, she decided rationally, this wasn't about them or whether they had a future together. It was about whether Jack would have one at all. And here she was, catatonic with self-pity as he drove directly into the mouth of the storm.

Tess sat up straighter.

There was only one way she could help him. Gil. Maybe he could provide some kind of backup for Jack, or even talk him out of doing whatever he was planning. Naturally, Jack would hate her for interfering, but that was a small detail compared to the possibility that he would die tonight.

She stood up and reached for the cell phone in her purse.

Flipping it open, she punched the speed dial button for Gil's number at work.

"This is Ben. You've reached my machine," said a voice that definitely wasn't Gil's. "Please leave a message and I'll get back to you." A long beep buzzed in her ear and she held the phone out, staring at it. *Ben?*

Frowning, she pushed End and redialed Gil's number manually.

"This is Ben," the machine said again. "You've reached my machine—"

Tess stabbed at the end button again, blinking in confusion. *Who the hell is Ben? And why isn't Gil's number working?* Uneasiness spread through her. She dialed Gil's home number. A series of clicks, the same ones she'd heard yesterday, ended with the same voice. "This is Ben. You've reached my machine…"

Tess punched Off and threw the phone down on the bed, staring at it in disbelief. Then she picked it up again and dialed the precinct.

"LAPD, Westside Division. How may I help you?" the dispatcher's voice asked.

"I'm trying to reach Detective Gil Castillano. I can't seem to reach his machine."

"Who's calling please?"

Tess hesitated. "Um…I'm…a friend."

"One moment please."

Tess frowned and waited. The line clicked and she heard someone pick up. "Gil?" she blurted.

"This is Captain Sullivan," a voice at the other end said. Disappointment flagged through her. Tess bit her lip, uncertain whether to reply or not.

"Is that you, Tess?" Sullivan asked.

Bill Sullivan had been Adam's commanding officer and was still Gil's. He'd handed her the folded flag at Adam's funeral and come by her house several times in the weeks that followed. She knew Bill Sullivan well, but the fact that he'd picked up the phone sent a chill of dread through her.

"Yes," she said quietly.

She could hear him shutting his office door. "You're looking for Gil."

"What's going on? Has—has something happened?"

"We couldn't get in touch with you, though I knew you'd want to know. There was an accident yesterday—"

"Oh, God."

"He's alive, Tess, but he's pretty banged up. He's in the hospital. It was a hit-and-run. They mowed him down right outside the damned precinct."

She went numb. This was her fault. All of it, her fault! "Which hospital?"

"University. It was touch and go for a while, but he's improved some today. I was just there. He's got some broken ribs, a busted arm.... He seemed worried about you. He keeps asking for you."

Oh, God...oh, God... She squeezed her eyes shut. Was she destined to lose every man she ever cared about? "Bill, I'm out of town, but will you tell Gil I'm coming? Will you do that?"

"I'll have one of the nurses tell him, Tess. I'll call right now."

"Thanks, Bill. Thank you. I'll, uh—thank you."

She stabbed at the end button on the phone and practically yanked out the drawer of the night stand to get at the phone book. She flipped frantically through half a dozen pages, then found what she was looking for. With a shaking hand, she punched in the numbers.

"Avco, we try hardest, how may I help you?" said the woman on the other end.

"Yes," Tess said. "I'd like to rent a car. Do you deliver?"

The name emblazoned on the ship's bow docked at Pier 49 read *Neo-Benedictus*. Eight days ago, Jack had learned that it was registered out of Colombia, and was part of a freighting fleet owned by a corporation called *Hilo de Arana*—in English, Gossamer. That corporation, in turn, was owned by a number of dummy corporations that ultimately and circuitously led back to a man named Carlos de la Arroya—one of Colombia's largest dealers in the heroin trade.

Jack took a sip of lukewarm coffee from the plastic cup he'd left balancing on the park bench beside him. All afternoon, unmarked semis had been off-loading wooden shipping crates full of cargo onto the pier. These had been systematically lifted onto the huge freighter by the towering crane poised over the pier, and had disappeared into the hold. Twice he'd caught glimpses of a man named Cordova, Saldovar's lieutenant and right-hand man. It struck Jack that Cordova must have been the one to betray his boss to the crime family. Jack had yet to see either Rodriguez or MacAvoy, and he wondered if Saldovar's sudden demise had thrown a kink in the plans for tonight. Jack had it on good authority that everyone would be here, including the top man.

Now, as dusk settled over the pier and evening fog was rolling in, he knew he was going to have to make something happen or risk losing it all.

A longshoreman carrying a large carton on his shoulder moved toward him, and Jack reopened the newspaper he'd been hiding behind all afternoon. He turned the page, pretending to read, until a certain picture pulled his focus away from the shipyard. The caption beneath a police portrait read "Westside Division homicide detective, victim of hit-and-run, hospitalized." Jack scanned down the page to the first few lines.

"In a bizarre and troubling incident, the Westside Division of the LAPD found itself the site of a crime scene Sunday morning, when fifteen-year LAPD homicide detective Gil Castillano became the victim of a hit-and-run driver near the building's entrance"

Jack swore out loud and kept reading.

"Police have declined comment on the detective's condition, other than to say he's hospitalized at the University Medical Center. Witnesses to the incident alleged that the unidentified late-model red hatchback seemed to swerve in to hit Castillano, who was opening the door of his own car at the time of the accident. According to sources close to the investigation, the driver made no attempt to brake or stop after Castillano was struck. Though police have no suspects in custody, a spokesperson for the Westside Division said today that they are following a number of leads.''

Jack stopped reading and shoved the paper into the wire basket beside him. It shouldn't have surprised him that they'd go for Gil. His friendship with Tess was common knowledge. But the bald arrogance of the move shocked the hell out of him. If they were desperate enough to take out one of their own right in front of the precinct, what else would they do? And what did Gil know that had made them rash enough to try it?

Jack jogged to the car and peeled out of the parking lot with a screech of tires. He didn't want to think about how Tess was going to take this. He knew already that she'd blame herself for Gil's involvement. He prayed she didn't get her hands on a paper in the next twenty-four hours.

As he merged onto the Harbor Freeway, he gripped the wheel tighter, thinking of how they'd left things this morning. The sick feeling he'd had in his gut still lingered. She hadn't made it easy for him. He'd known she wouldn't. That's who she was—strong, smart and independent. Those same qualities that drew him to her made leaving a messy business, and it was easier, somehow, to let her think that he'd used her than to reveal the truth—that he'd never let a woman come as close to his heart as Tess had managed to get. The fact that he'd even thought twice about what he had to do now proved that he'd let her get too close. He couldn't afford to go soft in the real world—it would likely kill him.

But as he fought the rush-hour traffic, moving in and out of lanes for optimum position, he allowed himself to think of her and imagine what it would have been like if he were a different sort of man.

Chapter 16

The elevator doors swished closed behind Jack as he strode down the hospital corridor. A rush of activity, like a river current, moved past him as he searched the room numbers for the one he'd been told was occupied by Gil. His stride slowed as he spotted the cop posted at the doorway up ahead. Gil's room, no doubt. He should have guessed they'd post a guard. Anyone with brains could figure out that the accident had been no accident and that Gil's life was still at risk.

Jack stopped at a pay phone and turned away from the guard, whose glance had just traveled in his direction. What were the odds that this cop was familiar with the APB that they'd put out on him last week? Low, he decided. This guy was a beat cop, maybe pulled in off traffic to guard over Gil. Jack had always been a gambler and that's exactly what he was about to do here. If he lost, he lost the whole damn pot. If he won...

He caught his reflection in the silver plate on the front

of the pay phone. Damn. He looked like he'd just been in a car wreck himself. He touched his busted lip gingerly and smoothed a finger over the cut near his eye. With a shake of his head, he gave a grim smile. Well, he thought, here goes nothing.

Jack turned and walked to the nurses' station, toward a pretty brown-haired woman who was doing paperwork. After folding a metal chart and sliding it into a holder, she looked up at him, taking in the bruises on his face. "Can I help you?" she asked.

"I'm here to see Gil Castillano."

"Oh, the detective. I'm sorry, but only family members are allowed to—"

"I'm his brother," he said without the flicker of an eyelash. He waited a beat, taking in the frown in her expression.

"His brother? He didn't say anything about—"

"If you could just tell him I'm here? Tell him Jack's here."

"Jack," she repeated. Her eyes took one more quick perusal of him before she smiled briefly and headed down to Gil's room. "All right."

Interminable minutes ticked by as Jack waited. The activity in the corridor stepped up as a new patient was rolled out of the elevator, surrounded by a half-dozen clinging family members.

"Mr. Castillano?"

Jack jumped slightly at the sound of the nurse's voice beside him.

"Your brother will see you now."

Jack nodded tightly. "Thanks." The nurse must have cleared Jack with the guard at Gil's door, because he gave him little more than a nod as Jack passed him.

Gil's eyes were closed when he pushed open the door, and Jack took a moment to study him. He didn't know what he'd expected Gil to look like, but he'd certainly hoped for less. The picture in the paper didn't capture the strength of his features or the handsome, boyish quality to his face. Jealousy shot through him as he thought of the affection in Tess's voice when she spoke about him. And he wondered suddenly why she'd overlooked Gil when it came to something more than friendship.

The detective had taken a pretty good hit from the looks of him, with his arm bound up in plaster, and bruises from head to toe. An abrasion down the side of his face contrasted with the pallor of his skin. Healthy, Gil Castillano would be a formidable opponent. In a hospital bed, he looked only slightly less dangerous.

Gil's eyes opened as Jack moved into the room, and he knew instantly the jealousy he felt was justified. From beneath the bandage on his forehead, Gil's dark eyes perused him with suspicion and something closer to murderous intent.

"Where's Tess, *Brother* Jack?" His voice was gravelly from disuse.

"She's safe. Far away from here."

"Where *exactly?*"

"A little place east of here called the Travelin' Style Motel. A friend of mine is with her. He won't let anything happen to her."

Gil glared at him. "I should kill you myself for getting her involved in this."

"Better get at the end of the line. But for what it's worth, I wish things could've gone down differently. Especially for Tess."

Gil leaned his head back against the pillows with a tethered expression. "Suppose you tell me why you're here."

"My reasons for being here are remarkably similar to yours. Because we both know something we're not supposed to. And because Tess told me I could trust you."

A small, sardonic laugh escaped him. "She did. Well." He sighed, staring at the ceiling. "That's just like her, knowing that I'd like to personally bury you."

"So, was she wrong?"

Pinning him with a look Jack suspected he'd honed interrogating murderers, he said, "I would never do anything that would put Tess in danger."

Jack smiled thinly. "That *is* a relief. Speaking strictly as the Antichrist, I'd say she's lucky to have at least one saint in her corner."

Gil's mouth twisted with a grudging smile. "Okay, so maybe I came on a little strong. But it doesn't change the fact that you've put Tess right in the middle of something very ugly."

With a sigh, he said, "If I'd had the choice, I definitely would've chosen another place to be that night than Angelo Canyon. As it happened, that decision was taken out of my hands. And Tess, being the woman she is, put herself on the line for me."

"She in love with you?"

Jack dropped his gaze to his hands and didn't reply.

"I guess I don't have to ask if the feeling is mutual. She's a remarkable girl. You'd have to be a goddamned idiot not to love her. But then, you may be a goddamned idiot."

"I didn't come here to talk about Tess," Jack said.

"What did you come here to talk about, Jack—or whatever your name is?"

"It's Ian. Ian McClaine. Lieutenant Colonel, U.S. Navy SEALS." He glanced at the closed door. "I want an information exchange. I tell you mine, you tell me yours. And maybe together we have a whole friggin' pie."

Gil nodded tightly. "You first."

Jack pulled a chair up to the bed and proceeded to tell him the story of Joe's murder and what he'd learned since.

As the details of what they'd done to him that night came out, the murderous look in Gil's eyes faded slightly.

"I'd already figured out that Rodriguez and MacAvoy were involved," Gil stated when Jack was done. "I did some checking after Tess told me about the two cops at the hospital that night. Turns out those two clowns have gotten a little careless. I lifted several prints off a bugging device I found in my home, and ran them through the computers. Naturally, everyone on the job has fingerprints on file, more for elimination at crime scenes than for criminal investigation purposes. But these were pretty and clear. And undeniably MacAvoy's. After I connected that, it was a matter of checking rosters and schedules to connect the two of them together on both the day of your shooting and that of several others, including Ramon Saldovar's."

Gil shifted uncomfortably on the bed and Jack handed him the glass of water from the nightstand. Sucking through the green straw, Gil leaned back in frustration against the pillows. "The bastards didn't do me themselves, though. I saw the guy for a second as I made acquaintance with the windshield, but I didn't recognize him. As far as the guy at the top, I've screened eighty percent of the brass at Westside and Santa Monica. But I'm not ready to go forward with it until I'm closer than that." His fist balled atop his thigh. "You say there's audio and video proof on that floppy?" Jack nodded. "Where is it?"

"Safe." Jack regarded him evenly. "If anything happens to me tonight, it'll find its way to a certain senator's desk. You're already in deep enough."

"My point exactly. I'm slogging in it. Which is why you need me."

Jack's deliberate and meaningful perusal of Gil said everything.

"Okay, so maybe I'm not running triathlons. But that doesn't mean—"

"Who do you trust?"

"Tonight?" he asked, glaring at the cast on his arm. "Nobody. I can't give you any absolutes. Only educated hunches. And I wouldn't bet my life on those. I'm your only man."

A nurse whose name tag read Summers waltzed into the room with a smile and headed for his IV. "And how are we feeling, Detective?"

"Oh," Gil said, "we're just peachy. Aren't we, Jack?"

Jack smiled, watching the nurse adjust his drip.

"Time to take your temperature," she said, poking a digital thermometer in his mouth before he could protest.

He yanked it back out. "Hey, could we have a moment here? We were right in the middle of a—"

She reinserted it. "I have schedules to keep, Mr. Castillano. It's very important that we get regular readings of your vitals. Keep that in." She turned to Jack, pulling a slip of paper from her pocket. "Oh, and I almost forgot. This was just called in for you at the desk."

The blood siphoned from his face. "For *me?*" No one knew he was here. *No one.*

"Your name is McClaine, isn't it? They described you right down to the shirt you're wearing—"

A sick feeling scratched the back of his throat as he grabbed the note from her. There was nothing but a phone number written on it. His eyes cut to Gil, who was dragging the thermometer out of his mouth again.

Jack shoved himself to his feet, grabbing the surprised nurse's arm. "Who called this in?"

"Well, that's what was so odd," she said. "The man must have been her husband, with same name and all. But he asked for you."

"Whose husband?" Jack and Gil said in unison.

"Well, that nice Dr. Gordon who came to see you earlier."

"*What?*" they both practically shouted.

"Y-you must have been asleep," Nurse Summers stammered, staring at them both as if they'd lost their minds. "She—she wasn't here long. She must have left with those two detectives I saw her with."

Jack blew out a quick succession of breaths and grabbed the phone beside Gil's bed. He punched in the number on the slip of paper.

"Is everything all right?" Nurse Summers asked.

"Would you excuse us for a minute, Nurse?" Gil asked sharply. "This is police business."

"Oh. Well. Certainly. But I'll be back," she admonished on her way out the door.

The voice that answered on the other end was a man's. "Nice of you to call, McClaine," he said without preamble.

"Who is this?" Jack demanded.

"That's not the important thing. I think you know what the important thing is. You've got the disk, we've got the woman."

His suddenly clammy fingers tightened around the receiver. "You're a goddamned liar."

"Am I? Maybe you should check where you left her. You have this habit of misplacing things."

The bones in his legs went soft. "You son of a—"

"Now, now, no need to get all excited. We can resolve this whole thing with a simple exchange. The disk for the woman. The warehouse at Pier 49 in San Pedro. Tonight. Nine o'clock. Come alone, McClaine, or all bets are off."

Jack shot a look at his watch: it was 7:45. "Nine! That barely gives me enough time to—"

The phone buzzed in his ear.

Dammit! In traffic, it would take him almost an hour just to get back there. And he needed to get to the floppy. He stabbed at the buttons again.

"*What?*" Gil demanded. "What is it?"

Seth answered his cell phone on the first ring. "Ian?"

"Is she there, Seth?"

"Hell no, she's not. She hasn't *been* there. The guy in the office said she left around noon after some rental outfit delivered a car to her. I waited for two hours for you to call, then I left. I'm on the I-10 just past downtown. Where the hell are you?"

Jack leaned against the wall with a curse.

"Ian?"

"They've got her, Seth." He slammed his fist against the wall.

"They've *what?*" Gil cried.

"Where are you now?" Seth's voice rang with panic. "I'm going in with you."

"I have to do this alone. They said they'd kill her if I didn't come alone."

"What?" Gil cried again, throwing off his covers.

"She's dead anyway," Seth told him. "You know that, Ian. They can't let either one of you go."

Cold fear puddled in Jack's gut. Of course, Seth was right. They had no intention of letting her go. And there wasn't a prayer in hell he would survive it, either. "Maybe so," he told Seth, "but I have to try."

"Who *is* that?" Gil demanded. "Who are you talking to? For crissakes, Jack, talk to me!"

Jack's gaze cut to Gil, who was struggling out of bed, clearly fighting dizziness. "What the hell are you doing?"

"What do you think?" he asked, ripping the IV out of his arm. "I'm coming with you."

He straight-armed him back down. "No, you're not. Nobody's coming with me!"

"Ian?" Seth shouted, from his end of the phone. "Who are you with?"

"Another casualty of this whole mess," Jack said, warning Gil with a look. "A cop friend of Tess's, here at University Hospital, thanks to his friends in blue. Look, I gotta go.''

''Think, Ian. This isn't a one-man op. Hey, pal, we've done this many times together. You need me. We're a team, remember? Tell me where you're going.''

Jack rubbed the ache stabbing him between his eyes. ''We *were* a team. You got a kid on the way, remember? What's the point of both of us dying?''

''Ian, dammit to hell! They're not gonna need to kill you, 'cause *I'm* gonna do it if you don't tell me where you're going!''

Jack knew he would regret answering. ''A warehouse in San Pedro. Pier 49. I can't wait for you, Seth. I'm going alone.''

''Don't go in before I get there, dammit!''

''I gotta go, PB.''

''Ian—!''

Jack lowered the phone onto its cradle.

Gil watched him from the edge of his bed. ''He's right, you know. They're gonna kill her. And you, too.''

Jack felt his throat closing up. ''Not if I can help it.''

Gil snatched up the phone and started dialing. Jack slammed his hand down on the button, cutting him off. ''What are you doing?''

''I'm a cop, Jack. Let me call for backup.''

''You show up with a squad of men and we're just as dead—only quicker.''

''You got a better idea?''

Jack glared at the phone. ''Maybe. Maybe I do.'' He turned back to Gil. ''But I'll need a few things. *Specialty* items. Can you hook me up?''

A grim smile spread across Gil's mouth. ''Do fire trucks have ladders?''

Tess tugged at the ropes chafing her wrists and tried to roll the stiffness out of her shoulders. The smell of ammonia and cleaning fluids was making her dizzy and nauseous. It felt like days since they'd left her lying in this dark closet of a room, hog-tied like a piece of meat. It couldn't have been more than hours, but how many was impossible to say. The cavernous warehouse MacAvoy and Rodriguez brought her to might as well have been a cave for all the daylight it let in. She guessed the sun was down by now.

A shiver of fear worked its way through her. There was no doubt in her mind that they intended to kill her. Nor was there any doubt why they'd brought her here. She was a pawn. They would use her to get Jack and the disk. It made perfect sense, and she'd walked right into it. Like a fool.

He'd told her to stay there. It was all her fault. If she'd only listened to him.

But it was useless to speculate. They'd forced her out of the hospital at gunpoint. If she'd put up a fight, innocent people would have been hurt. The two detectives had little to lose at this point. They were like wild foxes, scrambling madly to cover their trail with the hounds hard on their heels. Now she had to think of a way out before Jack walked into this to rescue her. And she knew he would, as surely as she knew that, outside, the moon had risen over the water. He would come and then they would kill them both.

She tugged at the ropes behind her back again. They'd tied them so tight her hands were getting numb. The crack of light coming under the door was enough to barely illuminate her surroundings. There were metal buckets and mops, brooms and cleaning supplies. Rags and towels stuffed into a box near her head still reeked of cleaning solutions. Oh, for a breath of fresh air, she thought, blinking her stinging eyes.

There was a shelf behind her, barely visible. She scooted toward it on her side to get a better look, finding it lined with more strong-smelling solvents and a jumble of brushes. Tess wedged her feet against a box and pushed herself up to a sitting position. From this vantage point, she could just make out the top of the shelf. Something metallic there caught the light. On her knees, she edged closer and shoved a box out of her way with her cheek. There was a matte knife, rusted with disuse and tossed forgotten into a corner. Her heart sped up. It looked too dull to be of much use, but it was something.

Tess turned around and tried to reach it with her bound hands, but the rope that linked her hands and ankles made it impossible. So she turned back around and, with a shudder of disgust, used her cheek to maneuver it until she could take it between her teeth. She dropped it on the floor, rolled down beside it. It took her a full minute to get her hands on it, but when she did, she worked it under the ropes around her wrists and began to saw.

Eddie Rodriguez pulled open the door to the janitor's closet and waved away the strong odor of disinfectant. It was dark in there and he couldn't see well. The girl was not where he'd left her, and he felt around the wall for a light switch. A moment later, light flooded the small space and Eddie found her curled on the floor toward the back of the small room.

"Hey *chiquita*," he called, from the doorway. "Wake up. It's show time."

The woman didn't move. It surprised him that she'd fall asleep, as ornery as she'd been when he'd locked her in here. But now, as he took in the sight of her lying there all quiet, with her lips parted slightly and her blond hair falling over her cheek, Eddie decided it was a shame they were going to have to get rid of *una belleza* like her. It went against his nature to pop a woman, but a man had to do what a man had to do.

He moved closer. "Hey, lady, wake up." He nudged her with the toe of his boot and got no response. Now that he was closer, he started thinking maybe she didn't look so good. Maybe all the fumes in this room...

A sinking feeling hit him in the gut as he hunkered down beside her, chucking her chin up for a better look. With a foul oath, he turned his head toward the door and shouted, "Lyle, you better get in here, man. This *chica* ain't breathin'!"

Whatever else Eddie had been about to say was lost in a grunt as Tess's knee caught him hard across the cheek with a vicious blow that sent him flying backward against the buckets and brooms. She was on her feet instantly, scraping off the remnants of the ropes she'd managed to cut through. The detective was scrambling over the clutter, still shaking his head, as she delivered a second well-placed kick somewhat lower. Eddie folded in half and gagged for air.

"Who's not breathing now, Eddie?" she snapped, as she wrestled the gun out of his hand and darted out the door. Out of the corner of her eye, she saw MacAvoy lumbering toward her. The warehouse was a huge, cavernous affair with stacks of crates lined up waiting for shipment, and Tess ducked behind a row of them before the detective could get near her. She ran, slipping among the crates, ducking into slivers of space between them as several men closed in behind her.

She had no idea where "out" was. The door they'd brought her through had been an almost invisible part of a huge wall of corrugated metal. Maybe she would stumble upon it accidentally. She had to believe that.

"Dr. Gordon!" Lyle MacAvoy shouted. "I don't know where you think you're going. We got all the doors guarded. See, you're just delaying the inevitable. You're only makin' it harder on yourself.''

Tess squeezed between two crates and listened to the sound of MacAvoy's voice. He was close. Twenty feet away at most and to her left. To her right she heard footsteps of another man edging closer. She brought the pistol up beside her chin and looked at it in the dim light. Was it even cocked? She'd never used a gun like this and wished she'd paid more attention when Jack had been handling Cara's pistol. Shoving the sliding cover thing downward as she'd seen Jack do took muscle, but she felt it engage with a click. She pointed it to her right, waiting for the man to step into view. Her hand trembled. No, it shook. But she was wedged in here too tightly to support it with her other hand.

It had taken them exactly two minutes to corner her here. She knew if she missed the man she was aiming for, she'd be trapped here with him on one side and MacAvoy on the other.

A shadow moved to her right and the man stepped into view. Tess tightened her finger against the trigger but hesitated a fraction of a second too long. He saw her. Her bullet plowed into a crate behind him as he dove out of the way. In the next instant, someone grabbed her other arm and was hauling her out the other side.

She yelped as she collided hard with someone's chest and was easily stripped of the gun.

"Dammit, Tess, you're becoming a regular problem."

She jerked a look up at the man who'd spoken, and for a split second, she knew a moment of hope.

"Bill?"

Dressed casually in khakis and a crisp navy polo shirt, with a gun holster wrapped around his shoulders, Captain Bill Sullivan glared down at her as he tossed one of the men the gun she'd been holding.

Chapter 17

Tess blinked, staring first at him, then at the man he'd thrown the gun to. One of MacAvoy's men. Her heart sank. "You *bastard.*"

Bill shrugged, grabbing her upper arm and propelling her unforgivingly forward. "Yeah, well, let's not resort to name-calling, eh?"

"I trusted you! I thought you were my friend!"

His expression was stony. "This never would've come near you, Tess. But you couldn't mind your own damn business, could you? No, you had to go out of your way to help that Rambo character of yours."

"He's not *mine,*" she pointed out hotly, "and I only did what any decent human being would do."

"That's not what I heard." He didn't even look at her as he said, "Thank God Adam's not around to see—"

Tess whirled on him with her fists, taking him by surprise, but it was only a moment before he wrenched her hard against him with his arm. "Easy, Tess. No need to get all upset."

It struck her then with the force of a sucker punch. "Oh, my God. Was it you? Was it you who killed Adam, just like you killed Joe McClaine? Answer me!"

"No," he said evenly. "No, Tess. I had nothing to do with that. Adam died in a legitimate street fight." He made her stumble, he was dragging her so fast. They reached a large clearing in the storage area with a table and two chairs. He shoved her into one chair beneath the industrial light hanging down from the ceiling.

"This—" he swept his arm before him "—didn't start until after all that. Believe me. I had nothing to do with Adam's death. Joe, on the other hand, was a casualty of war."

"War?" she repeated incredulously.

He smiled. "The war on drugs. Surely you've heard about it."

She stared at him with her mouth open, then looked at the other men, who regarded her as one of the enemy. Eddie Rodriguez, nursing a badly bruised face, was among them.

"I know you think I'm nothing more than a drug dealer now, Tess. But actually, I'm controlling the flow of heroin into this country. I know when and where the drugs are coming in. And how much I can afford to lose. I'm doing this country a favor. But whether you believe me or not, I really don't care. This is about my future. The future that my job won't secure. Surely you know as well as anyone about police pensions, Tess. They're a joke. This is just insurance for the future. Mine and my family's."

"Does Karen know you're a murderer?"

Bill's face darkened. "I don't think you're in any position to talk about my wife, do you?" He gestured to MacAvoy. "Tie her up again. And this time, moron, do it right." He looked at his watch, then clapped his hands behind his back, pacing around the table. "We wouldn't want her to turn up missing when Rambo arrives."

Tess stared down at the floor as the ropes MacAvoy tied around her wrists bit into her skin. But she hardly felt it. She was sickened by Bill and what he'd done. Never would she have dreamed him capable of becoming the twisted monster he was now. He'd fooled everyone, including her and Joe and Gil. And now he meant to kill her and Jack. And no one would be the wiser. *Oh, Jack! I'm so sorry!*

Jack moved silently across the asphalt-topped roof of the warehouse and knelt to place the last surprise in the access panel on the east side. He twisted the dial on the clock and set it, then glanced at his watch. Eight fifty-five. Five minutes to get to her.

Jack abandoned the access panel and made his way back across the roof, past the still-unconscious sentry he'd disabled, to the rope he'd left coiled and ready. He checked below for signs of another lookout, then dropped the rope and silently rappelled down. He tried not to think of Tess down there with those bastards. The shot he'd heard a few minutes ago had made his blood run cold. Then he'd seen them dragging her across the warehouse. She was alive. That was all that mattered. The rest he would deal with. Tucking his pistol into a hiding spot near the corner of the building, he gave his neck a crack, then headed into the lions' den.

There was a man posted at the door who centered his gun on Jack's chest as he approached. Jack raised his hands, and the man motioned him forward through the door set into the corrugated wall.

"Stop right there," the sentry instructed as another man searched him for weapons. Naturally, he found none. "Okay," he said, shoving him forward toward the light at the center of the building.

The skyline of crates parted to reveal them, standing beneath a stark white light dangling from the ceiling. Jack took it all in with a look: Tess in the chair, two men to the right, three to the left, cover a good fifteen feet away. He pulled his gaze back to Tess. Her eyes were locked on him and she looked scared and small sitting in that chair. He disconnected from that, knowing it would only hinder what he had to do. He had to concentrate. He'd trained his whole life for this moment. And despite the odds against coming out of this alive, it was the only shot he'd have.

"Ah, Lieutenant Colonel McClaine. How good of you to come."

With his hands still in the air, Jack regarded the tall man with graying temples standing near Tess. He had an air of authority that the others lacked, even without the gun he was holding on her. Jack hadn't seen him before, but assumed he was the man he'd been after. He tipped his head. "I could hardly refuse such a gracious invitation. I don't believe we've met."

"Sullivan. Captain William Sullivan," the man replied. "You look a lot like your brother, McClaine. Nice kid. Unfortunate timing."

Jack ground his teeth together and didn't say a word.

"I assume you brought the item we spoke about."

A humorless smile tugged at Jack's mouth. "You thought wrong."

Sullivan seemed unruffled by this. "*Did* I."

"Did you really think I'd walk in here and hand it to you, Sullivan? So you could do me like you did my brother?"

The captain's hand tightened on his gun. "Lyle?" With a tilt of his head, he ordered Lyle to grab Jack. The man twisted Jack's arm up behind him.

Sullivan moved closer to Tess with the gun. "I have no compunction against killing her. It's a shame, of course, but all in the name of money."

Tess's eyes widened and Jack saw her mouth his name.

The man behind him tightened his hold as Jack fought the urge to kill Sullivan with his bare hands. "I don't think you'll do that."

"Really."

"No. Because I have what you want. And unless you let her go, you and your little flunkies here get nothing. Except an express ticket to federal prison."

Sullivan let out a bark of laughter. "I'm not going to prison, McClaine. I assure you that will never happen."

"It will if the disk falls into the hands its intended for in the event of my untimely death. You take me, let her go. She calls when she's safe, then I take you to the disk."

"Jack, no!"

He didn't even look at Tess. "She's got nothing to do with any of this, Sullivan."

"I'm disappointed in you, McClaine. I half expected you to come in with a better plan than this. You see, we already found the disk you'd hidden in that airport locker, thanks to the key we found in your hotel room after MacAvoy and Rodriguez botched their job the first time. It was enlightening to see what Joe had gathered on us. What we didn't know was what you'd uncovered in your own investigation. My only reason for calling you down here tonight was to tie up the last two loose ends of our little problem. Tess, here, helped to accomplish that."

Jack smiled thinly, jerking at the grip of the man behind him. "Did you actually think I wouldn't make another copy of that disk? Gee, you're dumber than I thought, Sullivan."

The captain's mouth opened to respond, but the explosion of gunfire from two different directions made him duck. Jack threw MacAvoy to the ground and kicked the gun out of his hand. It went sailing toward a crate twenty feet away. He slammed his fist into the detective's jaw and saw his eyes roll back before he went limp. Now gunfire crackled from every corner of the warehouse as the timed charges Jack had set went off. The five men in the clearing dove for cover, leaving Tess alone in the chair. Jack was beside her in a second, dragging her by the arm toward the gun he'd kicked away. Sullivan and his men were busy returning the fire from the rafters as Jack dragged her into the shadow of a crate, then pulled her toward the entrance.

A bullet whizzed past his head, and Jack ducked, shoving Tess into a slender aisle between crates. He returned fire and watched Rodriguez fly backward with a cry, grabbing his chest. With her hands still tied behind her back, Tess sprawled in front of him as he stumbled behind her.

Jack hauled her roughly to her feet and shoved her out the other side. He turned back in time to see another man block the entrance from behind and raise his gun. Jack popped off a shot and the man crumpled sideways.

The diversion he'd set up on the roof would last another few seconds at most, and they were still twenty yards from the door. He swore as he moved out behind Tess. He grabbed her shirt and hauled her down the aisle.

"Jack!"

He looked back at her and saw a man running behind them, gun extended. Jack shoved Tess behind him and fired at the man. He missed and the man returned fire, the bullet pinging off the crate inches from his head. Jack's second shot caught him in the leg and the man fell, dragging himself behind a crate.

Behind him he heard Tess gasp. He whirled back toward her, only to find Sullivan holding her, with an arm across her chest and the barrel of a gun to her temple. The captain was backing up, gripping Tess against him like a shield. And suddenly the gunfire stopped. Jack pointed his weapon at Sullivan's head.

Sullivan looked around wildly, his graying hair spilling over his forehead and sweat disheveling his careful appearance. "Drop your gun, McClaine!"

Jack's fingers tightened on the trigger and he bared his teeth, gauging how much room for error he had. Exactly none. If he missed, Sullivan would kill her. Adrenaline rushed through him like a punch to the gut. "Don't do it, Sullivan!"

"Drop it!" Sullivan screamed. "Drop the goddamned gun! I'll kill her! I swear to God!"

"Don't do it, Jack!" Tess screamed. "He's going to kill me anyway!"

"Shut up!" Sullivan yelled back.

"Let her go and you can have me, Sullivan. Let her go! She's nothing to you now."

Sullivan eyed him wildly, overloaded by his choices.

"You kill her, I kill you," Jack said, sweat dripping into his eyes. "Is that what you want? This way at least you have a chance."

"Jack!" Tess breathed. "Don't!"

In the darkness behind them, they heard a door bang open and the sound of men rushing into the warehouse.

Jack swallowed hard. "Hear that? It's over. You have nowhere to go."

Sweat trickled down Sullivan's cheek and dripped off his jaw. "You just couldn't leave it alone, could you? Now look what you've done."

"Ian!" A voice echoed in the cavernous warehouse. It was Seth.

Jack waited, not taking his eyes off Sullivan. The shouts of men echoed closer. The captain's expression grew panicky, and he backed Tess up to a crate, still pressing the gun against her temple. His eyes darted to the entrance, then back to Jack. Tears were streaming down Tess's cheeks and her breathing was coming in ragged gasps.

Jack inched toward him, his hand out. "Give me the gun, Sullivan. You don't want to kill her. It's gone far enough."

"You're right," the captain said through gritted teeth,

tipping Tess's head back with the pressure of the gun. Tears streaked his face. "It's gone too far now. My wife...my daughters...they can never... It—it's all your fault."

For an awful moment, Jack believed he would pull the trigger. A silent prayer passed his lips. Then, suddenly, Sullivan's expression flattened and he cut his eyes to the SWAT officers coming around the corner of an aisle, thirty feet away. Sullivan loosened his arm, shoved Tess away from him and raised his gun toward Jack.

Jack didn't even blink. He put a bullet between the captain's eyes and watched him drop bonelessly to the floor. But all he heard was the sound of Tess's screams.

Gil settled a blanket around Tess's shoulders and sat down beside her on the crate. "You okay?"

She nodded, watching Jack talk with his friend Seth and a handful of SWAT officers who were still milling around. "Just a little shaky is all," she told Gil. "And you—" she pointed to his arm "—should be back in the hospital."

Gil sniffed and put his good arm around her. "Ah, those doctors. They're all quacks." He waited for a reaction, and when she rolled her eyes, he smiled. "You are a lot of trouble, you know that, Tess?"

She nodded, feeling tears gather in her eyes. She knew only too well how much trouble she'd caused everyone. "I'm sorry, Gil, for dragging you into this."

He gave her a brotherly kiss on the temple. "Shut up, will ya? And drink this," he said with a grin, handing her a cup of hot coffee.

Dan Kelso walked toward her, sipping coffee, too. Seeing him had been the biggest surprise. It seemed that he had driven down the hill after the incident with the body at Cara's, and had spent the afternoon trying to contact Gil. He'd been part of the team that had come in with Seth, because they couldn't keep him away. It meant more to her than she could say that he'd cared enough to do that, but she didn't know what to say to any of them. She just felt numb.

"Feeling better?" Dan asked, tucking one hand into his jacket pocket and regarding her with a worried expression.

She nodded. "I don't know how to thank you for everything you did. I owe you an apology, too."

Dan shifted uncomfortably. "Hey, don't. You did real well with a bad situation. I just wish I could have helped you sooner, but I understand why you didn't feel like you could tell me." He glanced over at Jack. "You were in pretty good hands, I'd say."

Tess shivered and sipped her coffee, wishing Jack would come over here and hold her. After he'd shot Bill Sullivan, Jack had grabbed her up and hugged her fiercely until she'd stopped trembling. And she'd prayed he'd never let her go. But the investigation had separated them and he'd barely made eye contact with her since. Now he was huddled with Seth deep in conversation. Apprehension was growing inside her. His parting words at the motel came back to her.

When this is all over, I want you to forget about me, Tess.

He couldn't feel the same way now, could he? Not after everything that had happened. He had every right to be furious with her after what she'd done. But she'd make it up to him. She'd find some way to—

Just then, he turned around and their eyes met. While the other men talked, he watched her over the rim of his coffee cup. Tess tipped up her chin and met his gaze squarely, no longer caring who knew how she felt about him.

Jack tossed his cup away and started toward her. Gil and Dan saw him coming and shared a communicative look. Gil got to his feet. "Dan, I think the lead detective over there is trying to get our attention. You take your time, Tess.''

She didn't even look at Gil as she nodded. She was already on her feet, walking toward Jack. They stopped a foot apart and Jack hesitated for a few long seconds before taking her in his arms.

''Oh, Jack,'' she murmured against his chest.

He pressed his face against her hair. ''You okay?''

She loved having his arms around her, even if he felt edgy and tense. ''I'm so sorry I didn't listen to you. I almost got you killed. Can you ever forgive me?''

''There's nothing to forgive.''

''I don't blame you for being angry.''

''I'm not angry.''

No, she thought a little desperately. It was worse than that. ''It was stupid and thoughtless, leaving the way I did. If I'd only done what you'd told me to—''

''Tess.''

''—none of this would have happened. And I haven't even thanked you for saving my—''

He dropped his mouth on hers and kissed her hard and long, putting an end to her babbling apology. She blinked up at him as he lifted his mouth from hers.

''I love you,'' he said softly, against her mouth.

The words sizzled through her like hot oil. Oddly off balance, Tess held on to him for fear of falling. ''W-what?''

He brushed a strand of hair out of her eyes and smiled at the shock in her expression. ''I said I *love* you.''

''Oh, I-I *thought* that was what you said.'' Tears welled in her eyes.

One side of his mouth lifted in a smile. ''Listen to me, Tess. I know what I said before, about forgetting what happened between us. But I was lying. I could never forget you. Not if I worked at it for the rest of my life. And more importantly, I don't want to.''

"Jack—"

He shook his head. "If I'm on the wrong track here, just...just hear me out before you stop me. I know I was a jerk back at the motel. I know I hurt you. I'm sorry for that. I have nothing to say in my own defense, except that I was totally unprepared for what I was feeling for you. I couldn't believe it could be real. It happened so fast. But I was wrong. As wrong as I could be.

"You know, I've fought beside some of the bravest men in this country, worked under the most brutal conditions, risked my life more times than I could count to complete a mission that somebody else thought was important. And I'd be a liar if I told you those things hadn't scared me. But they were all a cakewalk compared to what I felt when I heard that he'd taken you."

Tess's heart moved to her throat. Jack's eyes were lowered, and he was working hard to keep the emotion from his expression. He failed.

"When Sullivan pressed that gun against your head tonight—" he stopped, swallowing hard "—I found myself making deals with God. If He'd just let you live, I'd give everything up for you. I'd do anything, say anything I had to, to save your life."

"Oh, Jack—"

"'Cause you see, Doc, I can't picture my life without you anymore."

Tess exhaled slowly, hardly daring to believe what he was saying. She'd prepared herself for the worst. And she'd gotten something she couldn't possibly deserve.

"It's not gonna be easy. I'm not pretending it will, but I'm gonna make changes, Tess. I want to be a man you can count on. Not just now and then, but every day. And night." He looked at their hands, linked together, then lifted his gaze to hers. "I talked to Seth. He said there's an opening for me in Naval Intelligence with him. It seems the brass there are already interested in me. It's a real job, Tess. A new challenge. One I'd be good at. One that wouldn't have me living out of a duffel bag eight months of the year."

"But the SEALS—?"

"Hell," he said, rolling his shoulder with a grin, "I'm getting too old for all this 007 stuff."

She arched an eyebrow. "Oh, I don't know. You looked pretty good to me tonight."

"Atta girl. And don't remind me when my hair starts going gray, either, will you?"

"No," she said, reaching up to push it back from his face, "but I wouldn't mind being there to see it."

He smiled slowly. "For a long time now, I've been kind of sleepwalking, too. Like—I don't know—like there should be more. I guess it just took getting shot for me to find it. Marry me, Tess. I know it's fast and we hardly know each other, but—"

Now a tear slid down her cheek and she let it go. She pressed two fingers against his lips. "Shh," she whispered. "Do you know what I was thinking when I saw you tonight, standing there facing that gun for me?"

He shook his head, sliding his hands down her arms to gather her closer.

"I was thinking that you are the bravest, kindest…scariest man I've ever met. And I wouldn't change a thing about you. Oh, Jack, it wouldn't matter to me if you hung wallpaper for a living or…walked steel beams twelve stories up. Or if you stayed in the SEALS and kept jumping out of airplanes into the North Atlantic. I'll settle for you any way I can get you. You taught me so much about myself. You made me want to be a doctor again and helped me to believe in myself. I may not know Ian well, but I know Jack," she said, caressing his stubbled cheek with her thumb. "And I'm absolutely crazy about him. All the rest? That's just geography."

"Is that a yes?" he asked, tilting her head back against the palm of his hand and searching her eyes with his.

A slow smile full of promise curved her lips. "That is most definitely a yes, Lieutenant Colonel McClaine."

Jack grinned happily and swooped her up into his arms, carrying her past all the cops and the investigators and the stares. He took her outside under the canopy of stars, and when he had her all to himself, he kissed her deeply and well, loving the feel of her arms around him. He'd been alone most of his life and had never expected to find what he'd found in her. But he knew, with the instincts of a man who'd been to hell and back, that his time of solitude was over. Because for the first time in his life he understood what it meant to come home.

*   *   *   *   *

**Start celebrating Silhouette's 20th anniversary
with these 4 special titles by
New York Times bestselling authors**

Fire and Rain
by Elizabeth Lowell

King of the Castle
by Heather Graham Pozzessere

State Secrets
by Linda Lael Miller

Paint Me Rainbows
by Fern Michaels

On sale in December 1999

Plus, a special free book offer inside each title!

Available at your favorite retail outlet

V *Silhouette* ®
™
Visit us at www.romance.net

PSNYT

Looking For More Romance?

Visit Romance.net

Look us up on-line at: http://www.romance.net

Check in daily for these and other exciting features:

Hot off the press

View all current titles, and purchase them on-line.

What do the stars have in store for you?

Horoscope

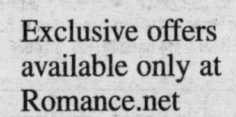

Hot deals

Exclusive offers available only at Romance.net

Celebrate Silhouette's 20th Anniversary

Don't miss Silhouette's newest cross-line promotion,

Four royal sisters find their own Prince Charmings as they embark on separate journeys to find their missing brother, the Crown Prince!

The search begins in October 1999 and continues through February 2000:

On sale October 1999: **A ROYAL BABY ON THE WAY**
by award-winning author **Susan Mallery** (Special Edition)

On sale November 1999: **UNDERCOVER PRINCESS**
by bestselling author **Suzanne Brockmann** (Intimate Moments)

On sale December 1999: **THE PRINCESS'S WHITE KNIGHT**
by popular author **Carla Cassidy** (Romance)

On sale January 2000: **THE PREGNANT PRINCESS**
by rising star **Anne Marie Winston** (Desire)

On sale February 2000: **MAN...MERCENARY...MONARCH**
by top-notch talent **Joan Elliott Pickart** (Special Edition)

ROYALLY WED
Only in—
SILHOUETTE BOOKS

Available at your favorite retail outlet.

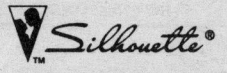 Silhouette ®

Visit us at www.romance.net

SSERW